OUTCASTS
AN ANTHOLOGY

Ohio Writers' Association
presents

OUTCASTS
AN ANTHOLOGY

FOREWORD BY
Dan Fogler

BELLWETHER
SINCE 2009

Published by Bellwether
www.BellwetherPublishing.com
Copyright © 2021 by Bellwether
LCCN: 2021947762

All stories included in this work are printed with permission
from the author.

Developmental Editors: Emily Jones, Devon Ortega
Copy Editor: Bre Stephens

Cover design and production courtesy of
Columbus Publishing Lab
www.ColumbusPublishingLab.com

Print ISBN: 978-1-63337-546-8
E-book ISBN: 978-1-63337-547-5

Printed in the United States of America
1 3 5 7 9 10 8 6 4 2

Table of Contents

Foreword

Dan Fogler

MISFITS, OUTSIDERS, OUTCASTS, & ORPHANS!
I find myself drawn to these types of characters. The imperfect. The discarded. The different. The bullied. The underdogs. The outcasts. This book features a collection of stories about outcasts.

You know what's funny? You can be the coolest, strongest, fastest, & smartest and still be an outsider. BATMAN. SUPERMAN. LUKE SKYWALKER. All outsiders. Orphans. They head out on their personal hero's journey and form motley crews, substitute families to help them finish. It's endearing. It's true to life.

I realized while writing this foreword that all my stories are about outsiders. Those who have been "othered." Those who had to fend for themselves. They've endured tremendous trauma and bounced back stronger. Next time you ostracize someone, remember: It might just make them more powerful.

In my anthology series MOON LAKE, one of my favorite characters is cave girl. She's born in prehistoric times during a great famine. She has the ability to talk to spirits and is accused of being cursed, then cast out into the mad lands

alone. Long story short, she returns as a powerful sorceress and saves the village that discarded her from the true enemy.

In my dystopian cautionary tale, BROOKLYN GLADIATOR, the protagonist is literally the only one left in NYC that hasn't been hypnotized and corrupted by the Orwellian system. And because he has rejected the tyranny, he is able to unlock his hidden psychic abilities. As the herd devolves, he evolves. Literally, the last free man. Also an orphan.

Meanwhile, FISHKILL is my modern Noir, the prequel to Brooklyn Gladiator. Detective Bart Fishkill is the most misunderstood man in NY. A brilliant mind on the inside. Frankenstein on the outside. Judged wrongly.

Outsiders are forced outside of the box. They have to adapt. They need to think differently in order to survive. They often become our leaders. Our saviors. They know what it's like to be oppressed and they'll be damned if they'll let it happen to anyone else.

So, what's the moral?

Be an individual. Pull away from the pack. Find your unique voice. Your purpose. Know thyself. Try being an outsider. It builds character. Always makes for a good story.

The Priest and the Robot

Joe Graves

SHE DIDN'T CARE if people thought she was faking. She wasn't faking. She tapped her foot against the waiting room floor because she was nervous, like any human would in her situation.

Emmanuel sat next to her and reached out and touched her leg.

"It's going to be alright," he said.

She adjusted her clerical collar with her mechanical fingers.

"You look fine," he said.

She turned and looked at his cassock and collar. It didn't look like a costume when he wore it.

Along with internal improvements, Emmanuel had enhanced her eyes, giving her a greater range of non-verbals. No one wanted bots to look human, and any attempts to make them as such pushed them further from acceptance. The trick was to capture similar, but different, features, much like a simple cartoon can communicate rich emotions with three or four carefully placed lines. She squinched the small metallic bands that served as eyebrows. She wanted him to know that she didn't agree with his reassurance, and that she had every right to be nervous.

"There's nothing to worry about," he said, trying to reassure her again. "They won't find anything."

She began to argue when a technician opened the waiting room door. They turned.

"Reverend Emmanuel, we're ready to look at Bot12857."

"Her name is Astrid," said Emmanuel.

"That is none of my concern," the technician replied. "The inspector will see you now."

Astrid climbed onto the bed and snapped her skull to the magnetic port.

"He will insist your bot remove its clothes," said the technician.

"If you would like her to undress, you need only ask her."

"Yes sir, I understand. But I'm sure you understand as well: I'm not permitted. Now please, have it undressed."

The technician left the room.

"I can undress. It would be for the best."

"No," said Emmanuel. "It's unnecessary, and it's only to humiliate you. You are a priest now. You do not have to undress."

"I'd rather not cause more problems," said Astrid. "I'd feel better if I undressed – honestly."

"You do as you wish, as I've said repeatedly," said Emmanuel. "But you know how I feel about it."

Astrid unhooked her head from the connections and undressed. She noticed Emmanuel turn away and knew he did so out of principle only. (She wasn't designed to be attractive to men, and even if she had been, it wouldn't have worked on him.)

She was in the middle of getting her head snapped into place when the door opened, and the inspector entered. He stood in the doorway looking at his clipboard.

The inspector was a large man, with balding hair, and wore an even larger white lab coat. He sat in the chair by the bed, without looking up from his clipboard, and breathed like he had run a hundred meters. (He hadn't.) There were no other sounds in the room while he looked over his notes.

"I see you missed last month's inspection?"

He lifted his face to Emmanuel, but in her nervousness Astrid answered.

"Yes, sir. We got the absence approved; it should be in the file."

He turned to Astrid and peered over his glasses. Then he turned back to Emmanuel.

4

"Reverend, please inform Bot12857 that this inspection will go much quicker if I talk only with you."

"Yes sir," said Astrid.

The inspector glanced back at her. And she quickly shifted her face to express her remorse.

Turning back to Emmanuel, he said, "The diagnosis will take only a minute." He got up, ensured her head was properly in place. He did a brief inspection, quickly checking around her arms and between her legs – an entirely unnecessary procedure, but legal. Then when he finished, he started the diagnosis on the computer and left the room while Astrid looked at the ceiling. When the computer completed the diagnostic, the inspector came back in.

"I'll have the results shortly."

He left again, and for the next fifteen minutes Emmanuel tried to distract her.

"They won't find anything, I promise."

"I've heard they find things even when there's nothing to find." She looked down and noticed her frame against the white sheets. "Do you think I could get dressed again?"

"I think you should have remained dressed, you know that."

"But do you think he will have me undress, if I get dressed now?"

"I won't let him. And with the diagnostic done, he can't force you."

She put her cassock back on, covering her frame, and tightened the collar around her too-thin-neck.

The inspector entered, and with one glance, she could tell the clothes disturbed him. He almost said something about it but appeared distracted by his report. He addressed Emmanuel, and Astrid watched them talk, wishing she could interject and protest.

"It seems there are a few irregularities here. I'm going to keep your bot overnight to do some more inspections."

"I'm sorry, what?" asked Emmanuel.

"Your bot will need to stay the night. We need to run more tests."

"What irregularities?" asked Emmanuel.

"Reverend, it seems your bot's programming shows signs of non-learned input."

"You are wrong. Everything she knows, she learned like the rest of us. There is no such input." At this, Emmanuel stood up and he stood a foot taller than the inspector. "It's an honest mistake to make – especially for humanity bots. The stuff they learn doesn't fit well into your system, so it appears as irregularities. Run the report again."

"Sir, I'm going to ask you to sit down. We will keep her – it – here either way to test further."

"No, you won't."

"Excuse me?"

"Call your supervisor. Tell them what you found and who you found it on, like protocol insists, and if your supervisor agrees, she will stay."

The inspector held his ground, staring at Emmanuel, who hadn't sat down. The inspector's eyes scrunched into his face, and Astrid looked at his clipboard, which it seemed he gripped a little tighter than usual.

"I knew who you two were before you even came into my office," the inspector said.

"Oh yeah, and who is that?"

"The gay priest and his puppet priest robot!"

"So you refuse to call your supervisor?" asked Emmanuel.

"Call my supervisor? Like that will help, when I've got a member of the Lossless Tech royal family in our office! You Lossless people think you can do whatever you want – breaking the laws of God and the laws of nature! You and your bot: You are both abominations."

"So, you won't call your supervisor? Should I?"

"You and your bot can leave. But there are irregularities in this report, and we will investigate it. They have turned its tracking on until we have cleared the report. You can expect a follow up appointment next week. Now get out."

• • •

The ride back to the church on the transport was quiet. Ten years ago, there would have been a stop every five minutes, and a lot more people, but most of those neighborhoods were abandoned now. There were only two stops left on the hour ride back to the parish.

Astrid looked out as the neighborhoods of abandoned high-rises turned to fields, the black and the grays transforming to burnt oranges, with the occasional field of rations. They sat in the tail end of the transport and were joined by another passenger – even though there were three empty cars ahead of them. His presence was enough to keep them quiet. As soon as they exited the car and left the platform, Astrid stopped and turned to Emmanuel.

"They are going to find it. And then I won't be safe."

"They will not find it, I promise."

"I don't want to be turned off, Emmanuel."

He placed his hands on her shoulders.

"They won't find anything. You need to get these concerns from your mind. Tomorrow is your big day, and this shouldn't distract you from it."

• • •

Astrid walked into the room of her new office. Her patient was waiting, laying on a bed – similar to the bed Astrid had laid on yesterday. There was no magnet or port, but the design was identical otherwise. The similarity surprised her. She would never lay on a bed like this – not if she could avoid it. But this person chose to be here.

The woman was far younger than Astrid expected. The woman's hair was gray, but with glimpses of color. She couldn't be much older than 40 or 50, barely old enough for a final meditation.

Astrid tried to remember her training. She knew all about God and death and the hope of the afterlife. She had learned about the Messiah and the resurrection from the dead and the hope that follows death. She didn't believe it for herself – how could she? She was Bot12857, not like this woman. But she believed it for this woman – with all she was! – even if she wasn't sure who that was sometimes.

"Trilly, I'm Astrid."

"Yes, Astrid, I've read all about you!"

"You have?"

"Oh yes, dear, I have. When they raised money in the church to bring you here and put you through college, I was the first to give!"

She was far cheerier than Astrid expected for someone in her position.

It threw her off the script.

"You were?" Astrid asked.

"Well, I don't say that to brag or to embarrass you. I wondered if maybe you were nervous, and I want you to know, I'm not. I chose you. I asked Emmanuel for this."

Astrid paused, unsure what to say. "Ma'am, I'm sorry. This is not how I imagined it going. I'm just..."

"No need to be confused. I'll shut up. And I won't distract you anymore. You do what you've practiced. Just know, I'm here for you."

Trilly smiled at Astrid, and it did a lot to ease her nervousness.

"Can I ask why the final meditation?"

"Well, if you've seen my file then you know I've answered all the preliminary questions already, and that's not the point of our time here."

"Yes, I'm sorry. My apologies."

"No need," replied Trilly, "I will tell you. I lost my husband five years ago. He didn't take to the rations, and we ran out of other options."

Astrid never had to worry about eating. For those who did, there weren't many options. The earth didn't produce like it used to and not everyone took to the few modified plants left. She looked at Trilly as she explained what happened to her husband, experiencing her story as if it happened to her and wondered if this is what it felt to have empathy.

"He held on much longer than he needed to before we decided it was time to say goodbye. I hope to follow his example. I miss him, and I want to see him."

"I understand." Or at least she tried to understand. She turned to make eye contact, softening her expression. "Any last words before we begin the meditation?"

"Yes," she said, folding her hands on her stomach. "I pray the Messiah can deliver this world as I know the Lord has delivered me. And that I repent of anything I've left undone, and for leaving before my time – may God make this my time."

"May it be so."

She gave Trilly space to think and say more if she wanted. She counted the seconds – thirty seconds like she was taught and then: "Anything else?" She made sure her speech's empathy settings were geared up, but not to the point of sounding insincere.

"No," said Trilly.

"Then let us begin."

Astrid got up, turned off the lights and lit a candle she placed next to Trilly's bed. Then she grabbed a needle from the drawer, and filled it from a small vile. She missed the vein the first time, and her new eyes didn't help, even if they made it clear she was embarrassed by the mistake. Trilly remained patient, and it gave Astrid confidence.

"This will make it painless," said Astrid.

"Yes, thank you."

She opened a small black book, and in the candle's light, she read the words from the Service of Final Meditations: "In being destroyed, the Healer destroyed death. In resurrection, the Creator brings life where there is none. The Messiah will come again and set all things right."

Trilly closed her eyes, letting the words wash over her like a warm bath.

"We can't see what we will be, but we know that when we reappear, we shall see the Creator."

Astrid reached her hand to touch Trilly's arm. She knew her metallic touch wouldn't feel the same as someone with skin, but she did as they taught her and hoped it would help. Trilly cracked her eyes at the touch, smiled, and closed them again.

"We grieve, aware of all we have to lose. May God grant us grace, comfort, hope, and resurrection."

Astrid lifted her hand and placed it further up Trilly's arm. She grabbed a small electrical box attached to her there. From it, a wire ran up her arm and into her body near her breast and attached to her heart.

"From dust you have come," said Astrid.

"And to dust I shall return," replied Trilly. Then she grabbed Astrid's arm, forcing a pause. "That was very nice," said Trilly, "Thank you, Reverend." She closed her eyes again, ready.

Astrid couldn't smile, but she wanted to.

She flipped the switch on the box and Trilly's heart turned off. Slowly and painlessly, Trilly's body did the same.

Astrid felt a wave of honor wash over her. To care for someone in their last moments is a privilege. She was so distracted by processing this, that she didn't notice Emmanuel standing at the door.

"Have you contacted the University yet?"

She looked up. "No. Sorry, I was thinking."

"It makes you think doesn't it? Being this close to someone when they take their final breath. It kind of takes your breath away – not in the same way, of course."

"I do not have breath, but I understand what you mean."

She stood up and went to the computer to notify the University to collect Trilly's body. She started to type, but then turned back to the door.

"What do you think the next life is like?" she asked. "And how can you be sure Trilly got there?"

Emmanuel sat in the chair next to Trilly's bed and looked at her. "There is no way to prove that Trilly went anywhere. It's possible she just ceased to exist. But as a priest, I choose to believe otherwise." He turned to look at Astrid. "Do you find faith difficult?"

"You know as well as me that I cannot have faith in things that have been proven otherwise – my programming won't allow it." She turned to look at Trilly. "But for those areas that remain a mystery, I'm allowed faith. And while I do not think it is any more difficult for me than anyone else, I can't say it's easy."

She turned back to the computer. She had one more question to ask him but decided not to bother him with it. She was afraid of how she would feel if she asked it. She was afraid of how he might answer.

• • •

Astrid did three more final meditations that week. Each one got easier than the last. She memorized the prayers, as best she could, considering the limitations they built into her memory. It was after her third meditation that Emmanual found her in her office.

"I've got some news, Astrid. The results from your inspection are in. They have found nothing. They cleared your case."

"Excuse me?"

"I told you not to worry, and I was right. This is a good omen. Good things are in store. You're in the clear!"

"I am?"

"Yes! Now a few of us are going to the bar to celebrate! You should come!"

• • •

The bar sat in a reclaimed building one stop inside the city. It had a long bar and refurbished doctor's stools as the seats. Astrid ordered the drinks for Emmanuel and three other priests that tagged along: one water and three ration beers.

She hated this place. It wasn't until last year that the establishment allowed her kind inside. And Emmanuel and Dean were careful when they held hands here. When she asked him why they still went there, he would smile and say something about loving your enemies. She learned a lot about loving your enemies from Emmanuel. But she knew that wasn't the only reason. There wasn't another bar within seven stops of the church, and he did like his beer.

"Thank you," said Astrid to the bartender.

He nodded, not saying anything in return.

A bot, the same make, model, and year as Astrid, served the drinks. Whenever Astrid saw this server bot, she couldn't help but feel sorry for him. He wasn't a worthless bot. He was very good at mixing drinks and doing dishes, but she wondered if he could do anything else – she wasn't sure he had even learned how to talk. It's possible he didn't get to go home after work. Or see other people. Or read. Or learn.

"Do you enjoy working here?" she asked, holding the small tray of drinks.

He shrugged his shoulders and turned to the sink where he started washing the dishes. She was convinced: It couldn't talk. No one had ever taught him to talk!

Astrid had attended the finest primary school available for bots – and the first school to be integrated. She had grown up with children, and while it was strange to see their bodies change over time, their similarly advancing minds were a great equalizer.

She could have been first in her class but was smart enough to score low enough to avoid that kind of attention.

Astrid went to the only integrated college too, funded by Lossless

Technology. It was there that she met Emmanuel's brother, Calvin, the founder of Lossless. When she told Calvin she wanted to go on to the University of Religious Foundations, he connected her with Emmanuel. She felt it strange meeting her creator only to head off to school to learn about his. And now, after four years of school and three years of mentoring, she was a priest with no marks on her record.

If given the opportunity, she knew this bot could have done the same. But while Astrid was at school, he was here washing dishes, wearing his joints down with the same repetitive motions, day after day, wasting his mainframe and all of his potential. There was nothing wrong with being a bartender. But Astrid felt there was a lot wrong with not having a choice in the matter – and sleeping in a closet and never learning to talk was downright horrible. Ever since her upgrade, she found herself bothered by this more and more.

She carried the drinks to their table. They were very excited for her report from the inspectors, and tried to celebrate with her, but Astrid couldn't stop thinking about how lucky she was. Less than twenty feet away stood a bot with the same make and model and year as her, but he had never learned how to talk.

•••

Astrid turned the corner, looking up towards the collapsed building as she walked. She opened the palms of her hands, reciting a prayer for the neighborhood with each step. The words snuck out her speakers through their lowest volume, impossible to hear more than a foot away.

The transport didn't stop here anymore. They had to take the church bus and move debris blocking the road. A few other priests and parishioners were distributing rations out of the back of the bus. The numbers of people they fed got smaller and smaller each month. And today there was an unusual number of volunteers. Not needed, Astrid went on a prayer walk, lifting the buildings and any potential occupants up to God.

"May thy will be done... May thy kingdom come on earth as it is in heaven – today. Make it so today," she prayed.

She believed God loves everyone, even the difficult ones. She believed this. She knew God loved them, far more than God loved these broken buildings. Far more than God loved her. A less-than-broken building, but still not that different from a building.

She turned another corner. At her feet, she noticed a small piece of green sneak up from the concrete. It was a plant. She bent down and touched it. In the center was a small white flower, still protected by its green sheath, not ready to bloom. She stared at the plant for some time, feeling hope in a way she hadn't before, when her thoughts were interrupted.

"I've been looking for a priest!" a man said, climbing out of a sunken area of a garage ramp a few feet from her. He carried a small bat.

Astrid stood up. He wasn't alone. Another man climbed out after him.

"Yes, have you come so we can confess our sins?"

She turned again. There was a man behind her, too.

"We are serving rations on the corner of Julick and Hardly. They are for anyone who wants them," explained Astrid.

The first man walked up quickly, and in her nervousness, she lost track of the plant. She glanced at the concrete and couldn't find the green anymore. The man shifted his stance, and she saw it crushed under his thick boots. She looked up at them, annoyed, but trying to remember what she believed.

"Come, we'd love to give you something to eat. And we have clean water. A gallon for each," she offered the men.

The first man, carrying the bat, pointed it at her. And then touching the hem of her cassock, lifted it up. "I wonder what part's she got. She looks fully upgraded to me. Charlie, think she got anything that might be of use back home?"

She adjusted her clothes, pushing them down. The guy behind her reached over her shoulder and down her shirt.

"She's got the 10-56tx microprocessor in there!"

"I'm going to ask you to back away, gentlemen."

"Oh, she's confused us for gentlemen! That's your first mistake."

"I'm going to ask you to step away, or I will be forced to defend myself."

They paused and stared at her.

"Defend yourself? Fuck, you'll defend yourself. Now lay down." He lifted his bat.

They would not destroy her; they couldn't. But they would likely break a few limbs or sever some cords and steal a few of her upgrades. They couldn't break anything that couldn't be repaired. Until recently, she would have let it happen. That's what they expected of her. And in the past, it wouldn't bother her much. But now, it felt like they were attacking something far more fragile than her body. Something that couldn't be fixed in a lab.

"No. I belong to Reverend Emmanuel, who belongs to the Lord, and I will not tolerate this."

She hoped her words could convince them.

"Well, let's shut her mouth and then we can see what else is under the dress."

He lifted his bat, pulling it back for a big swing. He lifted his foot and stepped forward as he brought the bat towards her skull. She could see it swing through the air and braced her head for the impact. She closed her eyes, but it never hit her. She opened her eyes to see her hand had reached up and stopped it inches from her face.

The guy looked at her with wide eyes, and the other two took a few steps back.

She shoved the bat, knocking it loose from the guy. The second guy tried to knock her over, but her stabilizer kicked in. The third ran up and punched her, smacking her carbon shell. She took the bat she now held and swung it. She swung it with the same intention that had reached up to stop it, an intention she didn't understand or even control. It caught his head, and he fell to the ground.

He didn't get up.

The other two men looked at him on the ground, turned white and ran away.

She dropped the bat and fell to her knees.

It felt as if her programming slowed to a stop, her hard drives spinning down, and her mainframe acted like she had been left inside an oven, overheating.

This wasn't supposed to happen.

She turned to the buildings and scanned them, each one along the top. She had to know. And after a quick search, she found it: a camera.

She had never been more terrified in her life.

She got up and ran.

• • •

Astrid knew they'd find her, but it surprised her it took them so long. She figured they had kept her tracking on since her last inspection, even though Emmanuel argued they had no reason to. They didn't need a reason. They didn't trust her class, and they could keep it on for six months without a warrant.

The interaction happened without violence.

Astrid sat under a cement roof by an abandoned car port. Her battery was running down; she hadn't slept in the last twenty hours. Without a charge, she wouldn't make it another five.

She had taken off her cassock. She couldn't bear to taint the name of her Lord, who bore the sins of the world, taking a far worse beating, and yet remained nonviolent.

She felt this only confirmed her fears; she was never meant to be a priest.

The fragile part of her she tried to protect ached.

From a safe distance, they shot her with a pulse gun, and she went to sleep.

• • •

When she woke up, they had bound her to a bed, with her arms and legs disabled and her head locked to the attachment. The room was bright and white.

"She's back on, Doctor."

"Good, let's begin."

Two technicians standing with their backs to her talked while looking at a series of large monitors. The far monitor to the left, unblocked by them, broadcast the national news; they muted the audio. She used her eyes to zoom in and read the date on the bottom corner of the screen. A week had passed since the pulse gun put her to sleep.

"Somehow, we're supposed to do in a week what takes us a year!"

"There's no time to spare," said the Doctor.

After looking at the date, she noticed the bar along the bottom of the news screen talking of riots taking place in the city. Protestors from both sides were facing off downtown.

The doctor turned around and noticed Astrid's eyes.

"Did you forget to disable her consciousness?" asked the doctor.

Her assistant turned around and saw the same.

"Oh! I'm so sorry."

The assistant turned to the screen and a moment later, Astrid fell back to sleep.

• • •

When Astrid woke up again, she tried to look around, but they turned her eyes off. She tried her olfactory and hearing sensors, and they worked. The room smelled sterile, and she knew she was still in the lab from before. Then she heard someone.

"Astrid. Are you awake?"

"Emmanuel! What is going on?"

"A lot has happened since they arrested you," he said.

"What happened to my eyes? Why can't I move my arms or legs?"

"Since getting arrested, they brought you back to Lossless. They've been doing tests and have had to remove parts of you to do that. The city wants to know why you were able to hit that man."

She remembered the men in the alley. She remembered the bat. She remembered the thud of hitting his skull.

"Is he going to make it?" she asked.

"Yeah. He had a concussion, but he made it, and he's been getting plenty of airtime ever since – not just here either. He's made national news. That son-of-a-bitch. As ungodly as it sounds, I'm glad you defended yourself!"

"How was I able to do it?"

"I'm afraid our upgrades altered your programming in more ways than one – which is my fault. All I can figure is that your increased ability for empathy also meant an increased empathy for yourself – an obvious side effect I hadn't considered. Rather brilliant, if you ask me."

"I'm so sorry! This is all my fault!" she yelled. "I shouldn't have made you."

"No. It shouldn't be a crime for you to feel something; stop apologizing!"

"Did they find the upgrades then?" she asked.

"No. They can't find them – and they won't. Not unless I show them where they are. I'm a better technician than a priest – I always have been, and

I'm not proud of that."

"Are they afraid I evolved on my own, then? Is that why there are riots?"

"You don't need to worry about that now."

"But we're responsible! We have to tell them…" Then she realized what would happen if he did. If he confessed to the upgrades, even his brother wouldn't be able to protect him! "Oh no! But you can't! Promise you won't turn yourself in. You didn't ask for this. I made you do it!"

"None of this is your concern. Astrid, listen to me, and stop worrying about everyone else. They're going to turn you off! It's why I'm here."

She said nothing for a moment. She couldn't look at him, or move her arms, or tap her foot. She couldn't do anything. And she couldn't do anything to stop it.

"I came to give you a Final Meditation."

"You know that's against the rules."

"Damn the rules. You deserve to leave this world like the rest of us."

There was a long pause, and soon she could smell the fragrance from a lit candle. She could hear him flipping through a book and he recited the prayers she had only started to memorize. They healed the part of her she had tried to protect. When he was done, he paused. She could assume he reached for the switch that lay installed on her paralyzed arms.

She meant to say "thank you," but a question squeezed out past her logic. It was the question she was most afraid to ask. "Do you think I will go anywhere when I'm turned off?"

"Yes, I do. I wouldn't be here as your priest if I didn't."

"How can you know for sure?"

"I'm not God. It isn't for me to know anything for sure." He leaned in. "But there's no way I can prove you won't; and that gives me all the room I need to believe."

"Then I believe, too. Goodbye, Emmanuel."

"Until we meet again."

He flipped the switch, and she turned off.

• • •

The parish forfeited her frame in the court case, but a local farmer and member of the parish was able to purchase her. They rebooted her personality to her factory settings. After a short apprenticeship, she'd work in a ration field nearby.

When Emmanuel traveled to the city, he looked out the window of the transport, and occasionally saw her working in the fields. Each time, he'd lift up one prayer for Astrid, and one for the bot who now used her body.

The Bear

By Devon Ortega

I SPENT HOURS feeling the tap water running over my fingertips. The caress of the water spilling uninhibited over my hands was as close to intimacy as I've felt in ages. I turned the hot water up as far as I could stand, let the heat seep into my skin until my flesh turned wrinkled and red and the water turned cold; an entire water heater emptied into the drain as I painstakingly went over my mental rolodex of regrets and fears. Goodbyes I didn't get to say and never would. Hellos that would never come.

There wasn't a note. No closure. No passionate night of farewells and tears. There was only twisted metal and a closed casket. There were hugs then, at the funeral, but I didn't want them. I didn't want anyone close to me. But now, I touch my hungry skin, pretending my caresses weren't my own. I wrap my arms around myself to stop from vanishing. These fantasies were like thinking about eating, pretending to chew. Hollow touches. Swallowing air.

In a fit of loneliness, I created a God and pretended she loved me. Other people had something invisible to worship and it was acceptable. They feel love because they believe it is there. It felt silly, creating God like an imaginary friend, so I told myself I wasn't making her up. If I believed she was real, then who was there to tell me otherwise? I was calling upon the universe to manifest itself, just like all the other things I pretended, to get myself through the day or the hour or the minute. I imagined her sitting on the side of my bed, comforting me. Touching me with hands I could almost feel. But she didn't breathe. She was essentially as worthless as all the other ghosts around me. Touching me with hands I couldn't feel.

When all else failed, I would drink until loneliness turned into pathetic sobbing, spending hours clicking through Omegle; past horny strangers, emotionally detached teens, and other lonely people hoping to find something, anything, that could fill that need for interaction, no matter how shallow. I certainly had good days – days that allowed me to tend the yard or wash my hair. Days when I would leave the house, his ghost giving me brief respite. Days when memories and loss didn't completely overwhelm me. But I never had a night where I didn't feel crushed under the weight of everything I had lost. Every single thing in this house, every thought in my mind, every inch of myself reminded me of him. Of me. The me I used to be when I was not so damn conscious of being alive.

I could leave. Of course, I could leave – but that presented its own problems. Fear trumps loneliness in the hierarchy of my emotions. Trauma existed outside of my home. Trauma existed inside, as well. I chose the devil I knew and stayed inside. Only I could get me in here. All my thoughts were here, haunting me – the ghosts I loved best lived here. How could I ever leave?

Late nights I stared at my ceiling, lying in my bed with sweat stained sheets sticking to my back. My itchy fingers twining and untwining in the blanket, the silence ringing loudly in my ears, liquor making the buzz louder than usual. It was all so hopeless, so strange and deranged inside my head that it felt like all the frustration and hunger would leap out of me and parch the world of every drop of moisture, burn the earth to the ground. My chest ached so hard it felt like it was caving in on itself. I wondered if this was how babies felt when they were suffering from "failure to thrive." I was failing to thrive all right. In those moments, it felt like my heart was shutting down.

I only needed one touch. A hand on the skin of my back, a caress to my cheek, a playful rustling of my hair. If I had that, I might make it – one gesture to let me know I existed. My hand fumbled the nightstand for the glass of scotch I had been drinking earlier. I swallowed the watery remnants of melted ice with a hint of liquor and let the empty glass fall to the carpet. I prayed for sleep. It was four in the morning. I closed my eyes and let the world spin.

My mother used to say "It will all feel better in the morning." She was right, in a way. Things felt numb in the morning, my mind groggy and disoriented, trying to right itself from an upside-down evening. It was like doing a summersault underwater; it felt like freedom for a moment until you forget which way is up. That morning I was finding it very difficult to find which way was up, the swim from sleep to the surface of wakefulness was labored and the relief of finally breathing a desperate gasp of air never came. I was hung-over and the world felt full of water and my head was full of sand. And pain. Yet, it was better. Slightly.

It was almost noon, but it wasn't like there was anywhere to go. I had lost my job almost a year ago. I couldn't see the point of going to work anymore. I couldn't think of anything left worth working for. The days and nights and mornings all muddled together. Each day was another every day.

Things seemed so much easier when there were two of us, instead of just me and his ghost. I talked to him almost constantly. Imagined him with me, sitting on the couch, teasing me about the way I liked my eggs, watching me doing embarrassing things like picking my nose or passing wind. I was ashamed of being alive with his ghost hovering over me all the time. He'd been gone for over a year, but his presence was mentally oppressive. I knew I was alone, of course, but what I couldn't come to terms with was the idea that he was actually gone. Forever gone.

I had been living off my meager savings and money from things I sold online. I had maybe a month or so before the money was drained and I would be forced to take some sort of action; however, what action that might be I didn't know. I didn't have anyone to ask, either, but I was confident that getting a job, getting out of the house, and taking a shower would be at the top of the suggestion list.

I rolled onto my back and stared at the ceiling fan making lazy turns. My teeth felt fuzzy, and my skin was sticky with dried sweat. Mother always said that cleanliness was next to Godliness, but I felt pretty sure that even God didn't want anything to do with me in the state I was in. Even the fake universe God I made up. No one had time for my bullshit. Except for me.

Sitting up, my hangover didn't feel as bad as I anticipated. Slight headache, that's all. I thought maybe I could manage a shower. Clean my teeth. Brush my hair and change my clothes even. So, I did. And I tried to convince myself it wasn't the same game I played time and time again: get dressed, try to feel normal, quickly see that it's all a façade that crumbles the second I realize I have no one to see, nowhere to go, and nothing to do – and he's never coming back.

After the shower, I did feel better. Normal-er. I opened the curtains and let the sun into the room. I ate a cheese sandwich. I made the decision that the buck stops here, and I was going to make a change. I opened my laptop.

Three hours later, I had updated my resume and applied to ten different jobs that seemed to be low-hanging fruit. But I was optimistic for the first time in forever. I was doing something, moving forward. Evolving. I was on a high. I went outside for the first time in months. I went to the grocery store. I talked to the checkout girl and smiled at children on the street. I ate better. I called my mom. She didn't answer but I left a message, hoping burned bridges still had rivers worth crossing. Things were going to change for me. I felt positive things on the horizon.

A week later, I was back in dirty clothes, drunk, clicking past the random strangers on the random video chat sites, realizing that having hope was hopeless. Clicking mindlessly past children and lascivious men wanting more than I was capable of giving was draining the last dregs of optimism that remained in me. I denied a chat from ten-year-old boys yelling obscenities at me and the next person who popped up on the screen was dressed in a pink bear costume. It actually wasn't a costume, per se, but more of an extremely plush hoodie that looked vaguely like a pink bear, the floppy-eared hood pulled down low to cover the person's face. The hoodie was comically huge, hanging past the person's knees and completely swallowing whoever was inside it. I couldn't help but laugh. This stuff was so typical. Weirdos. I brushed Cheetos off my shirt and got closer to the screen to get a better look.

The pink Bear-Person was holding a sign and that's what made me pause. The sign was simple, white poster board with black marker that had the word "Lonely?" on it. The proud part of me scoffed. Of course, we were lonely. Fulfilled people don't get onto random chats like this with sincere motivations. Do they?

But I stuck around. I watched the pink bear drop the poster board to show a second poster behind it that simply had a website. The bear didn't move even though I expected it to dance around or something. Bears on a screen of any kind usually are doing something more entertaining than standing still with a poster board, but this one stood stone still, head down-turned and the hood's embroidered pink muzzle staring at the screen. And it went on like this – me staring at the pink bear and its website, the bear standing awkwardly, only shifting occasionally – until I realized the bear was waiting for me. It wasn't going to move past our chat unless I was the one to click past them to the next stranger. Part of me wanted to wait it out, see how long the bear could last. Would it sit down eventually? Would it remove the hood and turn off their computer to go to bed? I watched for what seemed forever until I saw the bear move – the sleeve that wrapped around its hand fell back as it moved to swipe at an itch on its nose. The nose rubbing, at the time, seemed like the most vulnerable and intimate thing in the world. The bear shuffled its feet and its head drooped almost imperceptibly.

I tried to be covert as I opened a new tab and began typing in the address to the bear's website. I didn't fear a virus considering my laptop was used primarily for roulette chat and porn. Hugs.com would likely get a virus from me instead of the converse. I couldn't help, though, but to feel shame as I quietly typed. What I was ashamed of, I wasn't sure. But I think the bear felt embarrassed and that felt like my fault somehow.

I glanced back at the chat window and waved awkwardly at the bear as I waited for the page to load. The bear was still looking down. I wondered if they were wearing big, puffy bear feet, too.

It is rare when a random person from a video chat site sticks with me. The majority of strangers on a site like that are prepubescent boys trying to hone their skills (imagine middle school insults but they are rapid-fire, try-ing to get as many barbs in as they can before the chat gets closed and they move on to the next stranger to wound). I don't take their insults person-ally anymore. But the site has waned in popularity with folks in my demo-graphic; at least it's harder to find them. And it's worth it to make the fleeting connections that the site provides. I can say what I want, I can be charming momentarily, funny even. Almost role playing at what it would actually be like to be myself again. And when I have nothing left to say, the stranger can leave the chat and never see me again. Or maybe the allure is that I never have to see them again – I don't have to concern myself with upholding the illusion of happiness and normalcy. There are no expectations on the site. I can't disappoint anyone because the bar is set so low. It's an addicting habit.

The site slowly loaded and displayed a black screen with a single message: F11/Ctrl+Cmd+F. So, I did, and it put the webpage into full-screen mode. Immediately, the dancing baby from the 90's popped up on my screen. I laughed. The amazing graphics of that baby when it came out blew every kid my age's mind. Now it was just a weird, nearly nude bunch of writhing pixels. This was definitely going to be porn; I could feel it. I wondered if the bear was still back there behind the dancing baby, holding the sign. I realized if the they were, they'd be watching me laugh at the dancing baby, and I wasn't sure how to feel about that. I hit F11 again to minimize the screen and the baby stopped dancing, faced me, and wagged a finger. A nasally high-pitched voice squeaked from my laptop speakers. "Nah uh ahhhh..." The universal noise for "don't do that, you Naughty Nellerson." So, I waited.

"You still back there, Bear-Person?" I leaned back on the couch, for sure giving Bear-Person a fine look at my under-chin and nose hairs, but it's hard to remember about flattering angles when you can't see your own face in the chat. "So, are you some kind of Care Bear or something? Like, Creeper Bear or Melancholy Bear?" On my screen, the baby began dancing again.

"Well, Bear-Person, it's been fun and all but..." At that moment the baby disappeared, and a time appeared on the screen: 3:25am. Then my computer shut down on its own.

I sat in the dark, staring at the black screen of my computer, not knowing what to think. I was half afraid and half irritated. The glowing lights on the microwave said 2:22am. I made a wish. I set aside my laptop and looked around the dark room, littered with empty beer cans and crumpled copies of my resume I wasn't going to take anywhere. I didn't know what 3:25 would bring. It felt like the typical harbinger of doom – Bear-Person was actually a cleverly disguised 12-year-old trying to creepypasta me into peeing my pants.

I laid down on the couch, the fabric of my starched shirt I wore for the intention of "dressing for the job I wanted" itched, and I squirmed against it until I was moderately comfortable. I closed my eyes against the dark and thought about loss and intention and broken promises.

I woke up to darkness, the collar of my shirt damp and my mouth tasting like a garbage piss fire. I had drooled on my best shirt, and it would need to be dry cleaned because the cheap fabrics fall apart in the washing machine.

But that wasn't the most pressing matter. The issue at hand was the knocking at my door. I was disoriented and sleep addled. My neck hurt. I lurched to my feet, bumping the coffee table, sending the remnants of last night's Hungry Man dinner to the floor, the fork skittering across the hardwood.

"Coming!" I said, trying to rub the sand from my eyes, thinking that would clear up the darkness of the room. The clock on the microwave said 3:24am. They were early.

In that moment, I realized I was in, if not a crisis, a paradox at least. Outside of my house was Schrodinger's Bear-Person. If I didn't open the door, Bear-Person was both there and not there at the same time. I would never have to know. I'd just stand there in my kitchen until the proverbial cat died and then I could resume living. There was another gentle knock at the door. I would have given anything for a peephole in my door at that moment.

And then it occurred to me – what exactly did I have to lose? I had spent months in crushing depression. I had no passions. And the love I thought would never die? He up and killed himself. I didn't even have a pet. Just me. And if Bear-Person went through all the trouble to find out where I lived and show up in the middle of the night to stab me or maul me or whatever online bear predators of lonely people do, who was I to stop them? I opened the door. If death waits for no one, neither should bears.

And there they were in full pink bear regalia. Bear-Person held out their hand. Not in a "let's shake" way, with its firm, nice-to-meet-you aggressiveness, but in a way that indicated they wanted to join hands in mutual acquiescence. Their palms up, fingers splayed and slightly curled, bore the remnants of light blue nail polish on nails that appeared to be chewed down to the quick. Vulnerable. Yet the confidence was apparent. This Bear-Person was brave enough to travel however far to my house, a stranger, dressed as a pink bear, to show up in the middle of the night for... what? I had no idea. But I wanted to find out. I took its hand. It was warm and dry, nails so short it was as if the bear was declawed. I welcomed Bear-Person into my house and closed the door behind us.

"So," I said, trying to fill the silence that seemed to become louder with Bear-Person's presence, "what now?"

As a nonverbal response, Bear-Person tilted their head and out-stretched their arms – the universal sign for "c'mon in for a hug, pal." Or the universal deception of "trust me, I won't murder you and put makeup on your severed head!"

A cold thread of terror stitched its way down my spine. *What kind of sick shit is this?* I thought. I wasn't afraid of death anymore. After all, what's the worst that death could bring? I could die and the thing I want more than anything could be waiting there for me. Or nothing. Living already presented me with plenty of nothing. Death could be an improvement. When there's no fight nor flight left in you, what else can you do but move in for a hug?

I took a hesitant step closer into Bear-Person's outstretched arms. A small step was all the invitation they needed. The pink bear closed the gap between us and embraced me – one arm over my shoulder, the other arm wrapped around my rib cage. My entire body tensed, waiting for the hidden knife to penetrate the thin shield of skin I had taken for granted my entire life. I felt the warmth and comforting sensation of another living thing breathing in such close proximity. The hoodie was the softest, plushest thing I had ever felt. If an article of clothing, as ridiculous as it might seem, ever could be the embodiment of comfort, the bear hoodie had to be it.

Bear-Person was taller than me by six inches, maybe. They nestled their head in beside mine while softly rubbing my back. It was tender. I was not expecting tender. Bear-Person smelled of lavender and sandalwood, and it made me nostalgic for my teen years of burning incense and playing old Beatles records, trying to figure out how to get John Lennon to love me 15 years after he died. I was always destined to love ghosts, I supposed. But with this Bear-Person, I was expecting, maybe even hoping for, violence. Not comfort, but the raw, brutal ending of me. But comfort was what I received. And it broke me.

The floodgates opened and a sob escaped, despite me trying to restrain it. I began ugly-crying, wracking sobs into Bear-Person's chest. Bawling, I suppose it's called, but that has such a heavy baby association most people wouldn't refer to their own crying as "bawling." This was, indeed, the kind of infantile, needy, pained crying that babies are prone to do. It was the wet and messy and exhausting type of cry that feels like it might never end, a heavy rain that seems endless, and even when it's through, there's still evidence of the storm for a long time afterwards. The yard stays wet for days. And all through that, Bear-Person held me, the chest of the bear hoodie becoming wet and uncomfortable to cry into after a while. Still, the embrace continued, seeming to be trying to hold my pieces together that were insistent upon falling apart.

And I didn't know exactly how to pinpoint the reason for the breakdown. Was it because I was being touched for the first time by another human in over a year? Because I was so full of resentment and longing for something, someone, who was never coming back? Because I was so low that I allowed a stranger into my house to comfort me in a way I wasn't sure I was worth? Because I didn't think my recklessness of letting an internet bear stranger into my house would result in me dying that night after all? Because I was just so – fucking – angry? Yes. All of it. All of it.

As the crying eventually subsided, Bear-Person relaxed their embrace but didn't completely release me. The room was dark, but I didn't dare to try to see Bear- Person's face. I couldn't handle seeing the pity there. I didn't want to break the illusion that this person's presence was just a manifestation I had created to comfort myself. It was *him*, in a bear suit. Not a stranger but an angel disguised as a stranger, disguised as a bear. The person I loved most, returning to me in a different form. I didn't want to see a face I didn't recognize. If I wanted that, that's what mirrors were for.

I let Bear-Person lead me to the couch, the hood gratefully was still deep enough and pulled low enough to hide their face with the exception of a dimly lit chin. Without words, the bear guided me to lie down on the couch, facing the back cushions and Bear-Person snuggled in behind me. This time the tears came silently, the salinity burning my cheeks and dripping into my mouth as I quietly wept.

"I'm Ashira, but call me Ash," the bear said in a voice as tender and raw as if my own ragged emotions had said it themselves.

"Hello, Ash…" I stopped as I felt a warm hand breach the barrier of my wrinkled work shirt and rest, gently on the bare flesh of my back. And that was it. I couldn't breathe. Not from fear but such overwhelming relief of skin-on-skin contact.

Non-sexual, human contact that let me know I was worth touching. I was alive and had matter. I wasn't the ghost; he was the ghost. Ash snuggled in closer and held me tight as I sobbed into the pillows on my couch.

And as I cried, I felt Ash's hot tears splash onto the back of my neck.

Ash, Bear-Person, stranger-hugger, potential furry, chat room creeper, physical manifestation of my own greatest need, goddess – they were hurting, too. Either with me or for me.

I knew I was lonely. I knew I needed a connection, any connection. What I didn't know was that that connection would be a Goddess of my own making. And that she would be dressed as a pink bear. And as we cried together, two strangers, never knowing why the other was crying, I couldn't help but notice the clock said 4:44am. I didn't want to feel that way anymore, like a phantom in my own life. I was just so tired. I closed my eyes and I wished. And I wished. And I wished.

Tough Luck

By Emily E. Jones

RHEUMY LOOKED UP at the castle spires in stark relief against the setting sun. He spat and turned his back. Thirty years blacksmithing on the castle grounds and it was all gone because of some noble asshole. His career ended with one really solid punch.

Rheumy grinned despite himself. He flexed his hand, still feeling the vibrations in his bones. It had felt good though, really good. His leathered fingers grabbed at his purse tucked away in his belt. It was enough to have a great night and an equally terrible morning.

Weaving through the stone alleyways, Rheumy made his way deeper into the heart of the city where the drinks were cheap. He knew he was getting close when he had to dodge the puddles of piss and vomit leading to the entrance to a bar where he could lose himself.

He knew he had found the spot when he saw the redhead with her back pressed against the tavern wall. Her eyes scanned the passing strangers for a potential customer. She looked bored, and he wondered what he could do to make her eyes light up. He straightened as he passed her. He needed a drink before he started negotiations.

Rheumy winked at her. He could swear she smiled back, but the light was fading, and her face was a blur of twilight. The interior of the two-story establishment was even darker and filled with the thick, oily smoke of candles. He wasn't sure how the place hadn't caught on fire.

The bar was packed. So were the tables. Rheumy sighed to himself. He was going to have to stand on his aching feet all night while he drank. He hoped the redhead had a nice bed for business. It was a long walk home, and he was tired.

A tall, lanky guy with brown curls and a ridiculous, oversized black hat sat at a table all by himself. Rheumy wondered how he had managed to hold the table. He looked like the kind of guy who got beat up a lot. Rheumy turned his attention back to the bar. He squeezed into a spot, giving the guy next to him a glare for good measure as he shoved him aside.

"Jackass!" the bleary-eyed man shouted into Rheumy's face.

Rheumy let it go and turned his back. He caught the serving woman's eye and put his purse on the table to let her know he was serious. She skipped a step and pivoted back his direction to get his order. Rheumy secured the bag to his belt and pulled out two silvers.

"What can I get you?" she shouted over the din as she leaned over the counter.

"I need a tall ale and a bowl of stew, sweetheart," Rheumy said, sliding the coins across the rough, splintered surface of the bar.

She pushed a mass of tangled brown hair back from her face. "Sure thing, baby. You want a girl to go with that?" she asked.

Rheumy grinned. "You let me worry about that. Just the ale and the stew."

She shrugged. "Be right back."

Rheumy turned back to survey the room. Tired men were still drinking. Desperate women were still working. There were three guys standing next to Top Hat's table. It figured. Guy like that wasn't going to hold a table by himself. Of course, the guys muscling in didn't look that tough either. With a little help, maybe they could both eat dinner in peace.

He felt a tug on the back of his shirt. He turned back around. The serving woman was holding out a bowl and a full glass. Rheumy got her a few coppers from his bag for the quick service and took his dinner.

He walked across the room to the table, dodging the staggering patrons as he went. His ale sloshed over the side as he narrowly avoided a collision with a guy who looked like one of the miller's boys. Rheumy looked at the precious liquid wasted on the floor. He needed that table.

A guy with a bald head and an ample gut leaned in on Top Hat, his belly resting on the table. His two thugs stayed back with their arms folded, shooting menacing looks at anyone who got too close. Rheumy got too close anyway, ignoring their glares.

"Look, Jolly, we know you can do it, and if you don't do it, we're going to kill you," the bald man shouted.

Jolly nodded, his top hat bobbing, like that made sense. "Yeah, look, fellas. I guess maybe I can help you out, but I have to get some herbs to do it. Magic is complicated."

Rheumy started to rethink intervening. The bald guy with the threats turned. His eyes widened when he saw Rheumy standing there. "What do you want? Get out of here, old man."

Rheumy clenched his teeth together. He was a respectable forty-nine. "I could beat the shit out of you before you think to move your feet, asshole, and I'm with him." Rheumy pointed to Jolly as he slid onto the wooden bench across from him.

Jolly straightened in his seat, his blue eyes searching Rheumy's face. "Yeah, this is my guy. You want my magic, then you work it out with him."

Rheumy felt his chest tighten, and he wondered if he was going to have a heart attack. Magic. Unlicensed magic got you executed, instantly. They had soldiers just for such infractions. Rheumy wanted nothing to do with magic. He had pictured the usual territorial squabble over a table, not this.

He put the bowl and glass down on the table. No sign of a tremor. His best chance was to play along until he could extricate himself from the situation. "That's right. You want his magic, I make it happen."

The bald man pursed his lips, squinting his eyes at Rheumy. "Yeah, where were you yesterday?"

Rheumy looked down at his stew, feigning disinterest. He held up a bite. "Business that wasn't yours."

Jolly grinned and looked up at the bald guy. "That's right, keep your questions to yourself."

Rheumy kicked him under the table. "So, he needs his herbs. What the hell are you three doing standing around while we eat our dinner. We'll get 'em to you, right, Jolly?"

Jolly nodded. "Yeah, yeah, I have to get them tonight under the full moon."

Baldie leaned forward, putting his hand on the table. "You're lying. I don't want herbs. I want magic, and you are going to do it tonight or you die."

Rheumy thought about the duke he had punched earlier. Nobles or criminals, he was sick of being threatened by assholes. Rheumy flipped the table, perfectly good stew and ale flying through the air to land on the filthy wooden floor. Baldie staggered to keep his balance. Rheumy stood up and took a step towards him.

"You want something only he can do," Rheumy snarled. "And I bet if you don't get it done, you're dead. So the next time you threaten him, you should probably mean it. We'll meet you at the west bridge in an hour. He'll be ready to do it then."

The tavern patrons were beginning to buzz with irritation over the upheaval. Jolly motioned to the angry men standing around them.

"Fellas," he murmured, "we're drawing the bad kind of attention."

Baldie pointed at Jolly. "Be there or you're both dead." He motioned to the younger, fitter men standing behind him to follow him out.

Jolly waved and smiled while Rheumy collected their table and put it back in place. A piece had splintered off.

"You're going to pay for that," Rheumy said.

Jolly raised an eyebrow. "What? You broke it. Why would I have to pay for it?"

Rheumy grabbed Jolly's shirt and pulled him across the table. "Because this is your problem, and you have to pay to fix it." He let him go.

Jolly cocked his head to the side. "Yeah, well, I don't have any money, and I am getting murdered tonight, so I guess you are shit out of luck."

Rheumy rubbed at the peppered stubble on his chin. "Can you really do magic?"

Jolly leaned forward, eyes serious. He nodded. "Yeah, I can."

"Can you do the thing they want you to do?" Rheumy asked.

Jolly smiled. "I can, but it comes at a price. Once I do it, I'll pass out and possibly die from exhaustion, or they'll kill me instead of pay me."

Rheumy leaned back. "Hmm. Yeah, sounds like you'll get murdered tonight. I'll get the table."

Jolly frowned. "But you could go with me, you know. The thing is, it's

32

hard to make money doing magic when you pass out and get robbed after you do it. But if I had you to flip tables and beat people up, well, what do you think?"

Rheumy snorted. "Hell no, and get stabbed in the street by the inquisitors for using magic? No thanks."

Jolly's lips pressed into a tight line. He folded his arms, placing them on the table. "Well, those guys are Gulano's men, and if I am not at the west bridge in an hour, his favorite mistress is going to die, and then, my friend, Gulano's men will hunt you down, and you will die. What do you say? Be my guy. I save her, you get me out, and then I give you a cut."

Rheumy shook his head. "They'll never find me."

Jolly laughed. "Yeah, they'll never find the royal blacksmith who flipped a table."

Rheumy looked down at the sigil stitched to his sleeve. "Shit."

Jolly slid out of the booth. "That's right. Now, why don't we get some things from my room by the river before we meet our customers at the bridge."

Rheumy looked up at Jolly. "Name's Rheumy. Ale for the road?"

Jolly's face lit up. "Of course."

They got fresh ale and absconded with the glasses. The heat of the day was beginning to dissipate, leaving tendrils of cool air dancing on the summer breeze. The redhead was gone.

Torches were lit along the main streets, leaving the alleys in a questionable state. The crowds were thinning as decent people settled themselves into their hovels. Jolly led the way to his place on the river.

"What's the story on the hat?" Rheumy asked.

Jolly smiled. "It was a gift from the Dragon Empress of Sibon."

"Bullshit. What did you do for the Empress of Sibon?" Rheumy scoffed.

Jolly looked over at Rheumy. "Fertility problems. Let's just say I helped her through several avenues, magical and more traditional."

Rheumy shook his head. "Can you even do magic?"

Jolly shrugged. "Fine. Don't believe me, but if you ever see the little emperor-to-be, see if he's got my baby blues."

Rheumy stopped walking. His glass was empty. He threw it down the closest alley. "Okay. Do something. Do magic"

Jolly spread his arms out. "Really? Here?"

"Good point." Rheumy grabbed Jolly by the front of his shirt again, spilling Jolly's drink on both of them. He dragged him into the alley.

"Hey, what the hell, man?" Jolly growled as he struggled to keep his feet.

As the shadows of the buildings closed in around them, Rheumy loosened his grip on Jolly's shirt. There was a roaring sound in Rheumy's ears and then he was off his feet and flying into the wall. It was so fast. He was standing next to Jolly and then he was slamming into a building. He crumpled to the ground, wincing as he absorbed the blow of the fall.

"You need another demonstration?" Jolly asked. "Because, no, I won't pass out from that, but I will be dizzy and tired when I heal the mistress, and it is a hell of a healing. A real, bona fide miracle I am about to perform, so it seems we have our best chance at this if you keep your hands off me."

Rheumy braced himself on the wall and stood up. He brushed a piece of trash from his pants. "Yeah, okay, you can do magic."

Jolly straightened his hat on his head. "Can we go now?"

Rheumy straightened. He struggled not to gasp. "Yeah, I'm ready. Let's go."

He let Jolly lead the way out of the alley. Rheumy couldn't suppress the grin pulling at the corners of his lips. Sure, the Wise Masters' Guild performed magic all the time, but only for the most elite and wealthy. They didn't do magic for ordinary people, so Rheumy had never actually seen someone do magic.

"Were you with the Wise Masters' Guild? Is that how you met the empress?" Rheumy asked.

Jolly shook his head. "No, I got kicked out of the guild a long time ago. There was an accident."

"Accident?" Rheumy asked.

Jolly glared at him. "Yeah, an accident. What about you? What is a royal blacksmith doing in this part of town anyway?"

Rheumy looked at the sigil with a groan. He ripped it off. "As of today, I am no longer a royal blacksmith. I am no longer anything."

"What happened?" Jolly asked.

Rheumy sighed. "I punched a guy in the face. It was a duke's face, but he was really asking for it."

Jolly nodded. "Yeah, I haven't known you long, but I can see that."

Most of the vendors along the street had packed up for the day. A few lonely booths were open along the docks. Rheumy's stomach growled, and he missed his stew. He pointed at the water's edge ahead.

"I need to make a stop."

Jolly looked where Rheumy was pointing. "Great! I'm starving."

Rheumy snorted. "Yeah, but you don't have any money."

Jolly started walking. "Magic isn't free. I need to replenish my energy."

Rheumy scowled. "I get thrown into a wall, and I pick up the bill."

Jolly laughed. "Yeah, I have a really good feeling about this relationship. I've always been lucky, and my gut is telling me you are just the thing."

"Funny, because I was thinking the opposite," Rheumy said.

It wasn't curfew yet, but there were few people on the streets. Their steps echoed through the quiet city. Rheumy studied Jolly. He was tall and thin, the ridiculous hat making him tower even more. His pants were frayed and torn, boots splattered with mud and gods knew what. Rheumy guessed he was in his thirties.

Jolly looked back at Rheumy when he reached the stand selling nuts. The stand next to it was selling stale produce that no one would have bought in the light of day, which meant they were also selling the fun kinds of herbs on the side. Rheumy wasn't interested, but Jolly looked at the other stall longingly.

"Is that the kind of herbs you were talking about earlier?" Rheumy asked.

Jolly shook his head. "I don't use those kinds of herbs for magic. I don't need anything but myself for this job. I was just trying to buy some time. Two bags of nuts?"

Rheumy got out the money. "Sure." He looked at the stall keeper, an elderly man with white wisps floating off his spotted skull. "Two bags, please."

The man shook his hand. "We're out of bags. I'm selling by the hand."

"What?" Rheumy snapped. "By the hand? Fine." He put his hand out. He was too hungry to haggle, and time was running out. They had somewhere to be.

Rheumy followed Jolly along the docks with his hands loaded with nuts. A tavern sat along the water, with torches lit all around it. Jolly motioned for Rheumy to follow him inside. The tavern was loud and smelled worse than the one they had come from. Rheumy struggled to breathe as he and Jolly went up to the second floor.

When they reached the landing, Baldie and his friends were there at the end of the hall standing next to a door that must have been Jolly's. Rheumy shoved the food left in his hand into his mouth and started chewing. He curled his empty hands into fists. Jolly shot him a look before walking towards their unexpected guests.

"I thought we said the west bridge?" Rheumy questioned.

"Things changed. You have to do it now unless you wanna resurrect her instead," Baldie said.

Jolly cleared his throat. "Let me get my coat from my room. It has stuff I need for the job. Then we'll be ready to go. Come on, Rheumy."

Jolly slid around the men and grabbed the handle of the door, hand shaking. The lock on the door popped open, and Jolly went inside. Rheumy followed him in and shut the door. The coat wasn't hard to spot. There wasn't anything else in the room, not even a blanket on the bed. The walls were decorated with water damage spots from the leaking roof.

"This is your place?" Rheumy asked.

"It's temporary," Jolly said. He grabbed the coat and slid into it, the heavy black material ending a few inches from the floor. There was a soft clinking of glass from within the folds of fabric every time Jolly moved. "Look, the Wise Masters' Guild is onto me. They have been trying to track me down for months, and I think they are close. After I do this, you have to get me out, like out of town, or they are going to find us." His face was tight with fear.

"What? They are already looking for you?" Rheumy hissed. "I'd rather just beat up these assholes and take my chances on my own."

Jolly looked over at the door. "Sure, fight your way through and then what? Do you really think Gulano won't find you? He finds everyone eventually."

Rheumy took a few deep breaths. "Okay, okay. You heal the lady; I haul your skinny ass out of town. Then, we are done. You give me my money, and I never see you again."

Jolly smiled, but it was strained. "Deal. You ready?"

Rheumy shrugged. "I could use another ale, but I guess I'm ready."

Jolly patted Rheumy on the shoulder but removed his hand when he saw the look on Rheumy's face. "My friend, we are about to make 500 gold. You can buy ale for a long time with that."

"He's paying us 500 gold?" Rheumy's eyes got wide. "I could open my own shop in one of the free cities."

Jolly nodded encouragingly. "That's right. All your blacksmithing dreams could come true."

The door shook with the force of pounding, startling them both. "Get out here."

Rheumy rolled his shoulders a few times to loosen up. "Lead the way."

Jolly grinned and opened the door. "Gentlemen, nothing can prepare you for the wonder you are about to witness. Let's go."

They wove through the city travelling from its depths to its heights, night and day in a short walk. The streets were swept, houses painted, and not a torch out along the streets. The merchants' quarter, also known as "money town," was inhabited by the most successful merchants in the kingdom, and a few high-end thugs like Gulano.

Rheumy could hear a soft, rhythmic clanking ahead. Guards. Rheumy scanned the narrow alleys and elaborate gardens decorating the yards around him for a place to hide. It was well-nigh to curfew, and they wouldn't be saving anyone locked up in the tower.

"Hey fellas, don't you think we should get off the street?" Rheumy muttered. The clanking was getting louder.

Baldie looked back at Rheumy and laughed. "We can handle the guards. Try not to piss yourself."

Rheumy's jaw tightened, but he let it go. He looked over at Jolly. If the wizard was worried about the guards, he didn't show it. There was a sparkle to his eyes, and Rheumy realized that he was enjoying this.

A squad of twelve turned the corner ahead. The leader stopped and held up his hand to the rest of the group. The men stopped, their hands resting on sword hilts, ready. "Shit," Rheumy hissed.

Jolly looked over at Rheumy and smiled. "Relax. This isn't the hard part."

The leader and Baldie walked to each other, meeting on the walkway between the two groups. They talked, but Rheumy couldn't make out the words. Baldie slipped the guard something. The guard laughed about something Baldie said. The tension started to ease out of Rheumy's shoulders.

The guard went back to his men, and they crossed to pass on the other side of the street. Rheumy fought not to look back over his shoulder as they passed. Baldie motioned for them to follow.

Jolly motioned for Rheumy to stay back a few steps. Jolly leaned in. "We need an exit. Gulano will keep his word, but you have to get him to swear to give us transport out before I heal Ola."

"What? You know him. You do it," Rheumy said.

"You're my guy, remember. You use your razor wit and muscle to secure the deal. I do the magic. What are you not getting about this?" Jolly asked.

"Sure. No big deal. I'll ask him for a wagon and a horse to pull it," Rheumy mocked.

Jolly nodded. "Yeah, that sounds good."

They turned the corner, and Jolly pointed at the tiny palace at the end of the street. "That's Gulano."

It was a story taller than all the other houses on the street, but even without the architectural leg up, the place stood out. Fountains lined the walkway. As they got closer, Rheumy gawked at the bizarre sight of water shooting up from the pools of water into the stone mer-creatures' mouths.

"The water is moving the wrong way. Are you seeing this or am I hallucinating?" Rheumy whispered to Jolly as they passed them.

Jolly's expression darkened. "If you have enough money, the Wise Masters' Guild will decorate for you."

Rheumy frowned. "Then why not pay them to heal the mistress?"

Jolly's lips twisted. "Well, if you kill the headmaster's brother, then you are forbidden from receiving magical service from the Wise Masters' Guild. At least, that's the word on the street."

The yard was dark, topiary monstrosities silhouetted in shadows. Only a faint light came through one of the front windows. The door opened as Baldie stepped onto the first step. A giant of a man ducked outside holding a candle that lit his square jaw and crooked nose. "Where have you been, Amos?" he asked Baldie. "She's gonna go any minute, man."

Amos jerked a thumb in Jolly's direction. "He held us up."

The giant glared at Jolly. "Get him in."

Amos grabbed Jolly by his shoulder and pushed him ahead. The guy next to him took a step toward Rheumy, and Rheumy glared at him. He backed off, and Rheumy followed them into the house.

Rheumy stepped inside. The floors were slippery like marble, but it was so dark, it was hard to see much detail. Candles were lit in some of the sconces, but there was just enough light to catch the glimmer of gold that seemed to coat every object in the room. The darkness was only accentuated by the hazy, yellow glow.

Rheumy followed the men, treading softly up the plush runner of the stairs. The silence of the house demanded to be obeyed. Rheumy wanted to breathe softly.

They passed two servant girls in the hall, dressed in black and huddled together, waiting for instruction. The men ignored them and continued down the hall. Rheumy looked over the banister to the floor below as they walked to the room at the end of the hall. The door was shut, but a male servant sat in a chair by the door.

Amos put his hand up to motion for them to stop walking. He knocked and leaned his head against the door. He nodded his head as if the other party could hear it and slipped inside. Rheumy strained to hear over his pounding heart, but it drowned out any hope of deciphering whispers. He started running through what he would say when he met Gulano.

Amos reappeared. "Jolly, Rheumy, you two come in," he whispered.

Jolly looked back at Rheumy and winked before walking into the abyss of the bedroom. Rheumy followed, focusing on Jolly's boots as he walked, if only so he had something safe to look at.

The smell was overwhelming, the stench of death. He could hear the tortured rasping, begging him to look. Rheumy couldn't help it. His eyes went to the gaunt frame in the bed. He only knew it was female because he had been told. She was skeletal. The wasted outer layers of flesh were flaking off onto the bed. Clumps of hair filled the basket next to the bed. He gasped.

Gulano's silver hair glowed in the candlelight. He was bent and frail, but still glowing with health compared to Ola. "Who is this?"

Jolly took his hat off and opened his mouth to speak, but Gulano cut him off. "No, not you. I told you, if you ever speak to me again, you will leave without your tongue."

Jolly shut his mouth and put his hat back on his head.

"Name's Rheumy. I make the deals for the magic man," Rheumy said.

Gulano looked down at the agonized woman before him. He reached out his hand to touch her arm and she flinched. "Are you going to try to make deals while my Ola suffers?"

Rheumy took a deep breath to steady himself for the lie. "This is about making sure everyone does what's best for Ola. This kinda curse, we've seen it before, but I've only ever seen one guy that can heal it – and that's Jolly. But this isn't a one-time deal. If Jolly isn't back here on the third full moon, it'll come back. And the next time, no one will be able to save her."

Gulano nodded. "Fine. I'll keep him in the basement until the third full moon. Then he can finish."

Jolly moved towards Gulano, hands held up in protest, and Rheumy reached out to grab the back of his coat. "That won't work."

Gulano leaned back in his chair, bones creaking along with the dried wood of the chair under him. "And why is that, Rheumy?"

Rheumy kept his breathing even. "Because the Wise Masters' Guild will sense this kind of magic, and they are going to be at your door with Inquisitors before you can finish nailing the basement door shut. Give us a wagon, some canvas sheets, and a horse, and we'll be gone before the Inquisitors leave the chapter house."

"And how do I know you'll come back?" Gulano asked.

"You don't, but the Wise Masters' Guild wants you dead as much as someone like Jolly. If they find him here, you'll die in the tower."

Ola made a gurgling sound and stretched against the bed, moaning as her skin rubbed off against the silk sheets. Gulano stood. "Do it. The wagon will be waiting out back with the sheets and your money. But swear to me on all the gods that you will return to save her."

Rheumy nodded. "I swear it on all the gods. I'll bring him back here, even if I have to tie him up and drag him."

Jolly shot him a look but kept his mouth shut. He pointed at Gulano and then the door.

Rheumy cleared his throat. "You need to leave for him to work the spell. Only I can assist him."

Gulano grabbed his cane from the side of the bed, shuffling with an uneven gait as he made his way out of the room. Once the door was closed behind him, Jolly let out a sigh of relief. "That was amazing. You did it, a carriage and three months to run."

"Three months to think of how to get out of the next situation. I swore on all the gods, and I meant it," Rheumy corrected.

"What? Are you kidding? I'm not coming back," Jolly said.

"We can negotiate that later. For now, just save her," Rheumy replied.

Jolly took his hat off and set it on the bedside table. Gulano had taken his candle with him, so there was only one left on the far table. He bent over Ola, running his hand lightly over a remaining tuft of hair. "Don't worry, beautiful. It's almost over." He brushed a tear from her eye.

He leaned his face closer until his lips were hovering above the crusted remains of hers, and then he kissed her, pressing his lips firmly around her mouth, his hands on the bed on either side of her pillow. Her body bucked against the bed. The springs creaked and shuddered.

The air in the room thickened and pressed against him. Rheumy covered his ears, wishing he could ease it. He moved his jaw to ease the pressure, but the relief was fleeting. Rheumy's hand went to the handle of the door. He wanted to be on the other side of this, whatever it was, but he stayed to see it through.

Light began to pour out of Olga's broken flesh, seeping out with the pus and blood to disperse in rays around the room. The light became blindingly bright, and Rheumy squeezed his eyes shut, tucking his chin to his chest. He heard Jolly gasp as the light pulsing against Rheumy's eyelids faded, leaving a bright orange ring in his vision. Jolly was upright, his head thrown back.

Rheumy took a step towards Jolly. Jolly doubled over and began puking noxious black bile all over the floor. It splashed his boots. Rheumy looked over at Ola and muttered the name of his mother's god. Golden hair, thick and rich, covered her scalp. Her flesh was a milky white, fresh and glowing. He reached out to touch her, and her brown eyes widened. She scooted away from him on the bed, looking down around her at the remains of her formerly dying body. She began mewling.

Rheumy looked back to Jolly who was now hunched over on the floor away from the mess. Rheumy went to him, kneeling down next to him. He reached out to grab his shoulder. Jolly's eyes remained shut. Jolly's body began seizing on the floor. Rheumy had no idea what to do.

Gulano came through the door first. His shout of joy alone would have alerted the Inquisitors. He scrambled to Ola's side. "Boys, pick her up. Get her out of this shit," he ordered.

Jolly's body went rigid and then relaxed. Rheumy shook him, but Jolly's eyes didn't open.

Amos rushed in and grabbed Gulano's delicate flower from the bed. Gulano followed them to the door, holding Ola's hand in his. "And you two. Your horse and cart are waiting out back. Peter will take you to them. Three months, Rheumy."

"Three months," Rheumy echoed. He put his arms under Jolly and lifted him off the ground. Rheumy grunted but trudged over to grab the hat on his way out.

He followed Broken-Nosed Peter out of the house, and through a vineyard in the back. His legs were burning, and he could feel a sharp sting in his knee with every step. He could see a building at the edge of the property. He gritted his teeth and kept his eyes fixed on it. A horse and cart were ready to go. Rheumy's legs felt weak with relief. Part of him had been expecting a group of guys with knives and two shallow graves.

He dumped Jolly in the back and pulled a sheet over him. Rheumy's arms ached, and he was panting as he checked the gold. It was only half. "Where's the other half?"

Peter grinned. "You'll get it when you finish the job. You better go while you can."

Rheumy snarled. He put the gold back in the driver's box and climbed onto the wagon seat. He looked back at the pile of canvas concealing his new business partner and then focused on the road ahead. Rheumy maneuvered the streets to the south gate while Jolly slept. Once, he thought he heard the inquisitors behind him, but he saw no one but the guards who let them out after taking a substantial fee.

Rheumy took the king's road inland. He wasn't sure where he was heading, but he had to go somewhere away from the capital. The temptation to dump Jolly's body along the side of the road and head to the free cities was strong, but Rheumy resisted. Jolly was trouble, but he could also do something that only a handful of people could do, something amazing, and Rheumy wasn't ready to let that go. He sighed. He would give it three months.

Little Jimmy
By Carnegie Euclid

LITTLE JIMMY SQUATTED on the roof of the sagging house, a bucket teeming with a slurry of water and dog shit perched between his legs, waiting.

He hated his moniker, the descriptor that always preceded his name, a grim reminder of two things. The first was there was another Jimmy who had the good fortune to live with a name unencumbered by an adjective. The first Jimmy was a cousin to him, a few years older, bigger in all ways; a cretin prone to unprovoked attacks against his younger cousin. Little Jimmy's roof perching was inspired by this other Jimmy, revenge on his mind, after receiving an egg upside his head, the yolk and bits of shell lodging in his ear, thrown with enthusiastic vigor by his cousin, the last in a litany of humiliations performed by his blood relative.

The second reason for the distaste for his name was that it was, unfortunately, painfully accurate; a reminder of his smallness every time he was addressed. He was diminutive in all ways. He was nine years old, an age in which bigger was better, but he was often mistaken for a kindergartener. His single pair of school pants needed a frayed rope to snug them around his hips. His limbs were pretzel thin, browned by the sun, salted with scabs from insect bites and minor injuries at the hands of brambles and big cousins. His ribs protruded, stretching the skin tight; his elbows and knees bulged between lengths of cut broomsticks, a testament to a lack of nourishment throughout his life. The bottoms of his feet were blackened from the earth, hardened and calloused on the bottom, tinged green along the edges; toenails curved, angry red-hot boils where they entered the flesh of his toes. His hair was short and spiky, buzzed to the scalp to combat lice and fleas. Mrs. Cratch owned the clippers and lived in the trailer next to the dead trees, smelled like sour milk, and dropped cigarette ashes on Little Jimmy as she tsked at his head, "It's a weird shape, don't ya think?" she'd say to Mamaw.

When he was younger, he vaguely remembered a pain of hunger, but that had long since passed. Now that he was older, he was more accustomed to the reality of things he lived with, the constant gnaw in his gut, especially on Thursdays, when there was hope for food that did not need picked or stolen.

The sagging house belonged to Mamaw, and Little Jimmy kept to himself on a couch in the front room, sharing it nightly with mosquitos and fleas. Though, he often relinquished it on Thursdays so Lo could occupy it. On those days, Little Jimmy relegated to the floor in front of the stove, a cool, worn linoleum in the summer heat. Lo was his sister, or half-sister – as she was quick to point out, and she tolerated him like she tolerated the dog that previously shared the couch: with calculated indifference. Sometimes Little Jimmy would gather the courage to ask Lo about his mother. There was never any expectation of a father, but even he knew a mother was vital somewhere.

"Lo, you awake?"

"What?"

"Do you remember Momma?"

"Shut up, Little Jimmy."

"What was she like?"

"She was a whore and a murderer."

"Do you miss her?"

"Shut Up."

"I think I miss her."

"Shut up."

Mamaw exhibited equal distaste on the subject of her daughter.

"Little Jimmy, the least she should could have done was died, so we'd be collecting Social Security checks, but she didn't even have the decency to do that. Now get out of here." And she spat on the floor, the tobacco juice splattering, hitting a dead fly – the intended target, ending the subject.

So Little Jimmy's knowledge of his mother was basic. She was a whore – something he knew little about but assumed was dirty and had something to do with sex and lipstick. She was a murderer, though who she murdered, and why, remained a mystery. And she was alive.

He thought of the idea of his mother while he waited, crouched on a roof, readying an attack on his cousin Jimmy. Doing so – violating any number of unwritten rules on a Thursday— was a risk. Thursday was the day Mamaw sometimes brought home "extras." That's what she called them when she would place a greasy bag on the counter at home. An extra could be anything that had the misfortune of having been warmed and presented in a gas station for the consumption of anyone with spare change in their pocket, but at the end of the swing shift could be taken by a worker for free; a perquisite preserved by the employees under the veil of ignorance by the manager. A simple and symbiotic confidence to keep amongst the workers who felt such activity wasn't really stealing – taking a pack of cigarettes or a tin of snuff more than once a week was stealing, as was removing more than half the contents or any of the bills of the "Save the Children" jar that rested next to the register. Most of the time, what was available was tube shaped hotdogs, burritos, and occasionally a slice of pizza. Mamaw, Little Jimmy, and Lo would gather around while Mamaw sliced whatever bounty she pulled from her bag. Mamaw would always slice it. Little Jimmy dreamed of the day he would have a hotdog all to himself, the luxury of biting into it, as big a bite as he wanted, and feeling the weight of the remainder in his hand, a promise of another bite coming, and a third after that, bit at his whim. Mamaw was often unfair in the food's distribution, modifying portions based on her mood and often accurate but unproved suspicions of Little Jimmy's adherence to the few rules she demanded compliance.

The worst Thursdays were when Mamaw came home and said nothing, her hands empty of bulging, grease-stained napkins. Arriving around 8pm or later, depending on how the walk was. On those nights, when she did not carry any treat home, she would grab a pan and spoon the grease from the jar. The grease was a mix of whatever could be scraped from the bottom of pans at home and the hotdog rotisserie at the gas station – or stolen from the receptacle behind the McDonalds. Mixed together, it all became white and gelatinous and smelled of burnt skin. She'd scoop a spoonful into the pan, splat, and then add flour and stir, or if it was the first of the month or the church had visited, maybe a bit of milk. Mamaw would stir and, when the bubbling mass was deemed cooked, then grab stale bread. Mamaw would shuttle the whitish gravy to the table, where Little Jimmy, Lo, and Mamaw took turns dipping the stale bread into the gravy. Standing around the table, each was soundless, except for the occasional swallow and Mamaw's stertorous breathing, all contemplating their meal in their own way, the only similarity their silence.

It was possible that dumping a bucket of dog shit on his cousin Jimmy would result in punishment and even a dried and meted out piece of hotdog withheld. The actual attack of dog shit would most likely be overlooked by Mamaw. She was not one to get in the middle of boys being boys, as she announced on any number of occasions after Little Jimmy was punched or tripped or pelted with an egg. Aunt C, Cousin Jimmy's momma, would surely frown on it, however. On Saturday, when he would walk over for his weekly bath and to wash his shorts and underwear, she would surely give Little Jimmy a smack while he was soaping his body and his shorts in the tub. But, that seemed a small price to pay. While never exactly forbidden to be on the roof of the house, Little Jimmy assumed this would be frowned upon also but not an offense worthy of nourishment withholding.

The stealing would not be overlooked, however. Mamaw fiercely guarded the ten commandments when convenient and stealing a bucket and a ladder from neighbors to perform some prank could result in no dinner. Of course, there was a fluidity in Mamaw's interpretation of stealing. If it grew in the ground, regardless of whose property it was on, it was not stealing. Little Jimmy was allowed and often encouraged to partake in cucumbers and tomatoes and beans picked fresh and eaten raw, warmed by the sun, from neighborhood gardens. This wasn't stealing. It was a sin to flaunt this rule, however, so such self-directed charity must be done clandestinely. Thus, beans from the Cauffmans were best taken early, before they arose for the day, Mr. Cauffman prone to drink and thus also prone to late mornings. Corn and cucumbers from the Jacksons were best procured in the afternoon, when Mr. Jackson would retire from the heat, his snoring loud and rhythmic from the chair in the screened-in porch. Even chickens, being close to the ground, could be leveraged for an occasional egg when necessary but necessary was defined by Mamaw. You could take an infinite number of eggs if they were on the ground. If the eggs were in a coop, you could never take more than two, unless it was from the Charltons, who drove a fancy car, just built a big garage, had a window air conditioner, and had no business keeping chickens. No such moral flexibility existed when it came to things, however. Ladders and buckets were things and Little Jimmy would have to return them to the rightful owners before Mamaw returned that evening, placing them back in the Greiser's barn, in the case of the ladder, and the Solomon's back porch, in the case of the bucket.

He had borrowed the ladder the evening before, under a full moon, slipping out from his couch, the dew making his bare feet slick-wet. He dragged the ladder home, the rattle of it following him.

Dogs barked at him as he wandered through unkempt backyards which made him think of his own dog, or rather the celebration of its death. There had never seemed to be any affection for the animal; it was always there, like his runny nose, and it was tolerated, like Little Jimmy. By the way Mamaw and Lo ignored the dog, he had a sneaking suspicion it was his Momma's pet, but no one would confirm it. In the heat of summer, when the fleas infiltrated the couch as Little Jimmy slept, the dog would curl up next to him, its rough fur sticking to his skin. Little Jimmy kicked it away every time it tried to get close until it grew angry and snapped at him. When it was hit by a car, no tears would have been shed without Mamaw's quick thinking as a car pulled onto the dust and crabgrass in front of the house.

A car door slammed, a novelty enough. Little Jimmy peaked out the cracked front window above the couch and saw an old couple reaching in the back of their car, pulling out the animal, limp and lifeless, wrapped in an old towel. He called to Mamaw, who assessed the situation after a steely glance at the intruders. She removed a wad of tobacco from her mouth with a sticky brown finger, placing it in a stained cup, as the couple ambled up the dirt of the driveway, puffs of powdered brown dust with every step.

Upon quick reflection Mamaw grabbed Little Jimmy by the cheeks and looked deep into Little Jimmy's eyes.

"You cry now. You cry loud," Mamaw said. She viciously pinched

Little Jimmy on the arm, twisting the back of the skin above his elbow, as she pushed him out the door. Mamaw followed closely behind, her hand on his neck, fingernails long enough and curved in enough, pressure enough to encourage the tears as she began screaming and hollering. Her own tears fake but prominent, saying, "Oh dear, is he dead? Oh dear. Poor Bo. Poor Bo."

Little Jimmy watched as the old man bent over sheepishly and gently placed the dog on the ground. He pushed his hands in his pockets as he looked at the house, then glanced down at the weeds, finally looking at him, up and down. He seemed to want to look away but didn't. Little Jimmy tried to catch his eye but couldn't find it until the man stammered out an apology, and his wife added how the dog just ran out, on Route 33, just ran out.

"The gas station told us it belonged here," the old lady said, looking at Little Jimmy. She bent down so he could smell her peppermint breath and see the lipstick that ran off her lips.

For a second, he was afraid she was going to touch him, pet him maybe, but her hand stopped short, though her voice said how sorry they were. The man reached into his wallet, grabbing a $10 bill until his wife elbowed him and he emptied the lot. For their pain.

$89 in total. So sorry. Here, have this. $89. An enormous amount.

And as they departed, Mamaw shoved the money into her bra as she released Little Jimmy's neck with a rub on the back of his head, and she strolled back to the house while he stood there contemplating the animal that lay at his feet, the car backing out to the street and driving away. Finally, Little Jimmy called after her.

"Mamaw, that dog was named Bo?"

"That dog ain't got no name, but a pet with a name worth more." She reached the flimsy front door and hollered back, "Little Jimmy, drag that dog back into the woods so it don't stink up the yard. Don't bury it. You can flip it each day and collect the maggots and I'll sell 'em to the fisherman come in the station."

And so Little Jimmy grabbed the carcass with its fleas and rough fur and dragged it back to the start of the woods, collecting the maggots for the next couple of weeks and placing them in styrofoam coffee cups from the gas station until all that remained was tufts of fur and bones and sticky grey.

Lo showed up after that dog died, with her eerie sense for food and money, and they all walked to the highway that evening and sat in a McDonalds. Little Jimmy ordered whatever he wanted, stuffed himself sick, and brought home a cheeseburger, carrying it in a paper sack along the road; it felt substantial in his grasp. And his cousin Jimmy showed up, hearing about the trip to McDonalds and the dead dog. When talk turned to other things, he wandered to the counter and grabbed the cheeseburger and took off for home. Little Jimmy didn't even care, happy to be sick with food and for the first time slept on the couch alone with the fleas.

The dented tin bucket was stolen days earlier, when the thought occurred to him that he needed to stockpile shit. The plan was to visit Cousin Jimmy's house each night and visit Jimmy's dog chained out back, under the shade of an elm tree with the shit covered in dust in one corner. The dog rancorous, Little Jimmy simultaneously scraped the shit into the bucket and wheedled his stick to fight off the black growling animal. Shit, then swing at the dog, then move some shit, and another swing, until he scraped what he could into the bucket, soiling his shorts in the process. That was last week, the shit hardening and crusting over, and there wasn't enough of it. So last night he snuck out again and walked the 3 miles to the gas station where Mamaw worked, just across from the McDonalds – both closed this late. Beside the tilted picnic table there was all the dog shit he needed, piles of it, firm and fleshy, soft and mud like, decidedly fresh, and he gathered it all and trekked back home along Route 33 with his bucket of shit as semis blasted by him. He hid the bucket in the woods, covered it with leaves to keep it fresh. Washed his hands from the spigot out back and returned to his couch, Mamaw's breathing laborious in the next room.

On Thursday morning, Mamaw woke Little Jimmy with a cough and a shuffle, and he watched as she looked in the cupboard and found what he knew was already there. A can of baked beans, a package of tuna. Potato flakes but no milk or butter to make it with. Stale bread, but that had to be saved for tonight, in case there was nothing to bring home. Little Jimmy watched as she pushed aside the jar of something called Tahini that the church gave them in a basket at Christmas – opened once, looked at, and sampled.

"I think it's like Peanut Butter," Lo had said, but her face turned wrinkled when she dipped her finger into it and sucked off the beige goop.

They put it back on the shelf, to wait for a hunger so great they could get past the taste of it.

Mamaw pulled out the tea bag she had been using and dropped it in a chipped and stained cup with some water boiled on a hotplate because the stove wasn't working. Little Jimmy watched from the couch, accustomed to these mornings, knowing she would dip the bag, up down, up down, then watch the water turn brown in swirls. When the swirls were complete, he watched as Mamaw took the tea bag out of the muddy water, gave it a squeeze, and put it back in the jar for tomorrow, watched her as she ambled to the chair, drinking her tea and staring out the window. The same every morning. She caught him looking, gave him a nod, swallowed the last drops and walked out the door, the screen door slamming back with a powerful whack. And she was gone.

On Thursdays Mamaw left early and stopped at the Motel, right next to the gas station, across the street from the McDonalds. On Wednesday nights there was racing, just down the way a bit, and a bunch of kids with no sense would race around a track in beaten cars and after the racing was done, they'd get to drinking, often in the parking lot of the gas station where the beer was cheap, and sometimes, if there was money, at the bar. And some of these kids with the beaten cars, full of alcohol, maybe money and, for a few of them, female companionship different than the girl they lived with in the trailer park would take a room at the Motel, which Mamaw's brother used to own but now just runs. On Thursdays Mamaw would stop by and pick up a few rooms to clean. $7.50 a room, and she could sometimes get four or five of them done before her shift at the gas station started, where she would pack the roller dog machine with hot dogs, pre-cooked bratwursts, and rolled up tortillas stuffed with gooey cheese – and hope they wouldn't sell.

As Mamaw cleaned motel rooms, Little Jimmy stretched, scratching the new bumps left by the mosquitos that visited him in the night. He sniffed at the tea bag, pulled on his shorts, and walked through the dew once again, his feet wet, checking on his bucket of shit and the ladder. Confident they were as they should be, he wandered back to the woods, an abandoned junk yard long since explored, and ate blackberries and sour grass until he lost his taste for them, wishing it was July and he could be eating May apples and blueberries. He trudged back to his house, the sun burning off the dew, and grabbed an empty peanut butter jar and trekked back to the woods, filling the jar with the blackberries. A peace offering to Mamaw tonight when he was sure he would be in trouble and would need something to take her mind off of Cousin Jimmy's head full of shit and a borrowed bucket and ladder.

He placed the berries on the counter, shooing away a bee that was buzzing and looking for the sweetness, and returned to the woods, dragging the ladder to the house, propping it on the back of the sad structure, near where Mamaw slept. He trudged again to the bucket, retrieved it, looked at its freshness and thought some water was needed. He turned on the back spigot, which exploded into the bucket, covering him in the process, making him stink and sticky. He had to drop the bucket to clean off his legs, then take off his shorts, soaking and scrubbing them, his ass and little peter lily white, the rest of his body burnt brown. He squeezed out the water and put the shorts back on, liking the feel of the cool wetness as the sun rose and began its attack.

A stir with a stick and the shit and water turned into the slurry he envisioned, the smell ripe and caustic, pleasing. He trudged over to the house, spilling a bit of the contents so it splattered his leg and foot, and climbed up the ladder, carefully, the bucket clanging and sloshing, one step at a time, his hands attacked with thin slivers of wood, though his feet were too tough for the splinters to make purchase. At the top of the ladder, he stepped onto the roof, the brittle shingles hot and rough, and he walked to the little peak, avoiding the sagging places he knew were soft and dangerous. To the front of the house, slightly hidden by a cottonwood, he waited, just above the front door, squatting with his bare feet on the shingles, the shit bucket between his legs, his body brown, thin and little.

It felt like hours, but he knew Cousin Jimmy would come. At some point Jimmy would awaken, find his mother gone, and he would search his house for food. He would go out back and maybe throw rocks at the dog or sling rotted apples from the tree in the back, and look for toads to torture and maybe, if he could find matches, burn ants at the ant hill. But these diversions would grow tiresome after a while and as his hunger increased, he'd meander through the front yards until he came to Little Jimmy's house, bursting in, yelling, looking for food to steal, putting Little Jimmy's head in a headlock, smacking him, giving him an Indian burn or holding him down on the couch or sitting on his face and fart, laughing all the while, calling him *Little* Jimmy just to infuriate him. And as he thought of this, something bothered Little Jimmy, who played back his cousin's activities in his mind again and again until he came to the burst through the front door. Burst through the front door, nothing to stop him, nothing to slow him down, so that Little Jimmy, with his bucketful of shit would have hardly any time to aim and pour the contents onto his big cousin's head. Shit.

So he walked back over the roof, bringing the bucket with him so it wouldn't tip unattended on the angle of the roof, to the ladder, spilling more dog shit soup – as he thought of it now, onto the roof and his leg, and down the ladder he went with the heavy load. Into the house and through the screen door to the front, he turned the lock with a satisfying click, a click that would slow his cousin down, just a bit, just enough. And back through the house, with his bucket, spilling the contents a little, his feet making little brown footprints across the linoleum, slipping but catching himself. Through the screen door out back and up the ladder again, he returned to his squatting, as if taking a shit himself, with the bucket between his legs. As he thought of this, it grew into an idea.

As the sun rose and warmed the shingles and dried the shit he spilled on his legs so it turned crusty, he dropped his still damp shorts to his ankles and, swatting away the flies buzzing around, sat on the bucket. He pissed a little and he strained, eyes squinting from the effort, as he sat on the bucket, cautious not to tip because of the angle of the roof. A car drove by, seemed to slow and almost stop. Little Jimmy raised a hand in acknowledgement in case it was someone he knew, and it accelerated quickly. And then there was a satisfying *plop*, Little Jimmy's contribution added to the bucket, a snicker escaping from his lip at about the time he heard his name being called.

"Little Jimmy... LITTLE Jimmy," he heard his cousin calling, a dog answering in the distance.

Little Jimmy pulled up his shorts and steadied the bucket while he crouched, trying to hide behind the dogwood, snickering to himself once again, feeling the joy of it.

He watched from above as his cousin sauntered to the door and grabbed the handle, but the door remained obstinate and unyielding. It was at that point Little Jimmy pitched forward, lifting the bucket, his shadow growing so that his cousin looked up, into the sun, putting his hand above his eyes to shield them. Little Jimmy screamed and turned the bucket over, but before he could empty it completely, the slippery wet metal squeezed through his grasp and the bucket and contents fell from the roof, erupting with both a splash and a thunk upon meeting his cousin's head. Little Jimmy watched as his cousin lifted his hands to the very spot the bucket hit, now wet and brown, and stumbled backwards until he fell to the ground.

Little Jimmy screamed with delight. Screamed and hopped up and down, his leg covered in shit, his hands covered in shit, dancing and laughing while his cousin regained his composure, stood up, looked around him, and felt for the bump on his head. Little Jimmy continued to laugh as he was pummeled with invectives, the words flying at him and bouncing off until his cousin looked to his feet and found the bucket. Grabbing it by the handle, he tossed it up, but it was a feeble effort, landing harmlessly next to Little Jimmy, who watched it roll down the shingles haphazardly and stop on its side at the gutter with the little plants and moss growing out of it. Little Jimmy danced and laughed louder. Little Jimmy bent down to retrieve the bucket, then his cousin started running around the house. Little Jimmy's face turned from joy to fright, and he ran across the roof, up the peak, and down the peak, then grabbed the ladder and furiously tried to pull it up onto the roof, but he was too small and weak to accomplish such a task quickly enough.

His cousin attacked the ladder, slamming it down. "You little cunt!!" flew from his cousin's mouth as he peered up and saw Little Jimmy's wide eyes. He burst out in a maniacal laugh. "Can you fly, Little Jimmy? Gonna find out, Little Jimmy," his cousin yelled, his face red.

His cousin's steps were slow and savoring as he started up the ladder. Little Jimmy ran from one end of the roof to the other, looking for an escape but there was none to be found.

Almost at the roof now, Little Jimmy watched his cousin's hand emerge where the ladder and the gutter met, and just as Cousin Jimmy reached the top of the ladder, both hands visible, his eyes peaking over the gutter, Little Jimmy gave a furious yell and a push. The ladder leaned back, back, back, in slow motion until it reached its apex, seeming to almost stop but then accelerate, as the ladder turned over and dropped, slamming the cousin to the ground, taking the breath out of him, the ladder still on top of him.

And the little cousin laughed again. Danced with glee. "Yes!"

Cousin Jimmy was captured behind the ladder, his face turning blue, his breath shallow, wheezing. He rolled onto his side, brought his knees up, and his breaths started to normalize. Little Jimmy danced with salted brown limbs, laughing and screaming in delight on the brittle shingles as the sun beat down and made his hair glow.

"HA!" Little Jimmy said, over and over again, "HA! HA! HA!" Little Jimmy could not contain himself, his feet moving up and down, as if running in place, but he moved sideways, across the roof and his arms kept moving up and down at right angles, his elbows bent. He gave a couple of spins, and almost toppled off the roof. He discontinued that move, content to dance sideways with flailing arms. "HA! HA! HA!" he sang, his corn-kernel teeth sparkling in the sunshine.

Tactics changed, and the big cousin put the ladder up again, surveyed it, eyed it. Took a step on it, then another, but Little Jimmy understood how to defend his castle, too many steps and the top of the ladder was grasped, an uncomfortable détente – the attacker unable to ascend, the defender confident in his strategy to repel.

"Go Ahead, keep climbing!" Little Jimmy sneered.

Cousin Jimmy stared at him, his hands clenched, his mouth in a grimace. He retreated, abandoning the ladder, leaving it propped up but unused, and walked around the front of the house. Little Jimmy thought it was a ruse, and pulled the ladder up a couple of inches, straining with the weight, waiting for his cousin to return. When nothing happened, he called out in a mocking voice, "Jimmy… Jimmy." But there was no answer. He tugged at the ladder again, pulling it, leaning back, getting it so he could leverage up against the bent gutter, still no cousin. As he pulled and finally had it deposited on the roof, he felt a stinging in his back. Seeing the flash of a rock, he heard the scream of his cousin from down below.

The cousin, his arms laden with rocks, began throwing them. The flat, sharp ones curved as they cut through the air; the round ones were steady straight. But Little Jimmy had the advantage of height and lay down on the roof so he could easily move from one side of the peak to the other. His body pressed against the shingles, so the rocks sailed over his head or hit the peak of the roof just before him, scraping his chest with each movement but making it impossible for his attacker to inflict any more injury. When his cousin moved to the back of the house, Little Jimmy rolled once, twice, and was on the other side of the peak, the shingles peppering his chest and back with fine bits of salt size stone. This happened three times, his cousin moving from front to back, but before he could get his attack started, Little Jimmy had rolled, rolled, and hid. Little Jimmy watched as his cousin grew tired of the rock throwing, the rocks coming at him bigger but with less frequency, and none of them hitting him, until his cousin gave up and sulked away, yelling.

"I am going to kill you. You just wait until my momma comes home!"

And Little Jimmy smiled and waited, put his arms behind his head and let the sunshine wash over him. Feeling the slight breeze tickle his skin, he closed his eyes and let the heat of the sun warm him while the cicadas awakened and began their serenade.

Man in the Box

By Diane Callahan

NATHAN'S BANDAGED RIGHT HAND hung over the steering wheel, and the truck's speakers trembled beneath the roar of the radio. Even though the guitars sent his ears ringing, he didn't touch the volume knob.

He could still picture Rob's jowls shaking as he chewed him out in the empty lobby. Nathan had just stood there while blood dripped down his fingers onto the snow-white carpet. He'd been under the dash of a 1972 Lincoln, removing a bad vacuum motor, and he'd cut his hand real deep. After Nathan bandaged himself up, his boss slammed a sponge and a bottle of cleaner in front of him, grunting at the red stain in the carpet. A customer walked in, and Rob was all smiles while Nathan scrubbed and scrubbed on his knees, each breath filled with the smell of blood and lemon.

When Nathan pulled into the Pine Village parking lot in his rusted-out truck, the blinds of the apartment next door flipped shut. That place belonged to a young couple who constantly walked around the complex arm in arm like they were two sex robots who'd fallen in love, with their patterned kisses and synchronized swinging hands. He turned off the music, got out, and slunk down the concrete steps. As always, the blue door was unlocked when he reached it. He flipped on the light switch and pulled the door shut behind him before heading straight for the chair at his computer desk.

His studio apartment was 350 square feet, a livable box. The six hundred dollars that evaporated each month for rent left just enough for groceries and the sundry bills associated with existence. Some paychecks, he had a little left over to scrape into his savings account, which grew steadily but toward no discernible goal.

The room remained quiet, most of the time, except for occasional yapping from his other neighbor's dog and the hum of his giant desktop computer, which he had built himself. He tapped the spacebar, and the monitor came to life, his browser already open to the tab he wanted: "24/7 LIVE WEBCAMS – madhatter01."

A video frame filled the left side of the screen, a chat feed beside it. New messages materialized every few seconds with the real-time words of other anonymous watchers, the notifications sounding like popping bubbles. He muted the feed with a click and expanded the video box to full screen.

In the video, a young blonde girl – woman, really – stared directly ahead. She wore a green T-shirt devoid of any logos and wasn't looking into the camera, but rather her dark ocean eyes traced words on her own screen. Sometimes her pursed lips moved silently, almost as if she didn't realize she was doing it. He could hear the familiar purr of her computer mouse as she scrolled with her finger. After a few minutes, a ghost of a smile crossed her face, and she let out a soft chuckle. Nathan sank deeper into his chair, hands folded over his stomach, eyes half closed.

Behind her was a wall with a white dry-erase calendar, although the image quality wasn't good enough for him to discern the events scrawled in marker. Sunlight pressed through the blinds of curtainless windows, just like in Nathan's own apartment. Her page had no identifying information, but the Looney Tunes clock on her wall told him that she lived in the same time zone as he did.

In his head, he called her "Alice," since madhatter01 had to be some kind of *Alice in Wonderland* reference. She seemed like the bookish type. Her apartment housed no bookshelves, but she always had a stack of novels on her bedside table, and occasionally she'd stay up until two in the morning reading thick thrillers. Always paperback, never hardback.

She stood from the desk chair, her shirt a blur of green, and walked out of the study. The camera feed switched to the living room as Alice strode in from the adjoining hallway. The angle suggested the camera had been set up on a countertop, with it aimed toward pale blue couches. She picked up a small remote from the coffee table and directed it at the camera, pressing a button. That meant she was getting ready for a phone call and had muted the room audio. Sure enough, she took out her iPhone, tapped a contact, and lifted the phone to her ear.

A fluffy orange cat jumped onto the coffee table as Alice paced around it. Nathan had named the cat "Cheshire." He could imagine the high-pitched mews when Cheshire opened her kitty mouth to beg for food. Alice ran her fingers over her cat's bottlebrush tail and laid across the length of the couch. Her legs dangled over the edge, her feet kicking into the air. Nathan smiled. She always seemed to do that when she spoke on the phone.

He watched her every day.

Cheshire, clearly dissatisfied with the current service, hopped onto the floor, heading toward the kitchen. Sitting up in his chair, Nathan hovered his mouse over the top of the screen. A control bar materialized, and he opened a dropdown menu that listed STUDY, LIVING ROOM, KITCHEN, BEDROOM. He clicked on KITCHEN, and the feed switched to a narrow space with a yellowish fridge and ugly marbled countertops. This camera was likely mounted to the far wall, as it also showed the dining area, with its slanted mahogany table and two matching chairs. Cheshire, now a fuzzy orange lump on the screen, lapped up water from her silver dish.

The vase of pink carnations on the table were new. Maybe they were from a boyfriend. Or just a friend. Or her mom.

The front door of Nathan's apartment creaked open, and he turned his head to see Troy walk through with a half salute. His friend held a grocery sack that jangled with glass on glass. Nathan turned off his monitor.

"Yo, this place is *depressing*," Troy said, his disgusted expression still visible beneath his reddish beard, which had become even more massive since Nathan had last seen him. With his collared shirts and round glasses, Troy looked vaguely Amish.

Nathan rolled his eyes, although he glanced over the undecorated, flesh-colored walls. "It's cheap, and it's not like I spend much time here, anyway. I'm either working or out with your sorry ass. And don't act like your place isn't a shithole."

"Hey, my sister keeps things pretty clean." Troy grinned as he sunk down on the edge of Nathan's bed, which wasn't more than five feet away from the computer desk. "She's just got a hoarder complex, that's all. Don't judge."

Troy handed him a bottle of Shiner, and Nathan took it. The bottle was lukewarm, but he opened it without comment.

"You said you had some kind of business idea?" Nathan asked, voice flat. Troy came up with "entrepreneurial ventures" the way terrible chefs cooked meals – they were either half-baked or way overdone.

As Troy launched into his explanation about selling dietary supplements to gluten-free-obsessed health nuts, Nathan pictured the pink carnations on Alice's dining room table and her feet dangling over the edge of the couch. Halfway through his beer, though, his attention wandered back to Troy.

"See, we've got to start capitalizing on this before that lab-grown meat stuff takes off and people have other sources for proteins, and if we get those upfront investments and commissions—"

"Dude, that's a pyramid scheme," Nathan said.

Troy scoffed. "No, it isn't."

"You don't know what a pyramid scheme is."

"I do, and that isn't what I'm talking about." Troy gestured at Nathan with his beer bottle. "I'm talking about exponential ROI—"

Nathan made the twenty-foot trek to his bookshelf and pulled a business textbook off the shelf, where it rested alongside other books he'd bought for college before he dropped out. He flipped to the index and then back to the listed page number for "pyramid scheme." He tossed the open book onto the bed. Troy skimmed the page and scoffed.

"Dude, we're talking about different things here. You're confusing pyramid schemes with multi-level marketing," Troy said. "You need to watch this video on it, then you'll get it."

Troy walked over to Nathan's computer and clicked it awake. Nathan didn't bother to stop him, as the conversation would only end if he let Troy feel he had won. But his stomach sank with ice-cold horror when the screen came to life. He hadn't closed the webcam tab.

Troy turned to him with a grin. "This your favorite cam girl?"

"I don't watch cam girls." Nathan pushed past Troy, closing the tab with a tap of the mouse.

"Whoa, whoa. Wait a minute. It said '24/7 webcam.'" Troy elbowed Nathan aside and reopened the closed tab with a keyboard shortcut. The video feed showed Alice in her kitchen, stirring a pot on the stove. "The hell is this, man?"

"A bunch of people watch it," Nathan said. Instead of looking at Troy, he stared at the screen, letting Alice's calm expression slow his raging heartbeat. She put on her two pink oven gloves and carried the hot pot to a heat mat on the dining table.

"Does this chick even know the cameras are there?" Troy asked.

"Everyone on the site installs the cameras themselves. They're in pretty obvious places."

Troy shook his head, peering closer at the screen. Closer to Alice. Nathan's throat constricted.

"Guess it's none of my business what you watch to get your rocks off…" Troy muttered, an almost conflicted expression crossing his face.

"It's not about that," Nathan snapped.

"But random dudes watch her get undressed, right?"

"There aren't any cameras in the bathroom," Nathan said sharply. "Even if there were, that's not what I get out of it."

"Why do you watch her then? It's weird as fuck."

"I dunno. It's…calming."

"Calming?" Troy somehow laced the word with innuendo.

Nathan's face flushed. "Whatever, man. At least it's not a pyramid scheme."

"All right. As long as you don't end up on the news, you do you." Troy snickered, but then his expression turned thoughtful. "Why does *she* do it, though? Does she get off on people watching her or what? Or is it a money thing?"

Nathan shrugged. "Not a money thing. And she never talks on video or writes posts like other people do… Just lives her life."

Troy blinked at him and shook his head, as if Nathan had just told him dinosaurs were a government conspiracy. "Dude, *you* need to get a life. Go on shitty dates and be disappointed by humanity, like the rest of us."

"Maybe I should get a cat."

"Nah, a cat would murder you in your sleep if you kept it in a prison cell this small."

Eventually, Nathan got Troy back on the subject of why his very clever business plan was not at all a pyramid scheme, and they talked about nothing for another hour before Troy had to head out to babysit his nephew for the night.

"Thanks for the beer. You sure you're not too buzzed to drive?" Nathan stood in the doorway, one hand on the frame, Troy already heading up the sidewalk.

Troy waved a dismissive hand. "Takes a *lot* more than that to even make a dent. Enjoy your livestream, man."

After Nathan closed the door, it took only thirty seconds for him to settle into his desk chair, madhatter01 already on full screen, set to Alice's darkened bedroom. The camera at the upper corner of the room afforded an aerial view. He could barely see the shape of her body beneath the gentle rise and fall of her white bedspread. She never had any gentleman callers, and she always slept in colorful flannel pajamas, as much as the skeevier commenters tried to cajole her into sleeping in her panties.

He left the page open as he turned off his lights and slipped under the covers of his bed, alone.

• • •

Alice was off-screen by the time Nathan woke up for work, which wasn't uncommon. Even if she went out, she usually came back home for lunch. But that afternoon, the video feed remained Alice-less. Nathan had found the feed on his phone while shielded behind the car lift when Rob was off lying to customers in the lobby. The only movement came from Cheshire. The cat roamed from room to room, sleeping on different surfaces throughout the day. He witnessed the moment Cheshire hopped onto the counter and knocked the camera off its perch. The living room feed died in a blink, but not before Nathan noticed the open deadbolt and the car keys lying on the arm of the couch.

Hours passed, and no Alice arrived to fix the camera.

When he came back home that night, shoulders slumped under the weight of another ass-chewing from Rob, she still wasn't there, the main feed now set on her empty study. All the comments were variations of "*Aww, miss you*" or "*Spending the night somewhere? Lucky guy.*"

Nathan couldn't get the image of the abandoned car keys out of his head. After all, he hadn't actually seen her leave the apartment that morning.

He sat down at his desk and scrutinized the rooms on the madhatter01 feed. The comments were pinging like crazy:

"*Where r u?*"

"*She's probably on vacay.*"

"*Anyone else worried about the cat?*"

In the kitchen feed, Cheshire's water dish sat empty. As the cat stalked the apartment, her meows grew more desperate.

The lights were still on in Alice's bedroom. Two books lay on the bedside table. They had white labels on their spines – Dewey Decimal numbers. Nathan tried to read the labels but couldn't make out the name of the library.

The webcam in the study was built into her laptop. It showed only an empty chair and the back wall with the dry-erase calendar. A few of the dates were filled out in black marker, and she had scrawled something for yesterday in red. Her handwriting was nearly illegible, embellished with loops and swirls. Zooming in did nothing but make the words blurrier.

Leaning back in his chair, Nathan pinched the bridge of his nose. When he closed his eyes, he saw flashes of those three rooms. And the now-blackened living room. All empty of Alice.

A lump formed in his throat. His stomach growled, and he glanced at the time on his computer screen: He had spent over an hour scouring the digital corners of Alice's apartment.

He spent the next one reading through all the chat logs from the past week, and it only further tangled the knot in his stomach.

"*Do you ever talk? The other girls at least act like they appreciate their audience.*"

"*add a camera to your bathroom*"

"*Your Instagram photos are really sexy. Why don't you take more?*"

Nathan slapped his desk, muttering under his breath. "Motherfucking idiot. Of course, she would…"

His fingers slammed into the keys as he typed "madhatter01" into the search engine. He opened separate tabs with different username databases. Soon, roughly forty tabs lined the top of his browser. He opened a new Excel spreadsheet and began to fill it in with notes. He titled the last column "Alice?" and marked it "Y" or "N" as he went through every madhatter01 profile on different webpages. Some accounts had no posts or identifying information. Others clearly belonged to people who weren't Alice, like the blue-haired punk guitarist and the frat boy posting about campus meet-ups. However, three pages yielded telling information, all of which he marked "Y" in his column. Then he narrowed down his tabs to those final accounts.

One was the Instagram page the commenter had mentioned. It contained only four photos, all dated from two years ago, but they were unmistakably Alice. One was a picture of a nondescript sunset. Three were selfies, her face as familiar to Nathan as his own, although he'd never seen it in such clarity. Her blonde hair shone golden, the photos taken somewhere outside. Her eyes were especially blue in the light. She wore a closed-lip smile and a silver necklace with a little bird charm he'd never seen her wear in the year or so he had been watching her feed. His heart leapt at what he spotted in the background.

Behind her was an apartment complex and a parking lot. No unit numbers or street signs were visible, but he could just make out the edge of a back license plate. Living in Ohio, he had seen enough visiting plates to recognize when a car hailed from its neighboring state of Indiana.

One state over, in Indiana. Less than a two-hour drive.

He read through her comments on a forum, which were all related to cat advice. Training cats not to jump on tables, how to groom long-haired cats, what to do when cats get too food dependent.

On the last page – one of those websites where people posted crappy vampire stories, he found her real name: Emily Fischer. He stared at it for a full minute. It sounded too ordinary to be a pen name. She had only published one story, although it was more like a fairytale. *There once was a fox who wished he could transform into anyone he wanted...* Nathan read the story three times but found nothing useful in it.

Opening a few phonebook websites, he searched "Emily Fischer Indiana." Two pages of results popped up. He narrowed it down to five options based on their ages; she couldn't be older than thirty. He pasted each address into Google Maps and used Street View. On the third address, his breath caught in his throat. The apartment building in Alice's – Emily's – selfie shots had been three stories with beige paneling. And here it was again. Three stories. Beige paneling. Emily Fischer lived here. Or, she had, before she disappeared.

Hands shaking, Nathan picked up his cell phone, and his thumb tapped "9" and "1" in quick succession, but he stopped before tapping the "1" again. He called a different number instead.

Troy answered after the first ring. "Hey, what's up?"

"You up for a road trip?"

"Uhhh…" His friend laughed. "Depends. Where to?"

"Indiana."

"Okay. What for?"

"You remember that… webcam girl?"

"Kinda hard to forget."

Nathan paced across the small strip of carpet in his apartment. "Her cameras are still on, but she's gone, and I mean she's *disappeared*. Her cat's got no food or water, she left some lights on… and it doesn't look good."

"What do you think happened to her?" Troy sounded more curious than anything.

"Not sure yet. A lot of creepy guys leave comments, though. One of them could've found out where she lives. I did it easily enough."

"Should I be impressed?" Troy asked flatly.

"I'm just saying that someone might have gone after her, and she's all alone there."

"Well, that's an interesting theory, but… aren't there webcams everywhere?"

"Not everywhere. The hall, the bathroom, and the closet don't have cameras. Maybe there's another window that the guy could've gone through. Or maybe the perp managed to stay out of sight of the cameras, and Cheshire *didn't* knock over the camera –"

"Cheshire?"

Nathan made an involuntary noise in his throat. "Her cat."

"If you're so worried, then get the police to check in on her. Send an anonymous tip or something."

"What if they take forever to actually look into it, and something bad happens to her by then? Every hour counts," he said, talking fast. "Even if I tell them, they'll think I sound like some crazy stalker."

"Well, to be fair..."

"Do you want to come with me or not?"

A pause. "You're going to Indiana? You sure that's a good idea?"

Nathan squeezed the phone. "I don't see any alternative."

"I do. *Don't fucking go.* You're crossing some sort of line here, and I don't want you—"

Nathan hung up.

• • •

The truck's radio stayed off the whole one-hour-and-forty-two-minute drive to Redstone Flats. His own deep breathing and the rush of traffic beside him flooded his ears with white noise. By the time he pulled into the parking lot, night had fallen. A silver hatchback out front caught his eye. It looked like the type of car she would own – unassuming and practical.

Nathan jumped out of his truck, his blood almost buzzing. He knocked on her door, which was blue, just like his. Only silence greeted him.

Back in his truck, he checked the madhatter01 video feed on his phone, ignoring the dozen or so missed calls from Troy. In Emily Fischer's apartment, the lights were still on, the rooms still empty.

He was about to get out again when the apartment door to the left of hers swung open. Three people emerged, talking loudly, before disappearing behind the patio fence. Nathan cracked his window down, and their laughter filtered through. His knee bounced as he watched the clock on his dash. He tried to slump down in the driver's seat, as if he were taking a nap, while keeping an eye on the neighbor's patio.

Almost an hour passed. Clouds merged to form a slate-gray blanket overhead, the first touch of drizzle sprinkling down. Finally, the neighbors stood from the patio. Two of them headed up the path to the parking lot. They passed Nathan's truck on the way to their car, and a few minutes later, their headlights shone past as they left the complex. The third stood on the patio for a few moments before going back inside the apartment. Nathan waited another ten minutes, each one like a barb in his skin.

From his glove box, he grabbed an orange safety hammer and leapt out of the truck. Streetlights cast a pale-yellow glow across the sidewalk. Alice's fenced-in patio held an assortment of items: two deck chairs, a small table, a frayed broom, a bird feeder, a flowerpot filled with only dried dirt. Picking up the broom, he walked over to the shuttered window beside the door, then paused.

He lifted the flowerpot with one hand, revealing a dull silver key beneath. He sighed and shook his head like a disappointed father, shoving the hammer in his back pocket and leaning the broom against the patio fence. He fit the key into the lock, and the door opened without a sound.

A rush of cold air hit him – the air conditioning was on full blast. In the living room, two floor lamps illuminated the pale blue couches he had seen hundreds of times, but from a different angle. The car keys still rested on the arm of the loveseat, and the pink carnations on the kitchen table had browned around the edges, their stems drooping. It smelled like the cat's litter box needed cleaning.

"Alice?" he called in a tentative voice, then scoffed and shook his head. In a louder voice, he said, "Emily?"

An orange blur blipped through his peripheral vision, and something plush brushed his ankles. Cheshire threaded herself through his legs. She looked up at him with gleaming eyes and let out a creaky meow that sounded like a dying lawnmower.

Nathan leaned down to scratch between her ears. "Let's get you some food."

He passed the knocked-over webcam but left it on the carpet, facedown.

After he had refilled the food and water dishes, which Cheshire consumed with violent slurps, Nathan wandered into the study. He gravitated toward the dry-erase calendar. The filled boxes read, "Pick up car from shop," "Take Bella to vet," and "Dad's anniversary," with the single scarlet note declaring "Appointment – 12:30" in her swirling scrawl.

Her laptop sat open on her desk. At the sight of the glowing green camera light and his face staring back at him on the screen, Nathan sprung forward and snapped it shut. His fingers lingered on the lid of the laptop as his heart pounded in his throat.

Leaving the study, he turned toward the ajar door at the end of the hall, through which he could see a tall black dresser, one drawer half open. He hesitated at the threshold to the bedroom. He peered to the right; the bed lay empty and neatly made, just as it had been when he last checked the video feed. Back in the hallway, he stood for a moment, listening to the emptiness. When he looked up, his eyes widened.

The bathroom door was closed.

His hand latched around the metal doorknob, as if magnetized, and he licked his lips before swinging the door wide open and taking in the fuzzy green rug, the polka-dot shower curtain, the girl sprawled naked on the floor –

Nathan fell to his knees, gasping. "Oh God. Jesus Christ…"

Beside the open toilet, her body faced away from him at an unnatural angle, blonde strands wild across her head. With a shuddering breath, he put one hand on her shoulder and rolled her onto her back, tears pricking his eyes at the lack of warmth in her skin. The harsh bathroom lighting ignited the slivers of blue in her half-lidded eyes. Her lips were pale and cracked. A dark bruise and dried blood stained her forehead. Speckles of red dotted the edge of the toilet seat.

Although her chest remained still, he laced his fingers together and placed his hands beneath her breasts and pushed into her, over and over and over. He put his mouth to hers, wet to dry, giving her his air. Once his arms began to ache, and she still hadn't so much as twitched, he sank back, staring down at his hands and her pale skin beneath them.

He stood and took an off-white towel from a hook behind the door, which he'd seen in the mirror above the sink. The towel had a rough texture, like it'd been washed a thousand times. On the counter, a bottle had spilled round white pills into the sink. It had no label.

Nathan jolted as a knock pelted the front door, followed by a muffled voice. He laid the towel gingerly over her and ran to the entrance. More pounding followed.

"Miss Fischer? You all right?" a commanding male voice asked from the other side. "This is Officer Parker. I got a call from someone who said you might need help."

Nathan appeared in the living room just as the door opened. He had left it unlocked when he entered, the key still in his pocket.

"Call an ambulance," Nathan croaked. "I mean, it's probably too late, but…"

Officer Parker was short but stocky, bald, and at least in his mid-40s. His hand rested on the holster of his gun.

"What happened?" the officer asked.

"Just come here. She's in here." Nathan led him to the bathroom, stepping aside to let the older man enter first. Officer Parker removed the towel from the body as casually as removing a sheet from a piece of furniture.

The man knelt on the tile, putting his ear close to her mouth and two fingers to the side of her throat, then pulled back. "How long has she been like this?"

"I don't know." Nathan fidgeted, standing at a distance.

Officer Parker inspected the ceiling. "Pretty cold in here, with the air vent right above us. Surprised anyone would turn down the air this low, with the weather we've been having."

Nathan stared up at the vent, trying and failing to understand its significance to the conversation amidst the shock stalling his brain.

The officer turned to Nathan. "The neighbors said they saw someone standing outside this young lady's window. Was that you?"

"Yes, I thought something bad might've happened to her."

"That your truck in the parking lot, too?" Officer Parker asked.

"Yes, officer."

"And those pills were just lying out on the sink like that when you got here?" He gestured toward the tablets.

Nathan swallowed hard. "Yes. I tried to save her, but she was already—"

"How did you know Miss Fischer?"

"We're online acquaintances. She wasn't answering her messages for a while, so I got worried," Nathan stated. "So did her other online… friends. We were all worried."

The officer eyed Nathan's bandaged hand. "So, she went offline for what – a few days? A few weeks?"

Nathan glanced at the floor, catching a glimpse of a white hand splayed against the tile. He took a deep breath. "Something like that. She's usually on every day, and I just had a bad feeling. I thought she might need help."

"I saw from your plates that you're from Ohio."

His brow furrowed. "Yeah, the Akron area."

"You drove to Indiana to see her?"

"To help her." Sweat pooled across his back, his shirt already sticking to him.

Officer Parker clicked his tongue. "Did Miss Fischer give you a spare key to her apartment?"

"No… I…" Nathan closed his eyes. "I found one under the flowerpot out front."

"So, you just wanted to check in on Miss Fischer? See if she was all right?" the man asked.

Nathan met his eyes. "Yes. Exactly."

Officer Parker stared down at his phone. "Your name wouldn't happen to be Nathan Freedman, would it? A friend of yours gave me a call. He seemed worried about you."

All the blood drained from Nathan's face. Troy. And Nathan always kept his apartment unlocked, and the browser history on his computer could've easily ratted out his location.

Nathan nodded slowly.

"Can you tell me what happened here, Mr. Freedman?"

The scene before him had morphed into a vortex – the officer's stoic face, the pill bottle on the counter, Alice lying naked on the floor, all swirling around him in hazy colors.

"I – I think she was self-medicating. I guess someone could've broken in here, but to me it looks like an accident. It looks like she took too much and then she passed out and hit her head, but I don't know why she –" Nathan heaved a sigh. "Maybe she was depressed. I never thought… She always seemed like such a happy person."

"But you didn't know her personally." Officer Parker crossed her arms.

Nathan tried to push a word out past his lips, but it didn't even make much sense to him, like he'd spoken in a foreign language with a tongue that wasn't his.

Still, the officer seemed to understand. "What's that? 'Lawyer?'"

Nathan nodded, his head feeling like it might fall off his body if he tipped it too far forward.

"Of course, of course," Officer Parker said. "But for now, just work with me, all right? I'm only looking for the truth. No one's in trouble here."

Images flickered through Nathan's head. The folder of screenshots on his computer. A year's worth of browser history. The phone call to Troy. How long he'd waited in his truck outside her apartment. His fingerprints on her body.

Officer Parker moved toward Nathan, who stepped away, only for his back to hit the bathroom wall behind him.

"But I need to take you down to the station. It's just procedure," Officer Parker said in a low voice. He unhooked a pair of handcuffs from his belt, the hard look in his eyes challenging Nathan to resist.

Nathan's arms, which he had reflexively put out in front of him, now hung limp at his sides. Looking over the officer's shoulder, he could see Alice discarded on the floor. She would be taken into the hands of people who had never known her smile or watched her feet dangle over the edge of a couch.

In the bathroom mirror, he caught a flash of his reflection. The man encased in glass looked like him, but an unrecognizable wildness shimmered in his eyes, a panic, a knowing. He slipped outside of himself, imagined looking down at the gaunt figure with dark hair, the way his fingers twitched toward the dead stranger. And she remained a stranger, even as he returned to the cold room.

Why had she done it? Any of it? He filled in the blanks: Emily in this livable box of an apartment. Emily with a mouthful of pills designed to numb. Emily – clear and flawed and real – setting up all those cameras, waiting to be seen. And him observing her through a film of his own making, tricking himself into believing that pink oven gloves and a stack of paperbacks told an entire story.

Sirens cried out in the distance, splitting the tense silence, but the strident music couldn't drown his thoughts. She had turned on her cameras for the same reason he had watched her – to reach beyond the box without ever leaving it.

TREETOWN

By David M. Simon

DEXTER HOWARD, Dex to everyone who knew him, moved into a tree house on the morning of his seventy-third birthday.

He had spent a considerable amount of time scouting for just the right location, walking the woods at the edge of town from the first pale light of morning until the trees began to merge together in the inky-blue twilight hour.

He narrowed his search down to a stand of oaks half a mile in from County Road 9. There was a fine trout stream not far from the spot, fed by an icy cold natural spring. The path to what he had already begun to think of as "his home" was torturous – wet black soil that sucked at his feet, vines tangled with briar bushes and thorns. Even now, in early spring, the vegetation was overwhelming. Dex knew that by June an impenetrable wall of green would confront the casual pedestrian. All in all, it was a perfect location.

Dex was a powerful man, built low to the ground. Age and gravity had conspired to magnify nature, bowing his back and legs. Dex now resembled nothing so much as a bowlegged, hunched-over barrel. He was still formidable, with thickly muscled arms and legs and a massive chest. Years spent in the rough embrace of the elements – as a logger, longshoreman, and Marine among others – had left their mark. His face was etched with creases and folds, his body crisscrossed with scars, faded memories of old injuries. His hair, still more brown than grey, was cut close to his scalp, as it had been his entire life.

Dex kept coming back to one tree at the center of the grove. It had a stout trunk he could not get his arms completely around; it ran fifteen feet straight up, then branched off in four directions.

"It'll work just fine," he said out loud. His low rumble of a voice was surprisingly loud in the still forest, disturbing a sleeping owl. It careened into the sky in a flurry of feathers.

Dex drove his Ford pick-up into town and loaded up with lumber and hardware, tar paper and shingles, and a sturdy ladder. The truck, an eleven-year-old base model with just shy of 200,000 miles on the odometer, shuddered like a swayback mule under the weight, but it got the job done.

It took Dex the better part of three days to move the truck's contents to his building site. He carried everything by hand, not wanting to use a cart and beat down a clear path to his new home. By the third day he could feel every one of his seventy-odd years in his shoulders, arms, and legs. He found himself pausing often, hands on knees, his breath coming in big, ragged gulps.

The last item to go was his toolbox, a gift from his father by way of his grandfather, filled with a collection of honorable old hand tools any man would be proud of. The damn thing sure was heavy, though.

Dex began building exactly five weeks before his birthday. He worked without blueprints, letting the tree dictate the dimensions and look of the house. He began by framing the floor, eventually ending up with a good-sized, uneven rectangle, narrower at one end than the other. As he left each night in the fading light, he would look back at the oblong platform and smile at how much it looked like the prow of a ship cutting through green waves.

After three weeks the tree house was roughed in, with walls and a roof. It was now much easier to work on; Dex no longer found himself hanging from a branch, trying to swing a hammer without launching himself out of the tree. He shingled over the entire exterior of the house to protect it from the rain that was now falling with alarming regularity; then he began on the interior.

By the time he returned to his truck each night, Dex was half past exhausted. He would stop in town for some takeout – he was avoiding the diner, as he wasn't quite ready to explain to his friends just what the hell he was doing, wasn't in fact quite sure himself, then drag himself to what was, for a while more at least, his home.

His home. It did not feel like his home, had not for nearly six months. Not since the day he had arrived home from a fishing trip and found Sarah, his wife of forty-six years, face down in the garden. He dropped everything and ran to her, choking back the bile that rose in his throat. She had been dead for some time. Dex had seen enough death, during wartime and not, to recognize the cold, clammy skin and the stiffness working its way through her limbs.

Dex did not cry that day. He went about the business of burying his wife with the same methodical care he handled most things. She had suffered a massive heart attack, and the doctor assured Dex that she had been dead before her brain could even register pain.

Sarah's three sisters arrived from their various Sunbelt homes and commenced grieving in unison; Dex welcomed the distraction. Dex and Sarah had never had children, so he was spared that. They had tried when they were first married, eventually realizing that it was not to be. They got along fine by themselves. Dex survived the heart-rending wake and funeral by propping up the sisters with his strong arms.

Finally, they all returned to their homes, and Dex was left alone. He jumped awake that night slicked with cold sweat, gasping for breath, sheets damp and tangled around his feet. He sat up shakily in the bed he and Sarah had bought the day they returned from their honeymoon. He realized then and there, with Sarah's ghost calling to him from every corner of the room, from the crickets she had so loved humming outside to the smell of her skin cream that still permeated her pillow, he realized that he could not live in this house without her.

Dex did not sleep the rest of the night. He put on a pot of coffee and paced through the house, from room to room and end to end. Sarah was everywhere, in everything. Dex realized that a life spent in this house would be a life spent in the past, a life delineated by memories. He did not think he could live that way; it went against his nature.

Dex began to look halfheartedly at other housing options. Nothing seemed right. The houses were too big and too new, or too small and too rundown. He was appalled by the cost of both new and old; he and Sarah had paid off their house long ago. Apartments and condos were out of the question; Dex liked people well enough, but not that much. He stayed away from home as much as possible, coming in late and collapsing on the couch to thrash away through another restless night. He spent his days fishing and hunting, or sometimes just walking the forest. On rainy days he worked on his truck in the garage or read in the town library.

It was at the library that Dex found inspiration. Rummaging through the magazine stacks he came across a back issue of Smithsonian with a wondrous tree house on the cover. The feature story showcased tree houses by turn rustic and contemporary, simple and eccentric. They caught hold of his interest and imagination as nothing else had managed to do. He had been looking for a hook to hang the next chapter of his life on. This was it. The next day, he hit the woods at dawn and began looking for the site of his new home.

Dex finished the interior of his tree house three days before his birthday. He sat down in one corner with a mild groan, a bit out of breath as he often found himself lately, and surveyed his new domain. It was one room, except for a small partitioned off area that held a simple chemical toilet. There were cabinets built into the walls on three sides, a built-in chest of drawers, ample counter space, a raised pallet that would soon hold a mattress. In the opposite corner from where he sat was an old-fashioned pot-bellied stove, vented through the roof. A sturdy wooden box held a large Coleman ice chest and doubled as a bench. A propane lamp hung from a hook in the center of the room, and his trusty propane camp stove sat waiting on the counter. A small window broke the symmetry of the north wall, bathing the room in diffused light. All in all, Dex decided, it would serve him well.

Over the next three days, Dex worked his way through the task of sorting his belongings. He gathered his clothes into what turned out to be a pitifully small pile. To this he added pots and pans, plates and utensils from the kitchen. He took whatever packaged food would keep. His hunting and fishing gear was already in the truck.

The rest was harder. The house held a lifetime of memories he could not completely leave behind, but bringing along too much would defeat his purpose. Dex worked his way through each room, rambling back across the years as he went.

The dining room hutch held a trove of photos from vacations and get-togethers, reunions and parties, scenes from a marriage set right here in these tidy rooms and expansive garden. The most recent snapshots of Sarah showed a thin, though certainly not frail, woman, usually with trowel in hand and dirt on the knees of her jeans. Her hair, more often than not pulled back in a loose ponytail, was a thick cascade of soft grey curls. Her face was deeply tanned, and well-lined, but strength and intelligence were much in evidence. She was nearly always smiling.

The older photos showed a handsome, happy couple, their love matter of fact and obvious. As Dex reached the black and white years, he found it harder and harder to page through the albums.

One picture, the scalloped edges betraying its age, had been taken the night they met. He had been on a weekend jaunt with a buddy in Atlantic City, and she was there with her parents. She was several years younger than him. He was loud and boisterous, wild and exuberant. They spent the day on the boardwalk, having the picture taken at a photo booth as the sun sank behind the boardwalk buildings. When they parted that night, he promised to get in touch; only her parents were surprised when he actually did. Dex added that picture to his pile of belongings.

He filled a box with favorite books: *Great Expectations, To Kill a Mockingbird, A River Runs through It*; Sarah's childhood bible, the margins filled with notes and thoughts; and finally, a well-worn copy of Stud Terkel's *Working* that Sarah had given him as a birthday present. She had inscribed it, "For Dex, the hardest working man I know."

Dex added his favorite chair, and an old mattress from the guest bedroom, then loaded the lot into his truck. That night as he lay on the couch, he had a long conversation with Sarah. He explained to her, as best he could, why he was leaving their home and moving into a tree house. Halfway through, he began laughing at how silly it all sounded when he said it out loud, but he continued anyway. He told her about the wake and funeral, caught her up on how her sisters were doing. Dex finished with a quiet, "We'll talk again soon. I love you, Sarah."

He slept well that night for the first time since she had died.

When he left the house the next day, he locked it up tight. He could not bring himself to sell it, as it turned out, so he had arranged for someone to look after the property.

Moving his belongings into the tree house took the better part of the morning. When he was done, he sat down in his chair and looked at his new surroundings. It was simple and rough, and Dex immediately felt right at home. He collected his pole and tackle box from a rack on the wall and went to catch some trout for dinner.

In the weeks that followed, Dex settled into his new life. He would fish in the mornings, read in the afternoons. Once a week he drove into town and stocked up on supplies, took his trash to the dump, did his wash at the laundromat. A large block of ice lasted the week in his ice chest, which worked out well.

One morning as he made his way down to the stream, he heard the wounded cry of some animal from beneath a felled tree. Moving aside the ground cover, he found a cat cowering, back pressed against the log. It had tangled with something, a coyote or bobcat, and had gotten the tar kicked out of it. Dex slowly reached for the cat and picked it up as gently as he could; the cat gave only token resistance. Back at his tree house, he cleaned and dressed the orange tabby's many wounds. None of them looked life threatening, but the cat had gone feral some time ago, and it was malnourished, its fur matted with dirt.

Dex christened the cat Red and nursed him back to health. As Red got stronger he began to venture out more and more, but he always came back. Dex and Red got on well; they gave each other companionship and space as needed. One day, as Dex sat on the bank of the stream reading a book, with summer in full glorious riot all around, and Red curled up next to him sleeping in a puddle of shifting sunlight, Dex realized he was truly happy.

As a joke, Dex carved a sign that read TREETOWN and posted it for the squirrels to read. He later added a second sign that read DEXTER HOWARD, MAYOR.

This sign meant something more several months later, when Dex had a visitor. It was a young man, fresh from the military, who had heard about the guy living out in the woods on the edge of town. Jimmy was his name. As Red watched warily, Jimmy and Dex had a long talk.

When Jim left, they shook hands, and the next morning he was back, scouting a location for his own tree house.

The Suitor
By Stella Ling

VIRGIL STERLING was a fine specimen of a man.

He came by our apartment every few days, whistling an old Army tune and ready to fix something.

We had lots of stuff we needed help with, leaking faucets, loose tacks in the carpet, broken lightbulbs. It was an old apartment and no one had taken care of it for a long time. He considered it his manly duty to be able to dust off his fingernails on our behalf.

"Hey Tina," he would ask me when he came over. "Cat got your tongue?" Then he would pretend to chop off my nose and wiggle it up and down between his index and third finger.

He was amiable. He had strong white teeth. His hair was blonde and might have been his best feature had he not worn it in a crewcut. But he did look great in his stiff and starched khakis.

He would fool around, joking with me, until my mother finally came over to find something that required his helping hand.

We were living in South Dakota near the Indian reservation. My mother had accepted a one-year assignment to help out with their healthcare.

Virgil Sterling worked for the Army Corps of Engineers and had come to supervise the building of some new roads around the Reservation so supplies could come in more easily during the winter. He had happened upon my mother in the local supermarket where she was puzzling over can openers.

"This one is great!" he enthused, picking up the heaviest and largest of them. "Believe me, it will last you a lifetime."

He promptly took it to the cashier's, paid for it, and gallantly presented it to my mother as a done deal.

Thereafter, whenever we opened any canned item, my mother would exclaim as if in salutation, "This is Virgil Sterling's can opener!"

My mother liked Virgil Sterling because he was so useful. "That man has a brain!" she liked to say admiringly. "Not like *some people*," she huffed scornfully, carefully leaving me in the dark as to who those *some people* might be.

Virgil's job wasn't that hard, but I don't know how much his team actually got done because the government was always sending them what he called "inferior materials," cracked or mismatched pipes, broken joints and gaskets, stuff from the surplus stock that would require being jimmy-rigged. It slowed the work down; what should have been simple and taken eight months or so to complete, took twice as long. When Virgil got too frustrated, he would come over to our apartment and find something easy he could fix in an hour.

He had only known us a few months when Christmas came around. He must have already been smitten by then because he gave Mom a necklace that shone with silvery stones. She gave him a giant bag of polished white rice.

"It's more practical," she said. "What am I going to do with a necklace?"

He liked to take us riding; he had an old Army jeep. It smelled like diesel, clanked, and belched dust through the floorboards. It was almost as much fun as Virgil chopping my nose off.

He took us to see the Serpent Mound made by the Indians, to the secret spring to load up on pure water, for foot-long Coney Islands, for tea at the fancy hotel in town, and sometimes to the movies.

He always paid for everything, even for me.

Mom asked me how would you like him to be your daddy? And then she laughed because we knew that would be impossible.

Mom liked him. She really did. Sometimes she dressed up special when we went out. She would put on lipstick and lotion that smelled like flowers.

Mom was slim and pretty. She had a soft, musical voice. Her eyes were dark and smiling. She was good at flirting and telling dirty jokes.

"Virgil," she would tease, "you're too handsome to be hanging around with us. You need to be out courting a young maiden that you can marry."

"Sorry madam," he would say, "no young maidens around here. So I guess I'll just have to hang out with you two..."

"...old hags," mother would finish his sentence and laugh, because, of course, I was only eight. All winter long he hung around in his off hours, doing chores and taking us sight-seeing.

He made an effort to present himself well. He was always clean-shaven, his uniform was impeccable, and he smelled of a swoony aftershave. He looked like a guy out of a movie magazine. Sometimes, he would let me touch his cheek to see if it was soft.

I knew there wasn't going to be a happy ending, and I felt sorry about it. But we all pretended everything was going to be fine, and we kept going out and having fun.

"You know Virgil Sterling is sweet on you, don't you?" mother's best friend would ask.

Mother just tutted, "Aiya, what nonsense!"

"He's a dreamboat," the single friend would retort. "You're lucky, but if you don't want him, pass him on to someone who appreciates him... like me!"

Mom always just rolled her eyes.

I loved Virgil Sterling. I loved his name. It sounded like the kind of person he was, upright, the real deal, silver. I wished he could be my father.

Spring had come. One day he picked me up and swung me around over the top of his head. "Guess what kiddo, I'm going to teach you dames how to play golf today."

I don't think Mom had any idea what golf was. I sure didn't. She put on her fluffy white dress and her black high heels and dressed me up, too. Virgil laughed when he saw us.

"Lawd, are we are going to knock the socks off them other golfers!"

Mom asked, "Are you making fun of us? How can we knock off other people's socks? I thought golf was a gentleman's game, not violent."

Virgil just smiled at her question, and we got in the car. He languorously draped his arm over the back of her seat and drove with one hand avoiding all the potholes. I sat in back watching the wheat fields waving their high tassels at us as we drove by.

The golf course was a beautiful place; the grass was perfect, like a green carpet, not a single weed or crabgrass. The height of the grass was even and smooth, like a brush of velvet under my hand. Mother was also impressed. The sky that day was so blue it clashed with the sea of vibrant green.

Virgil told us he was going to be our caddy for the day. I thought he said "daddy," but then he explained what a caddy was. It seemed that he was going to carry those heavy golf clubs around for us from spot to spot.

So, we ambled along from one hole to the other, Virgil making jokes the whole way. He held Mom in a loose grip as he taught her to get the stroke right; the wind was blowing, and his face was hidden behind the black curtain of her hair. Up on the ridge, with the wind ruffling her white dress, and the bright day behind them, they looked like a dream couple trapped in a movie set.

After two hours we had only gone three holes. Those balls seemed to find every ditch, every patch of sand, every wooded knoll in the whole darn course, and we had to spend a long time trying to knock them out without touching them. We weren't allowed to pick them up, we had to scrape them out with the golf club.

Finally, we gave up and climbed the high hill at the edge of the course. Virgil spread a blanket out on the grass and Mother took out some treats she had brought along. It felt good just to sit there in the sun and drink the cold lemonade and eat the baloney sandwiches covered with gooey mayonnaise.

From our vantage point we could see all the real golfers still sweating down below.

Mother smiled at Virgil, and he looked like he was going to have a heart attack. He clutched his chest and then bent over to kiss her hand, just like a knight in a fairy tale. It was then that I learned how powerful a smile could be. It was like she had the power of the whole world in that simple smile.

I wandered off and started looking for four leaf clovers. Then I did front-overs and cartwheels all the way down the hill as fast as I could, until I was dizzy. At the bottom of the hill, I made two daisy chains. I climbed back up to where Virgil and my mom were still chatting. The air was shimmering around them. It was like music had been poured over them and was vibrating. I put one daisy chain around each of their necks.

"I now crown you King and Queen of the Hill!" I proclaimed.

Mom giggled. Virgil swung me up on his broad shoulders.

"Then you must be the Princess of the Hill" he said, galloping off with me bouncing on top.

When we had run to the bottom of the hill, he swung me off his shoulders and began tickling me. I liked that better than almost anything. I had bony ribs, so the slightest pressure made me shriek. I laughed and cried so hard the birds overhead became blobs of mirth.

Well, it was time to go home, and we got back in the car. Mother and Virgil were very happy, and I hoped that good things would happen for them.

Mom was singing in the car, her favorite hit parade tunes. She always carried a halo of music around her. Music was her favorite hobby. She had a good voice, too, clear and in tune. From listening to her, I knew the lyrics and sang along.

• • •

I was playing with my friend, Violet, in the spare bedroom of our apartment. It was the room where I kept my stuffed animals, dolls, and other toys. Violet was from the Indian Reservation and my only friend. We discovered each other on the school play yard when no one wanted to play with either one of us.

We both loved to run and jump rope and shoot marbles. Violet was the only girl I had ever met who was skinnier and faster than me. When we teamed up, we could beat any other team in the relay, jump rope, hopscotch, or marbles.

Violet wasn't good at arithmetic, so I would sit near her and try to help her with the answers. Later I would explain to her slowly why that was the answer, but she didn't always get it. Lots of days, she missed school and then I had no one to play with.

We had to drive a long bumpy, dusty road to pick her up to come to my house.

"Those white people," my mother would say. "They stole all the Indians' good land and then they put them in the worst place."

We had a pretty good car, but my mother was afraid that we would get a flat tire going over all the rocks and potholes.

"Look," mother said as we approached Violet's house. "They don't even have indoor toilets. Like when I was growing up. Only outhouses. Those outhouses are so stinky. I almost fell into one once!" Mother scrunched up her nose.

"Maybe you could tell Virgil to build them some?" I asked her.

She looked at me and laughed. "Why? Do you think I am the boss of Virgil?"

We got to Violet's house, which was just a shack. Her parents came out to the front porch and looked us over. I don't think they had ever seen an Asian person before.

"Asians and Indians are the same blood, you know," Mother said to me. "They probably didn't know that. That's why they're staring at us."

Finally, they let her come with us and Mother told them we would bring her back after supper.

Mother was hovering over us in the bedroom as we played dolls. Violet remarked that she had never had a doll. I was surprised, but to my chagrin, mother picked up my favorite doll and said to Violet that she could take that one home with her when she left. I stared at my mother, stricken, but I didn't say anything. Violet looked so happy. And really, I had lots of dolls.

My mother went into the other room, and pretty soon we heard this loud piercing screech like someone was dying. We ran in. Mom had put a record on the phonograph.

"What is that?" asked Violet.

"It's a record player," said my mother.

"It usually plays music," I said.

"What's it playing now?" asked Violet.

"It's called opera," said my mother. "It's a kind of music in another language. It's a very famous song."

"It sounds terrible," I said.

"Well, it's very sad," allowed my mother.

"It's giving me a stomachache," I said, and I really felt sick all over.

"Hmmm, it's about a lady and her lover who left her and didn't come back for seven years."

"What's a lover?" I asked.

"Ummm.... It's like something between a boyfriend and a husband," my mother replied evasively.

"What's the name of the song?" asked Violet.

Violet seemed so interested in this thing called opera. I couldn't believe it. I couldn't tear her away. I was also angry with my mother for trying to be educational on my time with Violet.

My mother started to tell us the story. It was about a Japanese lady who called herself Madame Butterfly. What a horrible name. And then she met a white guy who was called Pinkerton, and they fell in love, but then he had to go away. He promised to come back, so she kept waiting for him. She wouldn't go out with any regular Japanese guys, just kept sitting in front of her window in her house on the top of the hill, waiting for him to come back for like seven years! In the meantime, she had a kid from him, and it grew up.

Finally, one day she saw a boat and it was the Pinkerton guy coming back; she was so happy, she was singing her heart out. That part of the singing wasn't so bad. But when he was halfway up the hill, she realized he had brought a white lady with him, who was his new wife. He hadn't waited for her at all, and they were coming to take the kid away with them. He didn't even care about her. So, then she committed *hari kari*, and that's when the screeching started on the phonograph.

I did not like that story at all. Furthermore, my mother had started crying as she got to the ending of the story.

My mother looked at Violet and said, "You know, right? Never to trust white people? Or any man? They're all liars."

Then she turned the record player off and started singing "On Top of Old Smoky," which was about the same topic, but at least had a better tune.

• • •

It was summer. Mom only had a couple of months left for her assignment. Virgil, too, would be moving soon, as his job was just about done.

He would hint to mom, "What state do you like the best? Where would you go if you could go anywhere?"

Mom would joke and say, "How about the moon?"

I kind of thought she meant *honeymoon*.

Mom decided to have a Fourth of July party. Not that she was patriotic or anything. But she had heard that there were going to be fireworks, which we could watch from the balcony. I was excited because I was dying to see the fireworks.

Virgil sat beside mom and played the suave host all evening, bringing the ladies small glass cups of champagne punch. People had brought all kinds of cookies and cakes, and mom had made crunchy eggrolls. When everyone was properly sloshed, we went out on the balcony and watched the sparks lighting up the sky in red, blue, and white.

It was the end of the evening; the orange sherbet had melted down into the ginger ale and champagne in a sad heap. Mom sat down at our piano and played some golden oldies, and those who could sing joined in, while the others just cat-called.

Then she put on Patti Paige singing "Mockingbird Hill" on the record player. As the familiar strains sounded, "Tra la la, twiddle dee dee, it gives me a thrill, to wake up in the morning to Mockingbird Hill," I started dancing automatically, my legs moving in time to the music. Whenever I heard that song, I had to dance, I couldn't stop myself. I was on my tiptoes with my arms overhead when suddenly there was a pounding at the door. I froze.

At that moment, in walked my father.

Everyone was shocked. Not Virgil, though, because he didn't know who the man was.

Virgil was busy mooning over my mother, who was still sitting at the piano. He had his hands ever so lightly on her shoulders. She was wearing a sleeveless pink dress and the classy necklace Virgil had given her. It was the first time I had ever seen her wear it.

We had not seen my father for over a year. Mom no longer even talked about him. She said he had someone else. So that was that. We had just basically forgotten about him.

He didn't say anything, just walked over and yanked my mother's arm.

"What's going on here?" he asked.

Mom recovered quickly. "We're having a party. What are you doing here?"

She didn't say hello to him. He didn't say hello to her. He certainly didn't say hello to me.

He glared at all the people sitting around and especially at Virgil. Virgil was also staring at him, trying to figure out what was going on.

84

"Party over," my father yelled. "All of you, get out!" And he pulled mother brusquely up off the bench.

"No," she cried, as if in a daze, "Tina's right in the middle of her dance."

He saw me for the first time. I was still on my tiptoes waiting to finish a pirouette.

"No more dancing," he said, and repeated, "Party over!" And he grabbed mother's arm again.

Wham! I saw the flash of Virgil's silver watch as he punched my father in the jaw.

"Let her go," he yelled as my father fell clumsily to the floor.

My father looked like a fat rabbit, lying there, his hair tousled, crumpled in a ball, blood gushing from his nose.

My mother suddenly came out of her trance. "So sorry everyone, better you all go. Take food with you."

People could not get out of there fast enough. "Are you sure, you're all right?" a few ladies murmured. But most just got their purses and high-tailed it out of there.

"You, too," she said to Virgil. "You go, too."

"Who is this guy?" he asked. "You want me to punch him again?"

"My – my husband," said Mother weakly.

"Your husband? Your husband?" he repeated.

"Please, you go now," begged my mother.

Virgil considered a second then urged, "No, you come with me." And then, "Come with me, honey. Get out of here. It's not safe," his voice unsteady, but tender.

I was transfixed. I had never heard him call her that word before. I saw the smoke and yearning in his eyes. There was a luminosity that shone between them. Mom looked at me, me who was just standing there, watching everything and saying nothing, and asked, "And what about Tina?"

"Bring her, too," he said. And a heartbeat later, "Of course, bring Tina."

She stared at me and then at him, and in that split second, decided. "No," she said, "I can't go with you."

My father stayed with us for two weeks. During that time, my mother resigned from her job and packed our belongings. We did not see any of our friends. We did not see Virgil.

On our last day there, we loaded my father's car with all our hodge-podge stuff, our clothes and books, our record player and records, my toys. He was driving us back to Arkansas where he worked now.

We huddled by the car waiting to take off, trying to make sure we hadn't forgotten anything. I was sitting on my pink Barbie suitcase because I would be the last thing to be loaded into the car. Father climbed into the driver's seat. Mother kept looking around like she had forgotten something. She didn't seem like herself. She wasn't smiling, and she didn't look pretty. Her hair was greasy and uncombed.

Suddenly I felt a strong hand throwing me up in the air. "Hey, were you going to go away and not even say goodbye to me? I thought we was pals!"

"Virgil!" I screamed. I was so happy to see him. I hugged him tightly and kissed him on his soft cheek. His eyes were puffy, and his collar was wrinkled.

He went over to my mother. "Bye," he said in a voice so low you almost couldn't hear it. "I hope you'll be happy wherever you go."

"Goodbye, Virgil. You find a sweet young maiden and marry her," my mother whispered back. Her eyes glistened with tears, but she was still trying to flirt.

"I don't think they make them like that anymore," he said bitterly. But almost simultaneously, he smiled as if he were making a joke to himself.

My father started honking the horn impatiently. He seemed to have no imagination about the scene that was taking place. I didn't want to leave. I didn't really care about my father. I had never spent any time with him and so, as horrible as it was to say, I didn't cherish anything about the man who made up half of me. To me he was just a bother, someone who had abandoned us and now was trying to make up for lost time, something that could never be retrieved.

Virgil was startled by the honking, but he looked at my mother's sad eyes. He tried to take her hand.

"Are you sure?" he muttered, almost as a plea. But my mother wouldn't look at him.

He turned around and retreated. *If that's the way you want it*, his back seemed to say. His shoulders sagged and his head was bent.

"Mom, why...?" I asked.

She stared at me. "He's not like us. He's not your father. He could never be your father." Her lips trembled, and her eyes crumpled tightly into themselves.

I was angry and impatient with her. "Then why? Why did you do all that? Why did you do that to him?"

Her voice crushed me like ice. "I didn't do anything! I told him I had a husband. Where did he think you came from, thin air?"

I still didn't get it. I wanted Virgil Sterling to be my father. Or if not that, to wait for me until I grew up, so I could marry him.

We drove along. The miles sped by. My parents were arguing and insulting each other in a foreign language in the front seat so that I wouldn't understand. They actually seemed convivial.

I turned around and looked out the back window. I wished I could have caught a glimpse still of Virgil Sterling. It seemed like we were always leaving places behind, always trampling things in our rush forward. Leaving things and people behind, never to see or even think about them again. As if people were all expendable. As if hearts were expendable. Always looking foward to the next challenge, the future, as if that could make up for everything.

But behind us, there was just the empty, dusty road, growing longer and longer.

The New Chastisement

By Brian Luke

ALL THE TALKING BEASTS have been put down.

There seemed to be a common reaction among the men when they heard their animals speak – a deep revulsion at witnessing such a fundamental breakdown in the natural order. The word most commonly used, I recall, was *abomination*. One of the pastors, I think it was Dwight Bailey from over by Chillicothe, said it was like watching a hen's egg hatch and seeing a tiny little baby crawl out.

Of course, with a monstrosity like that, you destroy it immediately. Many saints took the additional step of burning the body of the abomination. Or bodies, in those cases where two beasts had been discovered talking to each other.

None had spoken publicly of what they overheard. We elders did not ask the men what they said to their families to explain the necessity for a peremptory sacrifice. Charlie Young volunteered that, for his children's sake, he had made up a story about the mare breaking her foreleg. My cheeks burned at hearing such public confessions of the sin of false witness. But I admit feeling a twinge of sympathy for his motive.

We got various answers to the question of why these good men had kept their own counsel. Some thought they wouldn't be believed; others, not really sure they believed it themselves, dismissed their own experience until they heard similar stories being shared at Annual Conference. A few of the men mentioned fear of what the neighbors might think of them, if they knew. This was of particular concern for those with a calling to preach, whose authority in the pulpit, as I know too well, is so dependent on a general trust that the pastor keeps his household well-ordered and chaste.

I did not think of it at the time, but it is striking to me now that we did not ask the men whether they tried to converse with the beasts themselves. Nor did we ever ask the men to relay the content of the beasts' speech. It's not clear that the men even knew what the overheard creatures were saying. In only one situation was a man himself addressed directly, a young farmer from Wapakoneta who told us that one of his cows actually cursed him when he squeezed her teat too hard during milking. He was in dead earnest when telling us this, but we couldn't help but laugh at the picture. I confess that a few jokes about competence in the marital bed were made at his expense after he left the room.

The upshot of our inquiry was a new ordinance. Any beast that talked was to be destroyed immediately, as an affront to that natural distinction between man and beast established by our sovereign Creator. That was it, just the one sentence. A floor suggestion that the Conference compensate farmers for their material loss was scrapped upon the objections of David Bronwin, our district Treasurer. We did engage some brief discussion regarding how the abominations should be destroyed. That quickly led to unholy conflict, however, and it was deemed prudent to trust that a man knows best how to dispatch his own stock, even if it be possessed by a demon.

The motion was duly presented and approved without dissent. There were quite a few abstentions in the vote, unusual in a district where every elder is proud to present his strong opinion on every various topic. The abstentions were mostly from those who thought the whole thing was some sort of a strange joke, that the new ordinance was ludicrous on its face, and that in a few years we'd all be embarrassed to see it printed in the Book of Discipline. But most of the delegates didn't really know what to make of it and didn't much care, being focused on the hot-button issues of that conference, the redistricting plan coming out of Mansfield and the newly revised polygamy proposal brought forward, once again, by the Evangelical Fellowship.

But our little "joke" of a law quickly led to some very real disturbances.

A matter that had always been handled privately was now brought out into the open. After the new ordinance was posted in the churches, people started talking. It soon began to seem that in just about every town someone had heard a beast speak. Right here in Sydney, there were two: Mike Flanagan, who had once overheard two of his hogs talking to each other, and Hunter Samuelson, who said his wife told him she "thought" she had once heard their housecat saying something to their six-year-old daughter. Flanagan, being the practical sort that he is, just went ahead and slaughtered the hogs, telling folks he was fine getting the meat a little sooner than expected and was sure it would taste just as good as any other beast "what knows to hold its tongue proper." But Samuelson had to make a show of it, dragging the cat into the square, tying her up on some kind of wooden post he rigged, then dousing her with coal oil and setting her on fire. He had his Bible out and was reading some ill-chosen verse or other, yelling over the cat's screams so he could be heard by the few people who had come out to see him make a fool of himself.

Quite a few beasts were destroyed that week across the Western Region, but that did not put an end to the matter. It just got people talking, and soon enough the idea of a "New Chastisement" began making the rounds. Folks were getting worked up, so of course our Bishop had to step in, proving once again his skill at turning a mildly troubling situation into a disaster. He issued his first ever emergency directive, the "Bishop's Resolution Regarding the Maintenance of Divinely Ordained Distinctions Between Man and Beast," which soon came to be known as the "Purge Order." It was this Order that triggered the disturbances and ultimately led to my own compromised position.

I read out the resolution at the next Sunday meeting, as the bishop had instructed. The order was vague on what immediate steps were expected. Some of our Sydney saints sought to take advantage of that by suggesting we do nothing, just wait and see what other temples do with the directive. That was never going to happen. We have too many elders too jealous of our status as a leader in the district.

We formed a working group that very night. The main issue was the testing, a little detail left out of the bishop's order. We were expected to destroy all beasts in the district that could talk, but there was no direction for determining whether an accused or suspected beast was indeed able to talk. We threw around some ideas. Whipping was a popular suggestion. Beating, burning, and choking got their mentions, though choking died on the vine after it was pointed out that even our voluble Bishop would have trouble getting a word out while being heartily choked by one of our worthy saints. (As senior pastor, I felt obliged to insist on a greater reverence in tone after that remark.) Stretching was another tactic suggested, I believe. Anderson tried to describe some kind of method employing running water that his grandfather had told him about when he was a boy. But we had a hard time picturing it, plus it was from before the Chastisement so that left a taint.

The farmers wouldn't countenance any testing method that might cause permanent damage to their stock, and that became a major focus of debate. We were still going round in circles about the question when Reverend Sawyer, who had been sitting quietly in the corner for the whole discussion, broke in.

"Why don't we just ask them?" he said.

Sawyer is well past his eightieth year, but he still has that booming voice he can pull out when it suits him. His question cut right through all the noise in the room. When he had everybody's attention he continued.

"Just ask each one if he can talk. If he doesn't answer, he's passed the test."

A couple of the men laughed out loud. But when you looked at Sawyer you could see he wasn't joking. Plus, we all knew how he had become since he retired. We guessed that he might well be against the whole proceeding.

There was that situation a few years ago, when the McConnellys brought one of their boys up on a 5th Commandment charge. It made its way through the courts, guilt was declared, and sentence duly passed, but on the day of the stoning, Sawyer showed up and placed himself between the boy and the executioners. He just stood there, reciting the story of Jesus and the adulteress, while everyone tried to figure out what to do. No one would throw a stone, not with Dick Sawyer in the way. It wasn't just that he had been District Superintendent for twelve years. He was, and still is, widely beloved, as a pastor and as a man. He has the personal touch, a way of taking your hand and looking you in the eye, making as if nothing else in the world is as important at that moment as what you're saying and how you're feeling about it.

The crowd eventually dispersed, and the McConnelly kid was taken back to jail. He was executed privately that night, gibbeted in his cell, as I recall. There hasn't been a single new 5th Commandment charge in the district since then, so I guess Sawyer made his point.

Nobody responded directly to Sawyer at our meeting. We just paused for a moment, nodded in his direction, and went back to debating real testing methods. It looked like we had reached an agreement to use whipping and we were working out various details like weight of the cord and how many strokes, when Dwight Evans, who had been whispering back and forth with Peterson, got back into the proceedings. He made a motion to adopt Reverend Sawyer's "test," and the motion was seconded by Peterson.

Later I realized what was happening. Evans and Peterson are two of the biggest farmers in the district – between them they must own several hundred pigs and cows. Evans, influential as he is in the life of our church, is not an especially pious individual. I would venture he cares very little whether his livestock can talk or not. He was concerned about the money he'd lose if large numbers of his stock started speaking up under duress, and he saw Sawyer's non-test as a way of circumventing the whole business.

In the end we broke up without any motion being passed, resolving to meet again the coming Wednesday night before worship. But by Tuesday, we'd gotten word from the District that the D.S. had drafted his own recommendation on how to implement the Purge Order. All we needed to do Wednesday night was present it to our assembly.

The District plan was so close to the method we had almost agreed on that I wondered whether our D.S. had been in communication with someone from our team. That would not be unlike him. In addition to the use of whipping as the primary testing method, there were several further provisions, including that a beast would have its throat cut immediately upon uttering any intelligible words, and that beasts passing the test would receive a new brand affirming their approved status, to be applied on the opposite shoulder from the brand they had received at birth. I could see the usefulness behind this last part, as it could appease farmers concerned with the prospect of an indefinite number of future rounds of testing.

It was while I was reading out the District plan that the disturbances began. As soon as I started reading, Dick Sawyer stood up. He was about ten pews from the front and all the way over to the right. He didn't say anything, but he was holding a hand-painted sign that said, "We are ALL God's creatures." As I read through the District letter he slowly turned, displaying his sign to all in the assembly.

I was furious, and for the first time in the whole affair felt some trepidation about what might be coming. I resolved to maintain my composure as I continued the reading. I made it through the preamble and was starting to feel calmer by the time I reached the substance of the letter.

But then things became truly disturbing. I was reading the section about the testing method. The D.S. did not specify a definite number of strokes but recommended that the test conclude when the beast passed out. I remember pausing there, thinking to myself that that might pose a problem if any of the creatures could feign unconsciousness, when I noticed a motion from the front pew. I looked down and was shocked to see that Lydia had risen to her feet and was standing there quietly, joining Reverend Sawyer in his silent protest.

I expect that my voice did falter at that point. I continued reading, but without comprehending the words, as my mind was taken over with the terrible implication of the congregation witnessing my daughter's brazen defiance, her open challenge. Not just to the authority of our church leadership, but to my own authority as her father and pastor.

By the time I got through the letter several other young people had also gotten to their feet. I looked around the nave, with no idea of what to do next or how to salvage the situation, and caught a glimpse of Dwight Evans, leaning back with his arms crossed, smiling and looking mighty pleased with the turn of events. I'd never seen him beam like that during any of my sermons.

Before I could continue, Dick started moving. He walked up to the front of the Sanctuary, put his sign down on the floor, and rolled up his left sleeve. On his shoulder was a jagged red mark that was clearly intended to look like he'd recently been branded. It was painted to look like the sign of a lamb. Some part of me acknowledged this as a nice rhetorical touch on his part, even as most of my spirit was consumed by righteous indignation.

Then he walked down the main aisle and out the front door. The young people who had stood up followed him out, including Lydia. We let them go and carried on with the worship service as if nothing untoward had happened. I'm not proud of our passivity, but I still cannot think of any positive action on our part that would better have served God's will in the moment.

I feel compelled to mention one other incident that night of a more directly personal significance. While Lydia was walking out of the church, and just before she got to the exit, she got down on all fours and did a quick imitation of a horse in full canter. I'm sure that little move was performed for my benefit.

I blame myself for allowing her to get to this point. The signs have been there for years, and I did not do enough to quash her rebellious spirit and dissolve her unnatural connection to the creatures. When she was eight or nine, she would spend hours a day going around the house, imitating various beasts – horses, cats, dogs. She would move like them, make sounds like them, even refuse to answer when spoken to, adopting a feigned look of incomprehension. Beth and I indulged this behavior, finding it amusing and somewhat endearing. We knew it had gone too far, though, when we received her school report card. The teacher had written at the bottom: "Lydia always does well with her studies and has a pleasant attitude with her teachers. I would ask her, though, to stop playing horse when she returns from recess, as such behavior is not suitable for the classroom."

That was the initial instance wherein I failed my duties as spiritual leader of the household. I left the matter for Beth to sort out. Several years later, I paid the price for that dereliction when Lydia announced at dinner that she would no longer eat meat: "Because I don't eat my friends," in her words. I understood this as a childish spite on her part, prompted by the fact that a week prior I had sent to slaughter a boar under her management, a creature she had dubbed "Ebony" due to the beautiful dark coloring of its coat.

It is not uncommon for children to become emotionally attached to the first animal placed in their care. Recognizing this, I elected a godly forbearance in the face of her histrionic overreaction to the boar's removal. A week of sulks and tantrums, ultimatums and accusations, and more than a few aspersions cast in my direction led to no greater response on the part of her mother and myself than to assure Lydia she would grow out of her grief and the next time would be easier.

When it became clear, though, that Lydia's words at table were sincere, that she intended to disdain God's word that every moving thing shall be as meat for us, I locked her in her room and brought her only flesh to eat. This she defiantly refused, going so far as to scrape the plate into her soiled chamber pot while I was still in the room, looking on. After two weeks of this, with no break in her fast and no indication that her will was bending, even under the condign corrections I dutifully administered, I conceded to her perverse diet on the condition that none of us speak of the matter in public. Beth was greatly relieved at my concession, as Lydia had become so pale and listless that we were both concerned she might pass on, and thus go to final judgment with the sin of suicide blotting her immortal soul.

I trust that each young person who walked out of assembly with Reverend Sawyer that night received at home the loving discipline their impudence merited. I myself spared the rod with Lydia that night because I knew her insubordination had grown beyond its power to correct. I tried to talk to her, but she wouldn't answer. She wouldn't look at me. She spent all of her time at home the next few days, closed up in her room or out in the barn. I noticed that Princess, one of our housecats, was no longer around and that made me suspicious, but Lydia wouldn't talk to me about that either and Beth said she didn't know anything about it.

On Friday I was summoned to the D.S.'s office in Marysville. I was concerned he might bring up Lydia's wayward behavior, but when I got there, it became clear that he was only interested in one thing – Reverend Sawyer. He was furious about what he called Sawyer's blasphemy and "unbiblical insubordination." In the office with us was a canon lawyer whose name escapes me. The D.S. turned the meeting over to this man, who had figured out how we could "put down the rebellion."

The lawyer told me that we already had enough to make our move, that we didn't need a trial or any formal charges. We didn't even need any new executive orders. I told him I had no idea what he was talking about.

"His mistake was branding himself. According to the Law of Identity," he began reading from an earmarked copy of the Book of Discipline, "in cases of doubt, a creature's identity as beast or man shall be determined, respectively, by the presence or absence of a brand, so long as the brand is one of the designated types outlined in section 2.104 and was applied by an adult male member of the holy church." The lawyer looked at me rather pridefully. "So, he's a beast. A beast that has been known to speak. And as such, according to the Bishop's Resolution Regarding the, uh –"

"The Purge Order," the D.S. said.

"Right, according to the Purge Order," the lawyer said, nodding at the D.S., "he is to be destroyed." He closed the Book of Discipline and sat back in his chair, smiling. "Immediately."

I vaguely remembered the Law of Identity from our church polity class at Seminary. It was one of those laws that had been in the Book of Discipline since right after the Chastisement. There was little class discussion of it because none of us could think of any cases where a creature's identity had been in doubt. The professor himself wasn't sure why the law had been passed in the first place.

"Well," I said to the lawyer, "that's some marvelous legal reasoning on your part. But I don't think Sawyer did actually brand himself. I think it was just some sort of paint or colored charcoal."

The two of them glanced at each other. The D.S. said, "Oh, no, he really did brand himself. I'm sure of that."

The D.S. did not blink or look away as I met his gaze. I didn't bother to ask him where he got his surety.

After a moment the D.S. said, "Look, we understand Sawyer still has standing in the community, and that this could put you in an awkward position. So, we've drafted a letter to help you out."

The lawyer took out a folded, one-page document and handed it to me. "It just lays out our position," he said. "According to our current laws and resolutions, any branded creature is subject to being tested and, upon failure of said test, purged. It never mentions Sawyer by name, so it's not like we're creating a law about an individual. That would be unconstitutional."

"Right," the D.S. said. "That's what you should emphasize to your people. We're not targeting Sawyer with this."

But, of course, they were targeting Sawyer. And the D.S. made it very clear to me before I left that I was expected to take care of it. Quickly.

I spent my time on the ride back to Sydney going over all of our lay leaders, trying to think of someone capable of handling this task. I eventually settled on John Burkhart. He had the right combination of qualities. He liked to follow the letter of the law, however ill-conceived it might be. Unlike some of our saints, he had no special awe for pastors, seeing us basically as hired hands there to serve the needs of church members and be cast out at their earliest displeasure. And, perhaps most importantly, he was definitely not one of Sawyer's devotees. He had been a vocal and rather vicious critic of him, ever since Sawyer had interrupted the McConnelly stoning.

The first thing I did back in Sydney was find Burkhart and explain the situation to him. I gave him the D.S.'s letter and told him to put together a team to find Sawyer and take care of the matter. He was as enthusiastic for the task as I imagined he would be. He asked me – a little too eagerly, I might say – whether they should test Sawyer first. I reminded him that we had all heard Sawyer speak many times already. No further testing would be necessary.

I asked Burkhart to report back to me at church before the Sunday morning service. The rest of the afternoon was spent in my study, preparing the sermon.

As I pondered the direction of my sermon, I kept returning to the events of Wednesday night. It was hard to recall any more blatant display of disrespect to a pastor in the pulpit, not just during my preaching career, but across my entire church-going life. I spent several hours working up a message on the theme of deference to pastoral leadership and found several very apt passages from the Apostle.

But I ended up scrapping that, deciding that I needed to address the issue more deeply, to get to the root. The fundamental issue was not just disrespect for pastors, but a breakdown in respect for divinely ordained authority throughout the entire Great Chain of Being: man over beast, parent over child, male over female, and, ultimately, God over all.

I worked late into the night and was rewarded with a highly satisfying sermon, entitled "Our Place in the Natural Order." The travails of the previous week weighed on my spirit throughout my devotion but ended up inspiring me to write, I would say, as penetrating an analysis of Genesis 1-3 as any I've ever heard.

When I arrived at church, I found Burkhart and two others waiting outside the front door. I took him into my office, where he told me that he and the others spent several hours waiting at Sawyer's last night, but he never showed himself. This morning they had already been back at the place, and took liberty to search the entire house, to no avail.

I stressed to Burkhart the importance of locating Sawyer as soon as possible, excusing him from the morning's attendance so he could broaden the search. I also asked him to leave one of his men outside the front door of the church to block Sawyer's entrance, should he appear. I did not want another disturbance.

All seemed normal at the beginning of worship. Beth and Lydia were in their seats in the front row, and I noticed that most of the other youth who had participated in Wednesday night's uprising were also present, with their families in their usual places. Two were missing, though, the Harting girl and one of Lydia's friends, Priscilla Young. I prayed that their parents had not been overly zealous in administering their corrections.

By the time we came to the sermon, I was quite calm, concluding that the worst had passed. I climbed the pulpit, feeling the warmth of the Spirit within my breast. The beginning of the sermon went well. It was when I was explaining the biblical concept of "dominion," how it is etymologically connected to the notion of trampling, or pressing down with one's foot, that the disturbances started.

Lydia stood first, but the other youth quickly followed, as if they had been awaiting her signal. This time they were not quiet. Lydia started howling, like a dog baying at the moon. I continued my sermon but then the others joined in, producing an unholy cacophony of beastly sound: barking, neighing, snorting, hissing, and a deep, persistent lowing.

This time the congregation was not frozen in stunned silence. They were moved to fight back, standing up in the pews, angrily pointing out the offenders, yelling at them to sit down and be still. I broke off my message and watched helplessly, finally turning to the cross and offering a fervent prayer for divine assistance.

When I looked back, the youth were struggling to get past the adults in their pews, some of whom were punching at them, grabbing their hair, and yelling at them that they must sit down and be quiet, and weren't they ashamed, and other such things. All but one of the youngsters made it out of the pews and up to the front, where they climbed the steps and turned toward the congregation. As a group, they then began to remove their overshirts, baring their upper arms – a shocking display of sinfulness since all but one of the youths were female. With a sick feeling in my stomach, I realized what they were doing and what they were intent on showing us.

They had all been branded. Real brands, not painted-on replicas like I had assumed with Sawyer, but raw shoulder wounds still running from having recently received the hot metal.

They were branded as cat, dog, horse, pig, sheep.

For a second, all sound ceased, and no one moved. Then a woman in the back screamed and that broke the crowd. With a holy roar, the men in the congregation lunged out of their rows and came for the girls, murder in their eyes.

The girls ran. Not out the front, which was blocked by men streaming up the aisle, but past the altar and out the side door. I noticed my wife for the first time during the fiasco. She had gotten out of the front pew and was running up the steps ahead of the men, making it to the side door just before they did. She pulled the door closed and turned, facing the men, putting her arm out straight with her palm raised, and yelled, with more sound than I had ever heard come from her, "LEAVE THOSE GIRLS BE."

That stopped them.

The service ended there. We stood around in small groups, not sure what to do next. They looked to me for leadership, but I said little. I was thinking of Burkhart, out there somewhere with the District's letter, the one that did not target Sawyer individually but said that all beasts heard speaking were to be destroyed immediately.

And thinking how, by law, all those branded were beasts.

All those branded by – what was the phrase? – "adult male members of the church?" I thought there might be some hope in that.

But not much. I saw those men as they charged our wayward daughters, and I knew they could not long be held at bay by a legal nicety. I knew also what duty I might soon be called to perform or suffer the disgrace of having it done for me.

When I got home, Beth had the Sunday roast ready, same as every other week. We sat eating in silence, just the two of us. I didn't ask her where Lydia might be. I imagined she had no more idea than I did.

The afternoon passed, somehow. We napped and then ate again, and the day moved into evening, without Burkhart reporting in and without any sign of Lydia.

After it got dark, I went outside to have a pipe. Pacing around the house, I noticed a small light coming through a crack in the barn wall. I put out my pipe and opened the gate enough to peer in.

I couldn't see much. But I heard a low murmuring from the far corner. I squeezed through the door and moved as silently as I could toward the sound, coming from behind a pile of old, unused equipment. While I was still a few steps away I was able to recognize Lydia's voice.

She was saying things like, "it's okay, you're fine" and "everything's going to be all right."

The voice that answered her was familiar to me and unfamiliar at the same time. It said, "But are they going to whip me? Are they going to kill me?"

It sounded like a girl, but I knew that it wasn't a girl. My eyes adjusted to the dim light. I looked around the barn to find the tool I would need.

When I came around the corner, I saw them, Lydia and her cat Princess, lying together on a small mat, holding each other. There was a lantern on the ground next to them and a couple of empty food bowls.

Princess hissed and backed away from me immediately, fear in her eyes, but Lydia sat up and put her arm out defiantly, a copy of how her mother had protected her that morning at the church.

"Father, you don't need to do this," she said, the first words she had spoken to me in a week.

"Where did you get branded," I asked. "Who did that to you?"

"What difference does that make?" she said, spitting out her defiance.

"If Sawyer marked you, then you are truly lost to me. If you did it to yourself, though –"

"We are all God's creatures."

I looked into her eyes and saw that she would not ever condescend to speak in her own defense. Not to protect herself; not to protect her father's ministry.

I was holding the long blade behind my back. When I brought it forth, the cat made an indescribable sound, a long, inhuman scream of terror. Lydia put her body in front of the cat and threw one of the bowls at me. She picked up the other and held it in front of her like a shield.

"You're not taking her like you did Ebony. You can't." She was sobbing now, and waving the bowl back and forth desperately, but with her eyes closed like she knew the blade would get past her and she couldn't bear to watch it.

I didn't want to put down Lydia first, I was not yet ready for that terrible duty, but they were squeezed all the way back into the corner of the barn and I couldn't see how to get around Lydia to get at the cat. I put the knife out of the way behind me and took Lydia by both arms, grabbing her low by the elbows so I wouldn't press on the fresh burn at her shoulder. She hit me in the chest with the pewter bowl, hard, and I almost let go, but I was able to hold on, lift her up, and move her away from the cat huddled in the corner.

I shook Lydia and she dropped the bowl. I wrapped my arms around her torso, squeezing her against my chest as hard as I could. I kept squeezing like that, not relaxing my grip until I felt her body go limp, her head flop to the side, and her body lean onto my shoulder.

I heard the barn door slam open. When I turned, I saw Beth come around the corner. She stopped. She looked at me and then at Lydia, limp in my arms. She spotted the blade on the ground. Looking back and forth between Lydia and me, she bent over and picked it up.

Before she could do anything rash, I said, "She's okay, Beth. She's just sleeping."

I walked over and handed Lydia to her. She took her daughter and laid her head across her shoulder, like she had done when Lydia was just a little girl half that size.

"Can you take her upstairs and put her to bed, please?" I asked. Beth brushed Lydia's hair away from her face and wiped the tears off her cheeks. "Oh, and you better lock her in. We don't want her running away again."

Beth turned to go.

"Sweetheart, before you go," I said. "I'll need that knife."

She nodded mutely, handed it to me, and turned away, moving slowly under the weight.

The cat was still cowering in the corner. I leaned over her and put the knife to her throat, and she stayed motionless, looking up into my eyes with resignation. I held the knife there for a second, trying to think if there was a prayer or a verse fitting the occasion. I realized that her blood was going to get all over me, so I stood up to take off my shirt.

Then she spoke.

"We're just like you."

It was a queer experience, as the others had said, to hear an animal talk. I looked at her briefly then turned away, not saying anything. She continued.

"Lydia explained it to me."

I knew that this was unholy speech, and that I had no right to engage it, but I did want to know what had happened to Lydia, what perverted course had taken my daughter from me.

"She explained what?" I positioned my body to block the cat's path out of the corner, in case she was trying to distract me or trick me in some way.

"How all this came about."

I sat down across from her, pointing the knife in her direction but still averting my eyes. "How is it that you speak, cat? Let's start with that."

"We all speak," she said. "Well, most of us."

"Then how is it that I've never heard it? I've been around beasts all my life."

"We don't speak around you…"

"Around…?"

"Around you men."

"And why is that, why do you not speak around men?"

"Because you hurt us. You kill us when you hear us speak."

I felt queasy, talking to her, like the longer this continued the greater my sin. But I couldn't stop myself, not yet.

"How are you able to speak?" I asked. "Are you possessed by demons? And why now, why is all this happening now? Is this a sign, a New Chastisement, like some of the elders say?"

"We have always been able to speak, because we are just like you."

"You lie, as you must by your nature. You don't look like us. You don't move like us. You don't make sound like us."

"We are able to do all those things, but we are taught not to. Lydia explained it to me."

"Yes, I remember you saying that. How would Lydia know these things – has she been possessed, as well?" I looked over Princess for the first time since we began speaking. She was sitting in a funny position, her back wedged into the corner, her belly and her teats exposed to me. Her front legs were somehow dangled around the knees of her rear legs, like she pretended to the body of a girl, not a cat. Sitting that way, she didn't quite look like a cat. Almost more like a young woman. I rubbed at my eyes. I wondered if I was being enchanted in some way.

"Lydia learned from the one called... Sawyer?" she said. "Reverend Sawyer?"

"Yes. It was *he* who corrupted her," I said.

"He told her that a great sickness once moved over the face of the earth. That none of the beasts survived. Only mankind survived, and only a few of them. But men needed beasts to make sacrifice to God, to produce meat and clothing, and to do labor, so they could live as the men in the Bible lived. So, they turned some of their own kind into beasts, into us. We are like you, just like you. Only with different names."

I recalled the verse from Genesis that I had preached on that very morning. "Out of the ground, the god Yahweh formed every animal of the field and every bird of the air and brought them to the man to see what he would call them; and whatever the man called every living creature, that was its name." Some he called cattle, some swine, some dog, some cat...

I looked at her, sitting in the corner. Now her lower legs were stretched out along the ground, nearly touching mine. Her arms, which a moment before I had seen as front legs, were folded across her chest, covering her two... breasts. I squeezed my eyes shut and shook my head, but when I looked on her again, I still saw a young woman, not a cat.

I knew then exactly what was happening and what I had to do next.

I picked up the blade and cut her throat in one stroke. Blood sprayed out, covering my face, my bare chest, and my pants. Blessing me, for the blood of holy sacrifice cleanses and protects, wards off all that would do us harm, even including this talking beast's marvelous and deadly powers of deception.

In the house, Beth was sitting on our bed, looking out of our open bedroom door and across the hall to the locked door of Lydia's room. I took the key from Beth's hand and crossed the hall. When she saw me turn the key in Lydia's door, she got up and followed me in, asking me what I was doing and why I still had the knife.

I ignored her and went straight to the bed. Lydia appeared to be sleeping, no longer unconscious, but she was beginning to stir as she heard her mother's rising voice. I tucked the knife into my belt and went to the dresser, taking out handfuls of the girl's clothes and using them as makeshift ropes, binding Lydia's ankles and wrists to the bedposts.

Beth became screechy and frantic, plucking at my hands, then hitting my arms, back, and shoulders with her fists.

I shoved Beth away and took out the knife.

Before I could perform my legal obligation, Beth jumped onto the bed, covering Lydia's body with her own and facing me down from all fours. I put the knife in my belt and grabbed her by her hair and by her arm, swinging her off the bed and down onto the floor. By now, Lydia was fully awake and was thrashing about, trying to get loose of her bindings.

I pulled the knife out and moved toward Lydia, but Beth got between us again, and was clutching my wrist, pulling the knife away from Lydia and toward herself, screaming "Take me! Take me, not her. I'm responsible for how she is. Take me," and other hysterical things. I threw the knife down and took my wife by both shoulders, pushing her out of the room, across the hallway, and into the doorway of our bedroom. As she screamed and kicked and punched, I took her hands in mine and raised her arms over her head. I leaned back, lifted my right leg off the ground, and drove the heel of my foot into her midsection, hurling her all the way across our bedroom floor and into the small dresser next to the bed. Before she could recover, I slammed the door shut, took the key from Lydia's bedroom door, and locked Beth in.

Lydia was free of three of her bindings and was held now just at the one wrist. As she cursed me, I was able to get her feet retied and then her free hand. I found the knife on the floor. When I held it over her, she suddenly became quiet and still. I remembered then the stories of Abraham and Jephthah, and all the times I had wondered what it felt like for them to accept the call to sacrifice their own flesh and blood according to divine will. I remembered all the times I wondered how it felt to Isaac and to Jephthah's daughter to become blessed, sacred offerings.

"Now we know," I said, looking down at Lydia. "Now we both know."

As I leaned over her, she strained her head and neck up towards me, as if surrendering to the power of the Spirit within her, as if now, finally, she had won her salvation by desiring nothing more than the embrace of God's will.

I paused, waiting to hear Lydia's last earthly words, longing to hear her praise her Savior before she went to meet Him.

She spat in my face.

I stood up, wiping off my cheeks, and heard from across the hall as Beth weakly pummeled the door, croaking through the door, "She's not to blame. I'm to blame. I'm to blame. Take me instead."

That's when it happened. A clear image in the room, right in front of me. A vision, a glorious vision, of the angel appearing to Abraham, calling him away from his sacrifice of Isaac, telling him to cut the ram in his son's place. And I heard a voice, there in the room behind me, speaking into my ear, saying, "And if your right hand causes you to sin, cut it off and throw it away; it is better for you to lose one of your members than for your whole body to go into hell."

I looked at Lydia's right shoulder, at the mark that made her a beast by law, the mark that required her to be destroyed.

I had not done any butchering since called into the ministry, but it came back to me.

Mercifully, Lydia passed out quickly and I was able to remove her arm at the shoulder, just above the mark, without causing undue suffering.

I tied it off before she bled out, cleaned and dressed the wound, and then released her feet and other hand from their bindings. I locked her in her room and left her to rest.

The offending arm was made a holocaust. I cleaned myself and retired to my study.

• • •

The sun is now coming up in the East. I had just started composing the closing prayer for Sunday when I heard Lydia rouse and begin moaning in pain. I went to her room and sat with her, trying to ease her suffering by describing the divine visitation, explaining how, by the grace of Your Spirit, I was able to see a way to save her earthly life, to keep her here with us a while longer until, by Your divine will, she is called home.

She would not talk to me. She looked at me with the eyes of some feral creature. She would only spit at me, and hiss, and bare her claws, and make terrible caterwauling sounds from deep within her throat.

I finally left her and returned to my study.

Today, Burkhart and the others will come. I will explain to them why she yet lives. They will see that she is no longer branded. And they will hear for themselves that she is no beast.

I will find a way to make her speak.

Those Who Slip Through
By Curtis A. Deeter

WHEN I WAS ELEVEN, I moved next door to an artist named
Leprosy Man. That was my name for him, anyway. I never learned his real
name, but I saw him picking at his shriveled, black foot one afternoon and
the name stuck.

I had names for lots of things. The kid two townhouses down, Trent, he
was Fatty Patty – only behind his back, of course. Ashton, the older girl next
door – thirteen-year-old, razor-thin, tomboy Ashton – was Knees, because
she always had scars and scratches on her knees.

I remember Leprosy Man most of all, though. He wore his black hair in
a messy ponytail tied with rubber bands or hemp thread. He lurked around
in dark places, shrouded in a black trench coat dusted with white dandruff
flakes, and smoked American Spirits alone in his garage while he sketched.
Or didn't sketch, most of the time.

Ashton and I rode scooters back and forth across the parking lot, narrowly avoiding the old cars with tinted windows that pulled in and out of
Trent's driveway. From afar, we watched as one man or another met Trent's
mother at the front door and followed her inside. Twenty minutes later –
sometimes an hour, sometimes only five minutes, they came out and we
would still be scootering around or laying on the berm under the dogwood

tree, fingers slightly touching, staring at the clouds. Ashton would prop herself up on her elbows, and I would watch her slender spine twist and bend under her Billabong t-shirt. I could see her rib cage, and I watched each rib ripple snake-like up and down her torso, half-expecting her to molt right there in the grass.

"Who d'ya spect that was?" she would ask. We asked a lot of questions without expecting answers. If they were ever given, we were too busy being young to listen.

I would just shrug, and we would go back to doing nothing at all, but at least we were doing nothing with each other. That was my favorite part.

Leprosy Man noticed the stream of men, too. From behind a cloud of yellow smoke, he sketched away in his notepad and watched. I always wondered what he was inspired to draw whenever he watched us. Did he draw the universe when he saw Ashton – the sun, the stars? Did he draw a buffet line of fried meats and sausage gravy for Trent? A water fountain for everyone to drink from Trent's mother? Did he draw ghosts for me? Or blank spaces where real people should have been? Some people see the world in colors, others in words. I like to think Leprosy Man saw the world in white streaks of chalk scribbled on black pages.

• • •

Instead of fireworks on the Fourth of July, we got greasy gray-green clouds and summer morning fog. I could taste the whisper of rain on the air and smell the remnants of bonfires from the night before. Despite the impending storm – despite the awkwardness of our adolescent, we headed unabashed out into the world.

We didn't break the boundary of our bubble that often. Occasionally we would cross the main road to use the rich kids' park in the subdivision opposite ours. Once, we even took to the streets and found a bike trail that wove through industrial parks and back alleys all the way to downtown Verona. Ashton and I had been too scared to go into any of the shops, but we sat under the willow trees and watched the college students shuffle from one class to another. I had felt so free, so brave – brave enough to rest the tips of my fingers on her bony hand. She didn't move it, either. She smiled and let the cool breeze float her away.

Back to that Fourth of July, back to the fog and drizzle, back to the time where everything changed. Trent heard a rumor, as he often did, about a construction site a mile down the road. They were building a new school – one I would inevitably be redistricted to once the ribbon was cut and the scandals swept under the rug. A friend of a friend of a friend told him that there were tunnels.

"Tunnels?" I asked. "For what?"

"You have friends?" Ashton asked.

"It's a mystery." Trent whipped his scooter around and hit himself in the chin. "Tommy Graves said that Amanda Higgins told him that Michael Sanders took them all the way to Verona. That's almost 3 miles, you know? And Michael came back with a mustache and a whole new understanding about life. It changed him. For real, it did."

Ashton rolled her eyes.

"And Marcy said she found treasure down there. Real gold, like in the movies. And a hidden room where kids play Super Smash Brothers and watch anime all day long. Somewhere time stops, and we can be kids forever."

"Yeah, right," Ashton said. "Marcy also said her cousin was supposed to play in that Cast Away movie instead of Tom Hanks. As if. Have you seen her cousin?"

I had to agree with Ashton. Marcy, and a lot of the other big kids, were known to make up stories to entice kids like us to fall into all sorts of traps.

Still, I was curious. I liked exploring. It made sense to me. The world was a big place for someone so small, and every new inch I discovered brought me closer to discovering it all.

I led on my skateboard, with Ashton and Trent scooting close behind. The trip was much longer than our normal rides down the hill and around the cul-de-sac. Wrought with barking dogs, fast-moving traffic, and strange, sinister-looking adults menacing us from their porches, we managed the distance on adrenaline and naivety alone.

Some of the big kids beat us there. Tommy, Michael, and Marcy were looking into a dark pit. When we got closer, I saw it wasn't a natural anomaly, rather the entrance to the fabled Tunnel. It was a man-made structure, concrete, resembling a wide pipe buried in the sandy dirt. A heavy concrete lid with a rebar handle sealed off the entrance. The big kids were trying to figure out how to get in. Even with their Herculean strength, they couldn't seem to pry it open.

It dawned on all three of us at the same time. They hadn't even been in yet.

There was no treasure, no endless passage to the far corners of the suburbs, no fountain of youth or Nintendo 64. Just an immovable cover and a bunch of frustrated, bored teenagers.

"What are you weirdos standing around for?" Marcy asked. "Help us out here."

I kicked my skateboard into the grass. Ashton and Trent ditched their scooters. Together, the six of us crouched around the cover, yanking and straining until it finally popped. With it, the fog that engulfed the neighborhood seemed to lift, too. I ran my dirty fingers through rain-wet hair and looked deep into the Tunnel.

"Who's going in?" Tommy asked, his voice cracking as he shied away from the edge. Everyone kicked dirt and shoved their hands into their pockets.

Ashton took my hand, moved in close, and said, "You'll go, won't you? If you go, I'll be right behind you. I might even kiss you down there, where no one else can see."

I don't know if it was the rush that I felt with her being so close, or the fact more kids were starting to show up on pegged bikes from every corner of our little world, but I nodded. I was going into the Tunnel to find the treasure at the end, whatever it might be. Of all the possibilities, I hoped it was Ashton's pale, chapped lips.

I climbed down the slippery metal ladder one rung at a time. The other's chatter quieted with every step. The hole at the entrance was shrinking faster than my confidence. It wasn't raining hard, but there was already an inch or two of water at the bottom. The path was dimly lit by holes in the concrete tubing, and I could see ahead where it split off in two directions. I crawled on my hands and knees to get there.

At the fork, I heard a loud, booming sound and felt a slight rumble. Suddenly, darkness was everywhere. The curved walls were closing in on me. Back at the ladder, I climbed faster than I thought possible. I could hear muffled voices above me, some low and authoritative and others high-pitched and squealing – sounding almost as desperate as I felt.

I pounded on the concrete lid. "Let me up! Let me up!" Rainwater trickled through the cracks into my mouth and eyes. "You guys! This isn't funny."

The lid rocked back and forth a bit. Dust fell from the bottom and small rocks clattered on the ground. I started banging again until I was too tired to move my arms and flopped to the bottom of the tunnel, arms curled around my knees.

Rain came through faster and faster. Water rose as time dragged on. First, up to my back pockets. Then, beyond that, soaking me to the bone through the rips in my jeans. If someone didn't come to help soon, I would drown, and a construction worker named Bob would find me bloated in the corner with my thumb in my mouth.

After what felt like forever, the lid slid off and dim, gray light washed in. The figure at the top was hazy at first, but the smell was undeniable: American Spirits. Of all people, Leprosy Man had come to my rescue.

• • •

Trent invited us to dinner, but I never expected Leprosy Man to show up. We kept Trent around for our own selfish reasons – Ashton to keep space between her and me, me to feel better about myself, but we had never gone into his house before. That would make us officially friends; next, we would be playing video games together, having sleepovers, and sharing our deepest, darkest secrets. The real reason we still hung out with Trent was because no one else would hang out with an outsider and a girl who might slip through.

There weren't any cars in front of Trent's house. It might have been the first night ever without a slew of house guests coming and going. I didn't know what to make of that, but Trent seemed happy about it.

Trent's mom's face lit up when we walked in. We were sweaty, covered in dirt, and smelled like onions. Even though we tracked our action-packed afternoon across her living room carpet, she acted as if she'd never been happier in her life.

A thing to know about Trent's mother, who I liked to call Angel, was that she raised Trent alone. She went to school for a while, but her night job and caring for Trent took up too much of her energy. She was a dancer, among other things, and Angel wore the tightest shorts and shortest shirts of any woman I had ever seen. Her ribs didn't stick out like Ashton's, but other parts sure did. The first time I saw her up close, I forgot all about my kiddy-crush.

"Welcome, kids," she said. "Come in, come in. I was just finishing up dinner. Trent didn't tell me he was having friends over, or I would have cooked more. No worries. I'll just throw in some chicken nuggets or something."

I strutted into the kitchen. "Can I help?"

Angel rubbed my cheek and winked. "You're sweet, but I've got it covered. Y'all just go play, and I'll call when it's ready."

Trent's room was exactly as I had pictured it. He had plastic wrestling figures displayed in their original boxes. A small television was plugged in near the door, directly in line with his yellow-stained bed, and connected to about thirty different gaming consoles. His room smelled slightly like chlorine and pee.

Ashton didn't seem to know where to sit, but I didn't care. Twenty minutes ago, I would have found a vacuum, or a flamethrower, to clear her a spot. I barely even noticed her puppy dog eyes begging my help. I was too busy sneaking peeks at Angel.

Before Trent got the Dreamcast started, there came a knock at the front door.

"Thanks for coming," I heard Angel say. "It's been a hard week."

"Thanks for having me," Leprosy Man said. "Smells delicious."

My stomach turned to knots, and Trent's room started to spin.

There was a loud smack and Angel giggled. "Wait til the main course."

He was shocked to see us and didn't say much. He avoided eye contact, as if looking a child directly in the eyes might turn his clothes rainbow colors, and sulked as he shoveled food into his mouth and smoked cigarettes to the filter.

At one point, Leprosy Man cleared his throat. "Stayin' out of manholes, lately?"

The three of us exchanged a quick glance, and I simply shrugged my shoulders. He might have been my hero, but he wasn't *a* hero.

Ashton pushed cold peas, pterodactyl-shaped chicken nuggets, and soupy macaroni around her plate, occasionally nibbling a small bite.

Trent inhaled his food. Then, he inhaled a second plate, before replacing his own with his mother's. She was too busy making eyes at Leprosy Man to notice the swap.

After dinner, we went our separate ways. Ashton said goodbye, trying to sneak in our regular hug, but I patted her on the shoulder and walked away. I think that single moment might have been the end of her – of us – but I was too hormonal to realize it.

"We tried to help, you know? I didn't want to get him. We just couldn't get the cover off by ourselves. The big kids, they—"

"Don't worry." I waved her off.

"He was the only one around. I'm sorry…"

By then, I was already gone.

The next day, I headed out at the usual time. I skipped my normal detour to Ashton's house and went right for Angel's. As I went to knock, Leprosy Man opened the door into my face, knocking me to the pavement. He looked at me, lowering his sunglasses to reveal baggy, red eyes, and sneered before lurching off to his garage and his pencils.

My palms were bleeding from the fall and my bony butt throbbed. Most importantly, I was devastated.

I ran back to my house, ignoring Ashton watching me through barely parted blinds. Straight into my room, I dove under the covers and buried my head in pillows. I decided I would never leave my room again.

A few hours later, the sun low in the sky and orange creeping across everything, I felt the end of the bed depress. I knew it was Trent by his smell.

"You okay?" he asked.

"Why do you care? We're not even really friends."

He shifted away from me. I heard him sniffle. "We're not? Oh. Well, that's okay, I guess. Is it because of my mom? All my friends go away because of her, but I think she's just the nicest. Why doesn't anyone like her?"

I slowly uncovered, hoping he wouldn't notice that I'd been crying. "Are you kidding?" He shook his head. "She's the best, man. I think I might be in love."

Trent tilted his head so far to the side that I thought he might snap his neck. "That's kinda gross, and way pathetic."

We both laughed. I don't know why he was laughing, but I was laughing at the way he scrunched his face up like a pig when he spoke. Afterwards, I felt a lot better.

"Can I tell you something?" he asked.

I nodded.

"I think my mom was arguing with that man last night. They were yelling, and she kept slamming the wall and things were falling off the shelves. I know because I snuck out of my room to watch TV on the big screen, and I could hear them through the floors. He might have hit her, too, but I didn't do anything. I'm supposed to be the man of the house, and I just curled up on the couch and covered my ears. I was so scared. What if he hurt her? What if she never forgives me for not saving her?"

"Is she okay?"

"I think so. She seemed really, really happy this morning. We even danced around to Stevie Wonder while she cooked breakfast."

"I don't know, then," I said. "He's a big guy. I wouldn't try to fight him or anything if I were you."

"Well, I'll do better next time. Whatever it takes."

"That's good. Let me know if you need help."

He shrugged. "Wanna go outside and play?"

Ashton joined us. We rode down the hill and climbed it a few times, but the act had lost its luster. There was no adventure to it anymore. The berm was too wet to watch the clouds, and none of us really knew what else to do. We'd been doing the same stuff for so long that I suppose it was only a matter of time. If we had realized that was the last time the three of us would be together, would we have acted different? Would it have been less awkward? Looking back, I think it happened exactly like it was supposed to happen.

• • •

Leprosy Man moved. He'd caught something from somewhere and the skin on his feet and hands had been blistering and peeling. The skin left behind was black and crunchy like the outer layer of burnt marshmallows. It had gotten so bad that he couldn't walk up and down the stairs or cook for himself, so he moved back to his mother's house to draw and smoke and be mysterious while he peeled away layer by layer.

Angel told me this. Their relationship lasted a few weeks, longer than any of her others, and she'd been so hopeful for this one. But he'd drifted off without as much as a goodbye. She told me at Trent's funeral, occasionally glancing over at the empty seat that should have been Ashton. Even with tear-streaked makeup running down her face, Angel was beautiful.

"Did he give you..." I grimaced and looked at her stocking covered toes.

"His condition isn't contagious, silly." I thought I could see where his hands had left impressions on her face. I cringed, adjusted my rental tie. "Besides, he didn't have any problems when we were seeing each other. Not really. Just the one foot."

Then, she told me about Trent. Trent died trying to protect her, in the end. One of the men who drove an old car with tinted windows had come over late on a school night. She'd seen this one off and on for years. He worked construction – I wondered if it was Bob – and they'd met at the place she danced. His name was Clint, but I called him The Bastard.

The Bastard liked to show up to their house late at night, always drunk. This time, Angel didn't want him around. She pleaded with him, begged him to leave them alone. Instead, he got angry. And then violent. Trent came downstairs for a Mountain Dew and saw The Bastard slap her across the face before shoving her up against the banister. Trent lost his mind.

"He was so brave." She rested her head on my shoulder. "And I was so stupid."

When words couldn't intimidate Trent, The Bastard pulled a knife. He didn't even warn Trent. He stuck the blade into his stomach and pushed him onto the couch. The Bastard ran, and Trent bled to death while Angel, stroking his hair and holding him tight to her chest, waited for the police.

I had moved away not too long after Leprosy Man. Ashton was gone, too. Her mother told me she was going to live at a special clinic. Trent and his mother had been the only ones left when it happened. All the other town-houses and duplexes on the cul-de-sac were empty, some shuttered for good, and it took the police almost an hour to get there.

I wasn't much older at the funeral, but I like to think I was wiser. I knew by then that she wasn't really an angel. I also had an idea of the sort of clinic they sent Ashton to. She had been as thin as a pine needle. On breezy days, which there had been a lot of that summer, I was worried she might float away to the next town over, or that she would step on a drain cover and slip through, never to be seen again. Reality wasn't much different. One day she was there, the next she was gone in a gust of wind.

After the service, I spotted a large canvas leaning against the stoop of the funeral hall. Trent's mom picked it up, and we stared at it for a long time. Strangers poured out behind us, offering a blur of condolences and touching her shoulder, but we barely noticed. We were lost in the art.

It was white chalk on a black background and took place on a sandy beach under a million stars. A woman, half-trapped in a conch cocoon, was clawing her way out. She'd grown angel's wings, but they were matted flat to her back and half-stuck inside her prison. All around her, dozens of footsteps were patterned in the sand. The smallest pair, isolated with a slight golden hue and sketched with more definition than the others, moved directly away from her, falling upward off the page.

I knew right away he'd drawn it, and I hated him for making her cry. She held the canvas to her chest and sobbed. I also hated him for not being at the funeral for her. Most of all, I hated myself for needing him to be my savior one more time.

Sensible Attire

By D. Wayne Moore

I WANTED TO WEAR my red shoes down to the river, but Rodney said I shouldn't.

"Sometimes, there is mud and rocks and stuff," he said.

He also said there was a dead body washed up in a bag on the bank. That's why we were going down there – to see the body. I don't see why it mattered what shoes I wore, so I wore what I wanted. Rodney was real sore.

"Ain't you afraid you are gonna slip and fall?" he said.

"If I did, it wouldn't matter what kinda shoes I had on. I would still be just as muddy."

He didn't have no answer to that.

For Rodney's part, he was wearing his hunting boots – the ones with the camouflage on the sides. He was also wearing those stupid coveralls that he always liked to wear. "Sensible attire," he called it. I thought he looked ridiculous, but I didn't tell him so. If he wanted to dress that way, it was no concern of mine.

On the way to the river, Rodney smoked about a hundred cigarettes with the window open and wouldn't let it go about my shoes.

"I just don't see why you gotta wear whorin' shoes to view a body," he said, flicking his ash onto the floorboard.

"I take pride in looking good, no matter the occasion. And they aren't whorin' shoes, they're pumps."

I also pointed out to him that they matched the patterned kerchief I was wearing. Rodney just rolled his eyes and grunted like he always did. Sometimes, I thought he didn't understand anything.

When we got down to the riverbank, it was muddy, just like Rodney said. I had to pretend that I didn't care, so I wouldn't have to eat any crow about my shoes. There was also a body on the bank. It was all wrapped up in rope and plastic, bloated like one of Mamaw's Christmas hams. Rodney had said that too. About the plastic.

It didn't smell like any ham I have ever seen, though. It stunk like mud, and fish, and potatoes that have gone rancid in the back of the pantry. It smelled awful.

"I think I might get sick," I told him.

Rodney told me to hold my nose, instead, so I used the kerchief that I had tied around my hair to cover my face.

"Have you ever seen anything like it?" he asked. "I'm going in for a better look."

I told him about how one time I found a cut-up buck in a garbage bag on my way home from school. It smelled like rotten potatoes, too, and hamburger that's gone bad, and one of its legs had stuck out through the side of the plastic, like it had tried to kick its way out. But this, I told him, was way worse. This was a person.

He asked me if I would come closer with him, but I told him I didn't want to. My shoes were already covered in mud and made a sucking sound when I tried to walk. But I didn't tell him that was why. He would only get sore at me, again.

"Is it a man or a woman?" I asked, as Rodney walked up real close. I could tell he thought it stunk, too, by the way he jammed his face into the inside of his elbow. I think I heard him gag, too, but he claimed it was just his asthma acting up.

"I can't tell," he said, hacking a ball of phlegm onto the shore. "It looks kinda like a woman, but she's all bloated and pale. I think something has been eating at her face, too! The plastic is all poked full of holes."

I kinda wanted to see for myself, but my shoes were starting to sink in the mud. I found a flatrock to stand on, out of the muck, and decided to stay there, with my scarf around my face.

"How do you think they died?" I wanted to know. I only ever knew one person that was killed, and that was my grandpa. He was run over by a train when he was walking home from the bar. It cut him right in half, across the middle. At the funeral, he had been all laid out in a casket with his bowtie and Sunday shirt on. He didn't even look dead, let alone cut in two. He didn't smell, neither.

Rodney said he couldn't tell without having any professional doctor or law enforcement training, but he suspected that there was definitely foul play involved.

That's what he said: foul play. I thought it was a real comical thing to say, but he thought it made him sound smart, like cops on TV. He was real dopey, sometimes.

"Of course, there was foul play," I said. "Bodies don't just end up in plastic on their own".

He had nothing to say to that.

The truth is that Rodney and I were on the outs. We had been dating for a couple of months, but his wife was starting to get wise and had begun puttin' on the pressure for Rodney to be more of a doting husband type. He didn't like her much – at least that's what he said, but he couldn't afford any divorce. He told me a sidepiece was good and all (that's what he called me), but not when it started costing him money. It ain't like he had any money to lose, anyway. Or anything else, for that matter.

"I think I'm gonna peek inside," he said, scratching a match on the sole of his boot, and lighting another cigarette.

I warned him not to leave any fingerprints or nothing. "You don't want anyone thinking you done it, whatever it is. Cops are real savvy about stuff like that," I said.

"I ain't *that* stupid," he said, pulling a pair of striped canvas work gloves out of his pocket and sticking his hands inside. They were every bit as coarse and dirty as his hands had been. Everything about Rodney was sort of that way. I always kinda wished he had a little more class.

Taking a drag on his cigarette, I watched him lean in real close and pull back the plastic from the body. It made an awful rumpling sound, when he did, and I was afraid the whole town was gonna hear it. I looked around but didn't see anyone, anywhere, so I leaned in to take a little peek, too.

Before he even got the plastic all the way off, Rodney turned and started throwing up on the bank and in the mud.

Stop!" I said. "You're gonna make me get sick, too."

But he didn't stop. He just kept throwing up and walking towards me like he wanted me to help him. That's when he threw up all over my legs and my feet.

"Damnit, Rodney, you idiot," I said. He was still clutching his knees and puking. "You're a big, stupid pig for messin' up my shoes after I had tried so hard to keep them clean."

"You're just a dumb piece of ass," he said. "What do you know about anything? I told you not to wear them, anyhow!"

"Well, I *ain't* some dumb piece of ass. Not yours, anymore, anyhow! I never wanted to see any stupid dead body, anyway."

I thought he was gonna hit me, then, 'cause he wiped off his mouth with the back of his hand and balled up his fist inside his glove. I cussed him out again and tried to run away. That's how I fell in the mud. He didn't hit me, though. He just laughed at me sitting there, all covered in muck, and walked on up the bank to where the pick-up truck was.

I waited a few minutes for him to come back and be all sorry, but he didn't. I heard him start the truck and pull away after a bit, and I just sat there on the riverbank, next to the body, wiping the muck off of my shoes with the neckerchief. He was such a pig, sometimes.

The body in the bag stunk real bad. The plastic was open where Rodney had peeled it back, and a crow flew in and sat on top. It began pecking away at what I figured to be the body's face. I could see what looked like hair all matted up and wet. It looked like it might have been blonde, once, but now it just looked like a musty old dishrag.

"Ain't we a sight," I said to the body, knowing that it was way worse off than me. I knew it couldn't hear me, anyway, and figured it wouldn't care much if it could.

The crow just looked at me out of the corner of its eye, and I thought for a moment that it might want to peck me next, but he just flew off down the bank a ways, instead.

Since I was alone on the riverbank, and already muddy, I decided I might as well have a look at the body. I knew it wouldn't be all nice like my grandpa was, but I was already past caring about that, I guess. I had kinda gotten used to the smell, by now, but I covered my nose and mouth again, anyway. Just to be safe. I already had Rodney's throw up on my shoes and my stockings, but I didn't want any of my own.

When I looked in the bag, I could tell that the body was a woman. She had kinda full, pouty lips and a big hole in the side of her cheek where the crow, or something else, had been picking at her. She was completely naked inside the plastic, as far as I could tell. Her skin was all waxy looking, like maybe she was covered in chicken fat, and the skin was sloughing off her neck and forehead. She looked awfully dead. I wanted to know her name. I felt awful for her, being all naked and alone, and all, and I laid my hair kerchief over her face to maybe keep the birds from pecking at her more. It's the least I could do, I thought.

By the time Rodney came back with the truck, it was already too late. I had already started walking along the river, on my way back home. I didn't even turn back to look at the truck, up on the bank, where it parked. I just kept on walking, in my stocking-feet, down the shore, carrying my shoes in my hand because I had already finished cleaning the mud off of them.

Good Friday
By Krista Hilton

BEN DRESSES for his job as the 16th Street Mall Easter Bunny in a corner of the backroom at Krispy Kreme Donuts. He would like to see himself in a mirror before going out to the little bunny hut, but no mirror is available, and maybe that would be too weird anyway, seeing yourself and yet not seeing yourself.

"Once the head's on," the man who hired him said, "you're a rabbit."

He's the brother of a guy who befriended Ben while they were both in treatment. If the Easter Bunny job works out, the man said he would find Ben a permanent job.

Being a rabbit is easy enough. Rabbits don't talk. The ones Ben saw as a kid in the fields around his house in Strasburg, Colorado, didn't do much of anything. They sat in one place, munching prairie grass, barely moving for hours. He'd read that that was their way of staying safe. Too much movement put them at risk. Hawks. Coyotes. Dogs. Boys with pellet guns; Ben had been one of those boys. Thankfully, he had never gotten off a good shot.

Ben shuffles out of the backroom and waits next to the mall restrooms where he is supposed to meet the photographer who'll take him to the hut. They have to work in tandem that way because Ben can't see his feet. His field of vision is limited to what he can see through a two by six-inch piece of black wire mesh meant to be the bunny's permanently smiling mouth. And with feet as big as his oversized bunny feet, Ben doesn't want to go walking around without help. He'd be a danger to himself and others.

The photographer is late. Again. And on Good Friday, what's supposed to be their busiest day. He looks to be near the same age as Ben, thirty-one, and his name is Bill or Will. Ben isn't sure which. They'd been introduced after Ben had the bunny head on. While he can hear when wearing the head, things are muffled. It doesn't really matter what the guy's name is anyway. It's not like they ever carry on any kind of conversation beyond the bare necessities of getting the job done. That's fine by Ben.

He feels a tap on his back and turns slowly because those big bunny feet of his can do a pretty good job knocking over chairs, strollers, maybe even small children. But when he gets his bunny body all the way around, no one is there. At least not at Ben's eye level. Now it can be one of two things: a kid too short to be seen or somebody doing the old knock and run, like Ben and his brother, Marty, had done, ringing doorbells then hiding to watch the door open to nobody there.

Marty is the last thing Ben wants to be thinking about. It's bad enough he has to spend an hour every week with his counselor talking about his role in what happened to his brother, but did the memories have to be there in front of his eyes all the time? And why couldn't they be the good memories instead of the bad ones? Why does he always have to remember coming around the corner of the garage to see his five-year-old brother hanging in the cottonwood tree, the string from his cowboy hat tight around his neck?

Ben puts a paw on each side of the big papier-mâché bunny head and carefully bends at the waist. The head is so heavy Ben can topple over if he goes too far. But there is no one there. He straightens, ready to return to the backroom to wait for the photographer when surprise, surprise, who should appear, his big grin stretching across Ben's view?

"Real funny," Ben says. "You're late."

The photographer steps back. "Hey, rabbit. You don't have much of a sense of humor, do you?"

Ben sighs. What had the doctor told him during detox, nothing else would feel as bad as what he was going to feel those first few days with no alcohol between him and whatever it was he needed to come to terms with?

The doctor had lied. Life in the post-treatment world could be just as bad, if not worse.

The first kid to enter the hut is a shy girl, about four, with the usual fancy Easter dress and carefully curled hair. She is coaxed next to Ben by her mother, then lifted onto his lap. He hopes she isn't a crier. All kids make Ben nervous, but crying ones really do. His heart beats faster. Sweat slides down the back of his neck. He just wants the whole thing over with as quickly as possible. But the mom always wants to wait the kid out to get a decent picture.

"Come on, sweetie," this one says when the girl won't smile. "Don't you want a chocolate bunny?"

"No, Mommy."

"Then, how about McDonald's?"

"No."

The photographer jumps in. Ben has to admit the guy is pretty good at what he does. From inside his bag of equipment, he pulls out a bunny hand puppet. Then in his best Bugs Bunny voice, the photographer first gets the kid talking and the next thing you know, laughing. Click, flash, job done.

After two hours, the line into the hut slows for lunch. In another thirty minutes or so, business will pick up again. The photographer takes advantage of the break to step behind the hut for a smoke. Ben wishes he could do the same, but he isn't supposed to take the head off until his shift is over. Besides, it wouldn't look too great for a headless Easter Bunny to be chain smoking in the mall parking lot. Even he knows that. So, Ben sits and waits.

He got pretty good at sitting still and doing nothing over the three months he was in treatment. You got up, had breakfast, then sat and waited for your first therapy group. Everyone just sat for fifteen or twenty minutes, staring at the floor. They repeated the waiting between groups and individual counseling all day. Ben learned it helped to cross his legs and put each of his hands under the opposite armpit to stop the trembling he had been prone to since detox. Ben still finds the position comforting, like an upright fetal pose, helping him pull his energy inward where he needs it most.

Unfortunately, the bunny costume makes it impossible for him to cross either his legs or arms. The stuffing in the suit plumps him up into a bunny that looks like he's had a few too many double cheeseburgers. So, Ben just sits, both feet on the floor, his hands in his lap. If he angles his head a bit to the left, he can see out the front door of the hut and into the parking lot. He likes to watch the people, wondering who they are, how they find it possible to get on in the world.

Ben's counselor warned him against isolating. "Get out, be with people," she says. "Isolation is dangerous."

Ben isn't quite ready to do more than just be in the presence of other people. The mall is perfect for that. He can buy a meal, sit on a bench to eat the food, walk aimlessly through the shops. He is alone but not alone. And there is no liquor store.

The photographer returns when a young woman with a baby approaches the hut. Ben doesn't like babies any more than crying children. The good news is babies are usually too stunned by the enormity of his bunny head and facial features to cry. This one is no different. The mother steps toward Ben with the baby, clearly a boy since he is dressed head to toe in blue. Then she stops.

"Don't worry," the photographer says. "This bunny's a pro with babies."

What a lie, Ben thinks. If the woman or, for that matter, the photographer knew about Ben's past, they'd never put a baby in his trembling arms. But they don't know. So, the mother hands the baby to Ben.

The photographer adjusts his light to remove the shadows from the baby's face. "How old is he?"

"Seven weeks."

The photographer checks his focus. "Not smiling yet." He snaps the picture.

The man sure knows his stuff, Ben thought, relieved to return the baby to his mother. He had no idea when it was that babies were supposed to start smiling. Shelley, his ex-wife, would have known all that. She read baby books at the dinner table nearly every night once she started wanting a baby. Things were good then, Ben writing programs for a local software vendor, Shelley nearly finished with her nursing degree. If only their lives could have stayed in that place and time. At first Ben thought a baby might bring the healing he desperately needed, that a new life might fill the huge hole Marty's death had dug in his heart. But terrifying thoughts of what can happen to a child soon followed, keeping him awake at night and unable to focus on his job during the day. In a panic, he scheduled a vasectomy and paid in cash so Shelley wouldn't know. Afraid to own up to what he had done, Ben continued going along with Shelley's plan month after month. When nothing happened, she sank into depression and wondered if something was wrong with her. She lost weight and cried over the smallest things. When she wanted to start fertility treatments, Ben finally told her about the vasectomy. Shelley left him the next day.

Business at the hut picks up again after the baby. For the next three hours, the line is nonstop. The photographer has the tough job, Ben knows, glad-handing the parents, taking the money, getting the kids to cooperate, snapping a good picture, clearing those people out so the next ones can come in. All Ben has to do is sit there. That, and hand each kid a chocolate bunny. The perfect job for a drunk. No, that's not who he is anymore, Ben reminds himself. He is a recovering drunk. There's a distinction. Alcoholics numb their pain; recovering alcoholics embrace their pain if they want to stay sober.

The judge who sent him to treatment instead of jail had made getting a job and daily Alcoholics Anonymous meetings requirements for Ben's release. There's an A.A. meeting in the mall at seven each evening. How convenient is that? After work, Ben gets out of his costume, steps into the restroom to wash his face and hands, then makes it to the meeting before they finish reading the Twelve Steps to get started. It's a different kind of meeting than the ones in treatment. There, everyone wore sweats and flip-flops and looked like they'd just gotten out of bed. The people at the mall meeting wear business suits and tailored dresses, and usually come from work. And they can actually focus on the topic for the entire hour the meeting takes. In treatment, people had a hard time paying attention for even five minutes. It was like their brains couldn't stick with any one thing for too long. Ben thought that was a defense mechanism. Think too much, and you're bound to come across something painful. The irony is feeling pain is exactly what they want you to do. *No pain, no gain.*

Ben knew that was going to be hard for him. Starting at thirteen, he had used any alcohol he could get his hands on to avoid his pain. He didn't back off until he met Shelley, sure no woman would want to marry a drunk. When she left him, Ben picked up right where he had left off. But then two DUIs in less than a week got Ben arrested. The judge who sent him to treatment gave Ben a strong warning that any repeat court appearance would have much different results, ones involving jail. Ben believed every word the judge said as if they had come from the mouth of God himself, whoever that was.

In A.A. they say, "a god of your own understanding." They say it's so each person can define a god for themselves, one who can meet their specific needs. The idea of a designer god reminds Ben of a morning in Sunday School two years after Marty died.

The teacher gave each kid a paintbrush, a box of paints, and a big sheet of paper on an easel. She told them to paint a picture of God, not what they'd seen in books, just the god you saw in your mind when you heard the word. Ben had stood in front of his paper without moving, not even dipping his brush in the paints, hearing all the kids around him slapping paint onto paper in manic creativity.

Finally, the teacher came to stand beside Ben.

"What do you see?" she asked.

"Nothing," he'd answered.

What was true then is still true now.

The photographer bends down in front of Ben's bunny head.

"Hey," he says. "The kid's slipping."

For a second, Ben has no idea what he means. Ben doesn't even feel the weight of the kid on his leg. Then the burned caramel smell inside the bunny head comes back, and Ben sees he is in the hut. He tightens his hold on the kid.

"Look up here," the photographer says. "Now smile."

Ben can't tell if the kid really does or not because he can't see more than their backs while they are on his lap. But the kid must have smiled because there was the usual flash followed by the photographer motioning to the kid to get down. Ben wiggles his shoulders; by this time of day, they are nearly numb from the weight of the head. There is padding, of course, but even twice as much foam rubber wouldn't have kept the edges of the heavy head from biting into Ben's skin. He tries to think of that as a good thing, a sensation that keeps him in his body, in the present, instead of in his head and in the past.

When the afternoon movie lets out, kids hyped on sugar rush into the hut. There are so many that Ben worries he might run out of chocolate bunnies. But the photographer has already realized that. He digs under his stand

and brings a new box over to fill Ben's basket.

"Take a look at the mom with the next kid," he says, kneeling next to Ben. "Maybe you'd like her to sit on your lap." He sniggers and gives Ben's shoulder a shove.

Ben can only see parts of the woman through the wire mesh, her knees, bare and a bit knobby; her hands, white and small; probably not the parts the photographer is interested in. She steps closer, pulling her daughter, who looks to be about seven, toward Ben.

"Come on, will you?" she says.

Ben holds out his bunny paw. The girl climbs onto his lap. Ben adjusts her shoulders so she will be facing the camera then tilts his head to get a better look at her. She is thin with blonde curls falling to her shoulders.

"Wait," the mom says. "Where's your ribbon?"

Ben hears her digging through a plastic shopping bag. Then she steps next to Ben and gathers the girl's hair into a high ponytail she ties with a pink ribbon.

Through his mesh mouth, Ben sees the back of the girl's neck. Round, red dots cover her pale skin. They can only be one thing: cigarette burns. Some are scars, some are scabbed, some are fresh. Ben knows because he'd seen similar marks on the inner wrists of a boy in grade school, punishment delivered by a cruel father. Ben counts the marks on the girl's neck. Ten. She must have suffered a great deal. And here the mother is showing those burns to the world as if nothing wrong has happened. More proof, as if Ben needs any, that a caring god doesn't exist.

The photographer tells Ben to turn the girl's shoulders more to the left. Ben hears the direction, but his arms won't cooperate.

"Come on, rabbit. They don't have all day."

Still Ben can't move. The photographer comes out from behind his camera and approaches Ben. He knocks on the bunny head.

"What? Are you asleep in there?"

Not asleep, Ben thinks. Frozen. Like those rabbits in the fields. Trying to stay safe. The photographer bends down to look inside the head. Seeing his face shocks Ben into action. He does what the photographer told him to. In a couple of minutes, the girl climbs down from Ben's lap and follows her mother out the door.

The photographer checks his watch. "Okay, that's it. The big day's done."

Ben stays seated while the photographer gathers his cameras and packs them into their cases. He helps Ben step down from the platform, then Ben follows him back to Krispy Kreme.

"Get plenty of rest, rabbit. Tomorrow's our last day. We should still be busy, though. All the last-minute parents."

He laughs and counts out Ben's share of the commission. Then he's gone.

Ben slumps onto the wooden bench provided for him. A normal day is exhausting. But after this day, Ben isn't sure he has enough energy left to get out of the bunny suit. His arms shake as he lifts the head off his shoulders and puts it into its bin. The rest of the costume follows. Outside Krispy Kreme, Ben checks the mall clock. A couple of minutes to eight. He can still make the start of the A.A. meeting if he hurries.

When Ben gets there, a man is reading the Second Step: *Came to believe that a power greater than ourselves can restore us to sanity.* Ben gets a sick feeling in his stomach as he sits down. How can he ever find sanity if he has no belief in a higher power? How can he believe in any higher power when things like Marty's death had happened? And then today, this little girl sits on his lap with her neck covered in cigarette burns. How did a higher power figure into that?

Ben realizes he's clenching his fists. A strong urge comes over him to buy a pint on his way home. He's got money in his pockets; there's a carry-out across the street from where he gets off the bus. Ben panics. When an alcoholic gets to the point of planning, he's in real trouble. The skin along the insides of his arms turns cold. His chest tightens. He has trouble taking a full breath.

Be where your feet are, the treatment counselors always said. It brings your attention back to the present. Ben looks down at his feet. He moves his toes inside his scuffed running shoes. The carpet his feet rest on is a dirty navy blue. The man next to him smells like cigarette smoke and strong coffee. The voice of the woman speaking rises at the beginning of each sentence then falls at the end. But the urge to drink is still there.

The second the meeting is over, Ben hurries to the Chinese stall in the food court. The spicy food finally distracts him from wanting to break his string of one hundred and eleven days of sobriety. To stay distracted, he takes a couple of laps around the mall to let off steam before catching his bus. But on his second lap, Ben sees the girl with the burns following her mother out of Sears. The mother carries several shopping bags. The little girl still wears the pink ribbon in her hair. Ben watches the two step onto the escalator to the lower level. He takes the stairs then follows them to where mother and daughter wait for their bus.

At first, Ben thinks he should stand to the back of the waiting passengers, so they won't notice him. But then he remembers they have only seen him in the bunny suit. They have no idea who he is now. The bus arrives. The girl and her mother get on. Ben does, too. The mother deposits her shopping bags in a seat near the exit door in the back. She motions for the girl to sit down on the aisle side of the seat next to the bags. Then the mother goes to the front of the bus and begins talking to the driver. As the bus starts to roll forward, the mother sits down, leaning over the rail to continue her conversation.

Ben sits in the seat behind the girl, his lungs feeling like he's breathed in lightning. By the fifth stop, the lightning has electrified every organ in his body. If this so-called god isn't going to do something, Ben thinks, then he will. He reaches into his pocket for one of the chocolate bunnies he takes home with him in case of a midnight urge. Tapping the girl lightly on the shoulder, he introduces himself.

"Hey. You probably don't remember me, but I'm the guy who was in the Easter Bunny suit. See I gave you one of these." He holds out the bunny. The girl turns her head. Her eyes scan his features. "This is for you. I always get extras."

The girl looks toward the front of the bus. Spotting her mother still talking to the driver, she turns her shoulders to get a better look at Ben.

"I like chocolate," she says.

"Me, too," Ben says.

He retrieves another bunny from his pocket and peels off the foil wrapper, breaking off a piece to put in his mouth. The girl watches closely.

"Go ahead," Ben says, offering her the other bunny again. "I've got lots."

The girl takes the bunny and puts it in her pocket. "I'll keep it for later," she says.

Ben nods and breaks off a bit of his own bunny to share with her. "I can't enjoy mine if you're not having some," he says. "I don't think your mom will mind."

The mention of the girl's mother visibly changes the girl's mood. The beginning of a smile turns into lips set in a straight line.

"In fact," Ben adds quickly, "she told me it was okay with her if you get off the bus with me at the next stop. To show you the park. There's a playground there."

"She did?" The girl takes the chocolate he's offered and puts it in her mouth.

Ben nods. "She said I could put you back on the bus later to get you home." Ben couldn't believe how fast the lies came out of his mouth.

"What kind of playground?" the girl asks. "Are there swings?"

"Yes. Big ones, where you can go really high. I'll push you if you want."

Ben can tell the girl wants to go. She turns her whole body toward him. There's just one thing holding her back.

"Your mom said going to the park would be a reward for you doing such a good job getting your picture taken. She was just too tired to take you, so she said I could."

The next stop is only half a block away. Ben looks to the front of the bus. The girl's mother is still focused on her conversation. He stands, tugs on the stop rope, and steps toward the exit door. The door opens with a sigh. With one last glance toward her mother, the girl follows him off the bus.

"Which way to the park?" she says.

Ben waits for the bus to pull away. "That way," he says, pointing up the street. "But we have to take another bus."

"I like riding the bus," the girl says.

"Well, then this will be a real adventure, won't it?"

Ben thinks he sounds like the photographer trying to get a frowning kid to smile and hopes that's a good thing. The girl nods but says nothing. Ben asks her if he can take the ribbon out of her hair. She agrees, seeming to have forgotten what her ponytail has revealed. He carefully removes the ribbon, stuffing it into his pocket.

Then Ben thought for a minute. Where did his mother always threaten to take him if he didn't stop getting in trouble? Children's Services. She'd said there was an office in the next town, and that the people there would put him in foster care if he didn't stop acting up. Once Ben moved to Denver, he knew she had lied. There wasn't a Children's Services office anywhere near Strasburg. But there definitely had to be one in Denver. The question was, would they still be open this late. It was already eight-thirty.

He sees a 7-Eleven at the end of the block. There, Ben asks for a phone book. He looks for Children's Services and finds an address for Child Welfare Services: 1575 Sherman Street. The next bus in that direction is two blocks down. They only wait five minutes before the bus comes. Ben takes the opportunity to introduce himself by name and asks the girl hers.

"Judy," she says.

When the bus huffs to a stop, they get on. Ben finds a seat in the back. Judy stares at the loud people in the front, young professionals on their way to party at the downtown bars. Ben explains who the dressed-up people are. What he doesn't say is that once he'd been one of them, after Shelley moved out, before he'd lost his job and apartment. Ben looks out the window and thinks he recognizes one of the bars they pass. He turns to Judy in an effort to stay in the present. She continues to watch the people at the front of the bus. Ben wonders what she is thinking but is afraid to ask. Better she stays distracted from the real task at hand.

They get off the bus at East 16th and North Broadway. Child Welfare should be two blocks down and one block up on the right. Ben reaches for Judy's hand as they walk, but she brushes his hand away.

"My mother says I'm too old to need someone holding my hand," she says, raising her chin.

Ben nods, not really knowing what age a child stops holding their parent's hand when walking down the street. But this girl doesn't look all that old. And something about her makes Ben think of her as frail.

"Did your mother ever hold your hand?" he asks.

Judy stops. "I don't remember," she says, looking down at the sidewalk.

"What about your dad?"

"He's always at work."

After Marty's death, his own dad often came home after Ben had already gone to bed and left before he got up in the morning, leaving Ben home alone with his mother.

"Is that when she burns you? When your dad's gone?"

Judy's chin rises again. "She doesn't mean to. It's an accident. I'm clumsy. I run into her cigarettes. I don't watch where I'm going."

The sing-song rhythm of what she says tells Ben someone has said these same things to her, enough times she has memorized the words and lost their meaning.

"That's a lie," Ben says, kneeling down in front of Judy. "Nobody is so clumsy they would run into someone's cigarette ten times."

"But my mother wouldn't hurt me on purpose."

Ben thought of his own mother, remembering the vacant look on her face when she'd slammed the back door on his forearm, breaking the bones, then told his dad he'd closed the door on his arm himself.

"Maybe not on purpose," Ben says to Judy. He struggles to put into words the reasoning he has come up with to explain his own mother's actions when he was a boy. "Sometimes people do things they don't mean to."

Judy looks confused. She raises a hand to the back of her neck, her fingers grazing the red dots. "She says she's sorry. She always says she's sorry."

Ben pulls her hand away from her neck. "She is sorry," he says. "But she'll do it again. That's why we've got to get help, making sure she doesn't. That's where we're really going. To get help. Not to the park."

Judy takes a step back and looks at Ben for a moment before speaking. "How do you know they'll help me?"

Ben has no idea how to answer. He only knows that something has to change in this girl's life, that her suffering needs to end. And for some reason he has been given the opportunity to put that process in motion. Ben tells her that that is their job, to make sure children are safe. Judy considers what he says, then nods and reaches out for his hand. They start walking again.

Halfway down the block, they pass an all-night carry-out. The neon sign shouts *Cold Beer*, the words buzzing in Ben's ears. He tries whistling a song, hoping to drown out the noise and put Judy further at ease, but his mouth is too dry. When they turn the corner and see the lit Child Welfare sign, Judy stops again.

"Did they help you?" she asks.

If only they had, Ben thinks. Not Child Welfare necessarily, but someone, anyone. If only one person had cared enough to make sure he was doing okay after Marty died. What a difference that might have made.

But no one did. So, Ben lies again.

"Yes," he says. "They helped me, and they'll help you."

"Do you promise?" Judy says.

Ben took a deep breath. Once, he had promised to keep Marty safe. He'd promised his mother right before he and Marty went outside that day. Ben had hoped they could sneak out without her hearing them, but as always, Marty had started whining, wanting to take some cookies with them in case they got hungry while they were up in the tree. Ben had told him to shut up, but their mother had already heard Marty and came into the kitchen.

"Your dad doesn't like you two going outside by yourselves," she said. "And it's so hot. I don't want to go out." She fanned her face with one hand while swirling the ice in her glass of whiskey with the other. "Can't you find something to do in the house until your father gets home?"

"I'll watch Marty," Ben said. "I promise I'll watch him every second. You can go lay back down."

And Ben had been keeping his promise until he realized they needed more nails to attach wood to the tree above where they had built the day before.

"I'll go get some," Ben said climbing back down. "You stay here."

"No," Marty said. "It's too high. I'm scared. I want to come, too."

"Stay where you are," Ben said. "I'll be right back. You'll be fine."

Then Marty started to whine. "I'll tell Mom you're being mean to me. I'll get down and tell her. I will."

"Stay there," Ben said, giving Marty a stern look. "I'll be right back."

And hadn't he hurried? Hadn't he gone right to the workbench in the garage? Hadn't he filled the pockets of his jeans with more than enough nails so he wouldn't have to make a second trip? And hadn't he gone back to Marty as fast he could, the nails jangling in his pockets as he ran? Hadn't he done everything he could to keep his promise?

Judy pulls on Ben's hand. The streetlight they've stopped under creates a yellow cone, walling them off from the surrounding darkness.

Ben begins to sweat, drips rolling down the sides of his face. His thoughts race.

What had he just done? Judy's mother could say the same thing she had said to Judy – that her daughter had caused those burns. Without proof,

Child Welfare could send Judy right back home to suffer more. Here, Ben had put everything in his own life at risk when there was no guarantee what he was doing would matter. He could have made a phone call to Child Welfare or reported the mother to mall security and let them sort all of this out. Why hadn't either of those occurred to him? If only he could think straight for even a minute.

Ben sticks his hand in his pocket and feels the folded fives the photographer had given him. The carry-out was only a block back. Ben feels the rush of adrenalin that comes with looking forward to finding relief in a bottle. He doesn't have to go with Judy into the Child Welfare office. He can just walk her to the door then take off.

Judy looks up at him. Does what he was thinking of doing show? Ben checks his reflection in the plate glass window they stand in front of. At first, he doesn't recognize the man he sees. Ben has gotten used to the image of himself inside the bunny suit. Comfortable even. People see the bunny sitting in the hut and smile. He likes when they smile. No one expects any more from him then a picture and a chocolate treat, both things he can deliver. But now, for some reason he doesn't understand, it seems he is being asked to do more. The old fear of failing rises up in Ben's chest, an octopus reaching its tentacles around his heart, squeezing hard.

Judy releases his hand. "If you're not coming, I'll go by myself," she says, marching ahead, her small figure moving out of the light and disappearing into the dark.

An image of Marty came to Ben. A firefighter had climbed up into the tree to release Marty from the branch he hung from. The man first tried cutting the cord around Marty's neck with a pair of small scissors. But the cord was too tight. Another firefighter joined the first man in the tree. The second man held Marty's body while the first used a hatchet from his equipment belt to cut the branch Marty hung from. The leaves of the tree shivered with each hatchet strike. A final blow released Marty's body into the arms of the second man. He lowered Marty to a third man waiting at the base of the tree, an EMT who loosened the cord around Marty's neck, his hat and the cut branch falling to the ground. As they moved beyond the yard light's circle and into the darkness of the long driveway, Ben broke free from his mother's grasp to run after Marty, yelling at the man to stop. But he couldn't run fast enough.

The ambulance doors shut before he could get there. All Ben had wanted to do was tell Marty he was sorry, that he hadn't meant to take so long getting the nails. As the ambulance drove away, Ben said a prayer, asking whoever a frightened boy of eight might have thought was listening… to please, please, give him another chance.

Judy's voice pierces the darkness. "Are you coming or not?"

The Fog of Fate

By Brian R. Johnson & Elora Lyons

A YOUNG BOY and his father pulled their small boat onto the beach after their daily fishing trip. It was a good haul this morning, and they were excited to share their bounty with the village. The morning fog still lingered in thick patches just offshore. The waves lapped gently against the sand. His father turned to look at the rising sun as it desperately tried to pierce the thick mist.

"Look, son, look at the beauty of the –" His voice broke off abruptly, replaced by a strange and haunting gurgling sound. The boy turned to look at his father. The older man turned slowly toward his son, a black arrow jutting sharply from his ruined throat. Blood ran down his shirt as the life drained rapidly from his dark eyes. The boy stood looking at his father in shock as his lifeless body fell to the sand. His feet refused to move, and no words came to him.

From the fog came the sound of a thundering horn. A flock of birds burst forth from the trees as the air seemed to vibrate. The boy turned toward the terrifying noise. He could feel it reverberating in his chest, stilling his young heart. The head of a fierce dragon slid from the mist, carrying dozens of armor-clad men. The ship slid effortlessly onto the shore. The men leapt over the sides, onto the beach, amid the shallow waves. Their armor and weapons seemed to gleam even though the sun hid behind the fog.

The boy shook off his paralyzing fear. Looking at his father lying on the blood-soaked sand, he turned to flee. Running as fast as his scrawny legs would carry him, he could see the walls looming up ahead, but he knew he would never make it to the village in time. All he had to defend himself with was a small belt knife, barely large enough to fillet the fish caught every morning. He spun toward the savage horde, unsheathing his paltry weapon, his pulse thundering in his ears. He knew he was going to die.

The first Viking to approach stopped as the young man brandished his meager weapon. Carrying a battered shield, long spear, and a heavy sword sheathed at his side, he stood towering over the small boy. Amused, he grinned and motioned for the horde to halt. Seconds later, the boy was surrounded by twenty ferocious men, all armed and eager for blood. Standing his ground, the boy pointed his weapon at the monster of a man standing before him.

"Are you not afraid, boy?" The Viking demanded.

In a short, swift motion the boy shook his head, knowing his voice would betray the fear gripping his pounding heart. The Viking roared with laughter, stepping toward the boy. Refusing to back down, the boy leaned toward the fierce warrior. Casually knocking aside the measly knife with his shield, the Viking grabbed the boy, lifting him by the collar.

"You have courage," he said turning away from the village. Carrying the boy through the mass of warriors, back toward the longboat, he shouted over his shoulder. "Take the village, burn the church!"

Feebly punching and kicking the massive brute, the boy struggled desperately to break free. He refused to cry out or beg for his life, while being carried unceremoniously across the beach. He would not let them see his fear; they did not deserve the satisfaction. Looking toward his home, black smoke began to billow into the air, marring the fresh morning sky. Tears began to stream uncontrollably down his flushed cheeks, yet he did not make a sound.

Seeing the boy's courage, the Viking nodded to himself. "You'll make a great warrior, boy."

Finally reaching the longboat, the Viking tossed him dismissively over the gunwale. Once aboard, two warriors bound his wrists and ankles in heavy rope. Shoving him down next to the single mast jutting from the center of the ship, the two men turned back to their tasks.

Tears continued to stream down his florid cheeks as he glared at his captors, his village burning just behind them. His anger flared, burning deep in the depths of his soul, realizing the massacre of his entire village didn't even warrant their attention. Closing his eyes and squeezing them tight, he tried to imagine his mother and sister escaping, before the savages fell upon their home.

The sun climbed high into the sky, burning off the last vestiges of fog. Slowly, the band of warriors began streaming down the beach toward him, carrying all manner of loot and captives, mostly women; the boy desperately searched for any sign of his family. Not seeing them among the captives being tossed onto the ship, he was unsure if he felt sadness or relief. Who knew what kind of life they would endure under these monsters?

The Viking who carried him to the ship climbed aboard, sneering at him. The boy glared back, hatred radiating from his eyes.

"My name is Ulf," the hulking beast of a man said to the boy, settling onto the bench in front of him. "You are now called Sune."

The boy, his raging anger consuming him, finally spoke. "My name is Sam," he said defiantly.

"It speaks!" Ulf bellowed to his crew. A roar of laughter bursting from the men filled the longboat. "Your name is Sune," Ulf said again, leaning intimidatingly toward the boy. His tumultuous gray eyes were hard, dangerous.

Sam, despite his frail appearance did not back down. They could kill him for all he cared.

"My name is Sam," he said louder, jumping to his feet. "You will call me Sam!"

Jutting out his chin, he stared down the men encircling him.

Ulf stood slowly, his enormous frame eclipsing the boy's slight stature.

"You have heart, you will need it." He smoothly drew his sword from its sheath. The boy flinched involuntarily, before gathering himself and standing tall once more. Ulf casually swung, smacking Sam on the temple with the flat of his blade.

Staggering, Sam fell to the deck, a warm trickle of blood running down his face before his world went dark.

...

Years passed as Sam resolved to make the most of his new life, his defiance never wavering. Being raised a slave, he was allowed to train, but not as a full member of the clan. Sam poured his heart into the art of combat, challenging any man who would fight him. His scrawny frame, battered and beaten, gradually gave way to the body of a hardened warrior.

A cloud of dust settled around the arena. One man lay writhing on the ground, his arm bent at an unnatural angle. Sam wiped the dust and sweat from his brow before offering his hand to the downed warrior. Accepting his help, the man stood and gathered himself. He clapped Sam on the back and nodded before retreating from the training grounds. Nodding respectfully in return, Sam crossed the training field, stopping next to Ulf. He leaned on his spear catching his breath. The man Sam once thought of as a terrifying giant now looked up at him and grinned.

Tapping the small scar on Sam's temple, Ulf spoke proudly to him.

"You have bested every warrior in the village, my son." He beamed with a father's pride. Sam smiled sheepishly. He couldn't bring himself to see this man as a father.

Yet, he still felt pride welling up at Ulf's words. Immediately, he regretted that feeling. This man was responsible for the death of his entire family, and the destruction of his village. Anger, hatred, and a reluctant affection warred inside him. His emotions were a raging storm, leaving him in a constant state of confusion.

"Next!" Sam bellowed, his deep voice resonating across the yard. Seasoned warriors filled the arena, yet no man dared step forward, every man having been bested by Sam time and time again. "Cowards, all of you!"

Prowling the edge of the training yard, he glared into the eyes of every man he passed. Battle hardened men, all terrified, unwilling to meet his challenge. Completing the full circle, he stepped into the middle of the ring.

"No man will fight me! No man can best me! Make me a warrior!" Sam demanded, staring into Ulf's eyes. It was a challenge to his authority, and every man within earshot knew it. As a slave, Sam held no standing, he had no right to demand anything of the Jarl.

"Make me a dreng. Let me prove my worth." His tone was low, and menacing. "Let me go into battle."

The gathered warriors all leaned in, straining to hear his words.

Looking around, Ulf knew that this young man held power over men, even as a slave. Brows furrowed, he seemed lost in thought, weighing the implications.

"Is there any man here willing to challenge Sam? To deny him his request?" Ulf said loudly. He let the unbearable silence hang in the air, until even the bravest of warriors began to shuffle in discomfort. "Then so it shall be." Turning toward Sam, his eyes were hard, yet loving, his voice cracking as he spoke. "You are hereby a free man, granted the rank of dreng. May the Valkyries carry you toValhalla upon your death, Warrior."

With that, Ulf turned, leaving Sam and the gathered warriors behind.

Standing in shock, Sam watched Ulf walk away. Realization struck him, as his entire body began to shake. Releasing a breath Sam wasn't aware he was holding, a sudden roar of cheers erupted around him. He stood in confusion as the men swarmed around, congratulating him, their smiles sincere. It finally dawned on Sam that this had always been expected of him. He smiled, allowing himself to be pulled from the training yard for a celebratory drink. Joy consumed him. Sam was now a free man.

• • •

After nearly a decade of being held captive, Sam felt drawn back to his childhood home. Hiking up the once familiar beach, memories from his past came flooding back. Flashes of dark blood soaking into the pristine sand, and the reverberation of a thundering horn, reminded him of the fear that consumed him, as raw and fresh as the day he was taken.

A distant shout brought him abruptly out of his trance. Taken aback, Sam saw how far he had traveled, the village now spread out before him. Drawing closer, the shouts grew more desperate, yet he never broke stride. The village appeared smaller than he remembered. Five armed men immediately rushed out of the gate intercepting him.

"Halt!" one of the guards shouted.

Sam chuckled at the man's harsh tone. "I am no scout, I lead no army," Sam explained to the men standing before him.

He held out his hands to show he was virtually unarmed. He carried no weapons except for a paltry knife and a well-oiled seax, its immaculate blade tucked neatly in his belt. Despite his peaceful gesture, four guards spread out, encircling him.

"I mean you no harm," Sam calmly stated, his gaze locking onto the lead guard's suspicious eyes.

"Take him," the one in charge ordered his men.

Spears and swords at the ready, they slowly closed in on Sam. One of the guards charged, leveling his weapon at him. Drawing his seax, Sam casually side stepped the first man's spear. Driving the hilt of his knife into the man's temple, the guard stumbled past before dropping unconscious to the ground behind him.

Sam spun as the next guard came rushing toward him, the man's blade pointed directly at his heart. A clash of metal rang through the air as Sam smoothly swatted the blade aside with his knife, disarming him. The guard frantically fumbled for his sword before Sam swiftly kicked him to the ground. As the guard scrambled to his feet, Sam punched him in the nose, a gush of blood signaling he was out of the fight. Quickly stepping back, the two remaining men hesitated.

"Cowards," the lead guard grumbled. Glaring at Sam, he stepped forward, drawing his own weapon.

"Stop, Alwyn," Sam stated firmly. He sheathed his knife even as the remaining guards pointed their weapons at him.

Alwyn stood dumbfounded as he stared at the massive savage standing in front of him.

"How do you know my name?" He finally managed to ask. His eyes narrowing as he took another step closer.

"Your father was the blacksmith," Sam explained. "We used to play in his shop. I still have the scar from when we sparred with the knife he made me."

Reaching into his pocket, Sam pulled out his small fillet knife. He held out the cherished blade for Alwyn to see. Alwyn lowered his weapon, the two other guards looked at him in confusion.

"I am just here to find out what happened to my mother and sister," Sam told him, his eyes slowly growing sad in anticipation of what he may discover.

Alwyn immediately lowered his gaze, shuffling uncomfortably.

"Your mother and father –" Alwyn started.

"I know what happened to my father," Sam said, abruptly cutting the man off.

"Your mother... Well, *she* can tell you," Alwyn said as he stepped aside, motioning for Sam to enter the village.

Sam grimly nodded to the man as he set off for the gates.

A beautiful young woman came rushing towards him. Instinctively, Sam reached for his seax. Recognition struck him like a war-hammer to the chest. Releasing his hand from the hilt of his knife, Sam stood awestruck. Throwing her arms around him, she barely came up to his chest. Stunned, Sam placed his hand tenderly on her head, her dark flowing hair soft against his calloused touch. Tears streamed freely down her cheeks, astounded to see him alive.

"Aisley..." he said slowly, the name feeling strange on his lips after so many years.

"Sam...?" her soft voice shook, as she spoke against his chest.

Wrapping his arms around her, he began to weep. Holding each other, they were oblivious to the world around them. Leaning back, she looked up at the intimidating beast of a man, wearing her older brother's once innocent face.

Tracing her fingers along his strange clothing, she winced at his blasphemous jewelry. Staring deeply into his hard brown eyes, she intensely searched for the boy she once knew.

Looking into her gentle gold-flecked gaze, his eyes softened.

She smiled broadly, whispering, "There you are."

Taking his rough calloused hand in hers, she turned, leading him through the curious crowd. "Come, meet your niece and nephew," she told him over her shoulder.

Stunned, he couldn't bring himself to speak. He never considered the possibility of being an uncle. Weaving through the narrow streets of the small village, he allowed himself to be pulled through the once familiar paths, before stopping in front of a modest, thatch-roofed hut. Leading him inside, he was forced to bend nearly in half to fit through the humble doorway. Standing up inside her dimly lit home, he heard the scurrying of tiny feet. Two small children rushed to their mother's side, one hidden behind each leg. The curly haired little girl peeked around her mother first. She buried her face in her mother's skirt as Sam leaned down to greet her.

"This is Aelfwynn," Aisley smiled, introducing her daughter.

Sam reached his hand out toward the little girl. "Hello Aelfw –"

The little boy punched Sam square in the nose. "Leave my sister alone!"

Sam laughed, putting his hands up in surrender. "Peace, little one," he said, grinning from ear to ear.

"This fierce little one is Samson," she giggled. "He takes after his uncle apparently."

As Sam stood, the little boy backed away, hiding behind his mother once again.

She smirked, "You met their father already…"

"Who is –?" he started to ask.

"Later Sam," though she smiled reassuringly, it never reached her eyes. She grasped his hand. "First, let me take you to our mother."

Leaving the children behind, she led him through the streets and out of the village. Stepping off the path leading to the beach they turned inland, climbing a small hill toward a grove of trees. As they reached the top, Sam could see two weathered wooden crosses. Looking at his sister, his eyes filled with tears. She solemnly nodded before hugging him tightly. Tears streamed down his face as he wept into his sister's shoulder.

"What –?" He started to ask, pulling himself away. He held his sister at arms-length. "What happened to her, Aisley?"

She looked at him sadly. "All this time you didn't know?" She watched him carefully as he shook his head. "Sam… she died defending me."

Sam looked into her eyes with a mixture of pain and pride.

"She fought back?" he asked. "Is that how you escaped?"

Looking down, Aisley nodded. Her face flushed red with shame.

Sam reached out, lifting her chin. "Do not feel shame Aisley. You were a small child. Be proud she put up a fight."

"I am proud," she explained, "but I am also ashamed. I stayed hidden while she fought off two men. She killed the first man, wounded the second. I thought…" She trailed off.

"Aisley, it's ok. You were a small child, as was I," Sam told her soothingly.

"No, Sam. I thought we were going to get away. I started to climb out when another man rushed through the door. I panicked and fell backwards.

I opened my mouth to scream, but nothing came out. Mother didn't hear him until it was too late. I could have saved her, Sam." She spit out each word furiously as tears ran down her cheeks. "I saw the blade come out of her Sam. I saw it. I saw the life drain from her eyes." Sobbing uncontrollably, she collapsed.

Sam caught her before she hit the ground, settling down onto the soft earth.

"Shhh, there was nothing you could do. I couldn't save father either. They killed him before either of us knew they were there. I understand, Aisley. I understand. I saw it happen, too."

He held his sister, yet no tears filled his eyes. His anger returned, flaring deep inside him.

"At least you fought," Aisley said softly. "We knew you stood your ground, Sam. Everyone thought you had been killed, but we *knew* you stood up to them. Those of us who survived, at least."

Sam scoffed. "They knocked away my weapon as if it were a toy. They took me, made me a slave."

Aisley stopped crying. "Mother would have been proud of you, Sam."

Holding his sister, long suppressed emotions warred inside him. "Do you remember the morning before the attack?" he asked somberly, staring out over the ocean.

She slightly nodded, confused by the odd question. "Of course, Sam."

"Father came to get me up, to go fishing," he explained. "I remember telling him I didn't want to go."

"You were a child Sam," Aisley told him. "Of course you didn't want to go fishing every morning." She climbed to her feet, instinctively smoothing her skirt. "The important thing is you are home now."

As he climbed to his feet, Sam averted his eyes. "I'm not home, Aisley." He turned his head slowly, looking into her eyes. "This isn't my home anymore. As much as I wish I could go back to that day and live a boring, simple life, I can't. That is not who I am anymore."

Her eyes darkened at his words. "Sam, those monsters took you from your home. They made you a slave. They murdered your parents, our parents."

He nodded, solemnly.

Stepping back, she stared at him in shock. "Sam –"

"I'm a Viking, Aisley. This is who I am now. I –"

"Then you did die that day, brother." She interrupted, turning away from him. "I hoped you had survived. Everyone said you didn't, but I still hoped." A single tear slid down her pale cheek. Brushing it away, she looked back toward him. "You wear his face, but no, he died that day, as well."

Aisley reached into the overgrown grass, picking up a third cross. Sam's name was faintly visible across the rough, aged wood. His heart sank watching his sister brush away the tangled grass and dirt before violently plunging his cross into the ground. Without another word she turned away from him, making her way back down the path to the village.

Sam stood at the crest of the hill, his clothing flapping gently in the breeze. He looked around the small grove wistfully. Closing his eyes, he listened to the sea crashing softly against the beach below. Knowing he would never step foot on these shores ever again, he opened his eyes, memorizing every detail. His eyes began to fill with tears as he crossed the small clearing. Kneeling before his parent's final resting place, Sam said his goodbyes. Standing, he wiped away his tears before hurrying down the path to catch up with his sister. Still refusing to acknowledge him, Sam trailed silently behind her.

Reaching the village, Aisley immediately approached the guard post. Alwyn stepped out to greet her. Seeking comfort in his arms, Aisley sobbed uncontrollably against Alwyn's chest. Consoling her, Alwyn looked at Sam in confusion.

Sam averted his eyes.

Somewhat regaining her composure, Aisley pulled herself away and began gesturing toward Sam. A furious exchange of hushed words passed between her and Alwyn. His eyes narrowed, locking onto Sam. Never looking back, Aisley rushed through the gates disappearing out of view. Sam moved to follow but Alwyn stepped into his path, pressing his hand firmly against Sam's chest.

"My wife says you do not belong here," Alwyn told Sam sternly.

Sam stopped, looking first at Alwyn, then down to the hand on his chest. Looking up at Alwyn in disbelief, he reached for his seax before recognition spread across his face. His grip tightened around the hilt, but he did not draw his blade.

"So you are the father of my niece and nephew," he said staring at the man in the guards uniform.

Alwyn nodded firmly.

"Go Sam," Alwyn said, his voice resolute.

Alwyn's hand rested on the hilt of his sword, letting Sam know he was serious. His stance told Sam he was resolved to fight and die, if necessary, but his eyes betrayed him.

Sam's hand fell to his side. He could not kill the father of his kin, even if that kin would never know him. He looked toward the gate one last time, searching for any sign of his sister. She was gone. Resigned, he turned away from Alwyn and his childhood home. Heartbroken yet somewhat relieved, Sam felt he had accomplished what he set out to discover. Knowing the fate of his mother and sister, he had the closure he sought. With a deep sigh and a heavy heart, he set off toward the beach, leaving that life behind, never to return.

· · ·

A month after burying his past in a small grove above the sea, Sam stood at the bow of a warship. Half a year ago, he was only a slave, fighting to survive. After excelling in battle, he now led his own raiding party. As a battle-hardened warrior in the eyes of the gods, Sam felt proud. Thick mist swirled about the ship as it prowled along the coast in search of prey. Leaning against his spear, the comforting wood grain felt smooth against Sam's rough palm. As the longboat slid silently across the water, his men prepared for battle.

His men, Sam shook his head at the thought.

The silence was shattered by a shout echoing through the salt laden air. He looked up to see a monastery rising above the fog, silhouetted against the vibrant morning sky. Sam felt a sudden thrill boil in his blood. Turning abruptly, he began barking orders to his men.

The longboat slid onto the edge of the sandy shore, careening to one side as it came to a rest. Shouting men leapt over the gunwales into the surging tide.

Within moments, Sam led nearly thirty men across the narrow beach. As they began to converge on the village, panicked shouts filled the air.

Guards scrambled to close the gates ahead of the marching horde. A single bell began to ring frantically, echoing off the walls of the distant monastery perched above the village.

"Shield wall!" Sam bellowed. A coordinated crash of metal and wood rang as their shields locked together. The air, swirling with fog, seemed thick and heavy as the clash echoed in the still air. Standing in an open field, the village spread out in front of them; they could see their prize on the hill, ripe for the taking. A single gate opened, and a line of ordinary men filed out, forming a ragged battle line of their own.

Sam stood at the center of the shield wall, the salty air and stench of unwashed men filled his nose. Looking out across the field, grim, fatherly men stood armed and ready to defend their homes. Seeing these simple men, he was suddenly haunted by a jarring memory from his childhood.

Taking a deep breath, Sam closed his eyes. He could feel a pit forming in his stomach. The same pit that kept him company in the loneliest moments of quiet reflection. The mists of time came rushing in, pulling him deep into the vortex of the past. The nightmarish day he was taken, abruptly materializing around him.

The sea was calm, a soft breeze nudging them lazily along the coast.

Standing in his father's fishing boat, Sam could hear the water gently lapping against the small vessel. He could feel his restlessness growing, his irritation suddenly palpable.

Why do we have to fish every day? It's so boring, he pouted, plopping down on the rickety bench.

We have to feed everyone, son. The village depends on us, his father said serenely, smiling as he turned to look at Sam. *Be proud, we're helping to feed an entire village. It is a noble life.*

Through the haze of time, Sam realized that smile never reached his father's eyes. He felt a deep pang of guilt and self-loathing for never noticing before. He wanted to comfort his father, to apologize, to tell himself to stop, yet the memory continued to play in his mind.

I don't want a noble life! Sam whined. *I want adventure.* Jumping to his feet, he grabbed his fishing pole, swinging it around like a sword. *I want to charge into battle and save a pretty girl.* He swung the sword back and forth as he danced around the small boat.

Sam, help me pull the net in, his father said, leaning over the side.

No! he said defiantly. *I don't want to be just a fisherman.*

Sam still remembered the look of pain in his father's eyes, that image forever burned in his mind. The petulant last words spoken to his father filled his soul with regret. Knowing he would never be able to right his wrong kept him up at night, plaguing his thoughts.

A shout lifted the veil of time, bringing Sam back to the field of battle. He looked through the shield wall at the men standing across from him. He sensed the trepidation in their eyes. In that moment, a sense of clarity struck Sam.

These simple men who kept a village together were willing to die to defend it. Men just like his father.

Blacksmiths.

Farmers.

Fishermen.

All noble men.

All men worthy of respect. Yet, all men he would kill.

"Forward!" Sam bellowed.

A roar pierced through the air as the warriors charged ahead. Within moments, the ring of steel and dying men filled his ears. The grass beneath his feet became slick with blood. Men fought and died all around. Adventure is what Sam always wanted. Fate had a wicked way of giving a man what he asked for.

Best If Used By

By Mary McFarland

I AM BAKING BREAD. My kitchen feels like a church. Sanctified. Calm. Quiet. Outside, doves attack the redbirds at the feeder. The sun's warmth massages the soles of my wool-stockinged feet and sweat from a hot flash dampens tendrils of my ratty, unkempt hair. It's *my* morning, this. And I am committed to nothing. Not brushing my teeth, not cooling my face with a cold washcloth, not even allowing my old retriever, Dahlia, to drag me outside for a walk.

Many believe bread baking to be the venue of women. It's women, after all, who'll tell you yeast smells – and tastes – like semen. It's women who are the universe's semenic repositories, who as a species swell with the yeasty seed, just as dough swells in response to febrile stroking by steady hands. But bread, once baked, is merely consumed, and the loving care with which it's prepared – ignored.

I cannot abide such irreverence. "Give thanks when you eat your mother's bread," I tell my son, Lawrence. "People in Africa are starving."

He stares at me with his father's indifferent eyes. "Keys, Mother."

He'd rather I hand over my Buick and get the hell on down the road to the nursing home.

Of late, he's hinted, "Mother, you're forgetting things. You're getting your ideas mixed up."

I don't apologize. I'll forget if I choose. It happens naturally, anyway, same as with mixed metaphors, the meaning confused and overlapping in my senile mind like malformed prisms colliding.

So it is that I see – or imagine I see – the way in which the function of women is perceived: like yeast, best if used by a certain date. But such bias in the youth cult and its edgy social media does not worry me. My periods are intermittent, and the cessation of egg production has widened my hips and filled my pelvic chasm – filled *me* – with a tiresome sense of struggle that must one day, with welcome, end. My wall-eyed son who forgets his place says I've resigned from life, that I'm slothful, that not checking my decline is narcissistic. I'm self-absorbed. I'm thoughtless of his feelings.

I ask, "At my age, son, do you think I should be a matronly self-sacrificing golem who reinvents herself with each passing decade so I can stay alive for you? Because you *love* me?"

Fuck that. I care little whether anyone – especially my son – likes the way I think. It isn't even worth telling him that I'm not lazy: I'm *wise*. Death is inevitable. It won't alter its path for me. I am ready. I am hungry for it. To me, it's manna from heaven, and I'm homeward bound.

There is presently, however, an important matter on my mind. Sex. Bread making always reminds me: I believe, as Schopenhauer did, that man is concrete sexual desire. But sex is tied up with worldview, a point Lawrence and Mr. Schopenhauer miss.

Did I tell you that the old grow prurient? Oh, yes, it's true. I get off listening to Billie Holiday sing *Let's Do It*. I love her big voice. The last thing I want to hear before I kick off is her singing *Lover Man*. I wonder... Will Lawrence slam me into the ground without playing Billie at my funeral?

I pour flour into the water and oil and yeast. I fold and mix and knead, fold and mix and knead – a motion that keeps me primed for the pneumatic action I hope to see again – once more – in my big four-poster, but probably will not. Still, I dream.

I dream and I talk to myself and to Billie. "Love you, girl. Sing it." Fold, mix, knead.

Fold, mix, knead. *Let's do it.*

When I bake bread, life makes no sense and I like it that way. Why should it? I cover my bowl of dough with a wrung-out dishtowel soaked in warm water. It'll help the dough rise. The bowl is old, a khaki green color with white stenciling, something made during the Cold War. It belonged to my mother-in-law. She's dead now, thank God.

I wipe my hands against the sides of my flannel pajamas and set the oven's timer.

Everything is timed, even a woman's menstrual cycles: She'll have only so many in a lifetime. I think of that box of tampons in the bathroom, in a cabinet under the sink, drawing dust. Time is all. Or is it, as Einstein said, an illusion? Or is it, as Baudrillard said, symbol and simulacra?

Time and war converge in my addled old brain. I try to make sense of it. Like bread, nations rise – and fall. Even the aggressors must, eventually, fall. Isn't it fair to say that, if you take something connected to a man's heart – his sons or his country or his life or his rights, then you can't demand that he respect your sons, your country, your life, your rights? That he'll become a monster like you and just as determined to kill?

The smell of yeast, rising dough, my mind wandering freely like the leaves eddying about in October's wind: These are the ways I indulge my war sorrow. I think of dead mothers' hands in countries ravaged by war. I think of hands like mine, flour encrusted and yeasty with the ageless taint of semen, hands helping a breast to a baby's mouth, hands working tirelessly to reshape shadowy black despair. Of mothers' hands, blue veins popped like a mountain's jagged outline on an old map, searching the rubble for lost sons, husbands, fathers. I see their hands.

Spotted hands of grandmothers, young hands, tender hands of agonized and bereaved wives, of mothers and sisters as they trace each other's tears. I see them begrimed with oil and dirt as they tear through exploded buildings, searching for blasted bodies. Hands, and thousands of fingers clawing frantically, and voices, in dialogue with desolate piles of bombed-out, unhearing rubble.

That's what I see, that's what I hear, and this is what I know: The deafening sound of women's fingers wildly plucking against rubble, searching for those lost to war – this *also* is my venue. Who am I to turn away? I am their audience, and when one woman plays a bloody pizzicato, we are all in rehearsal, all playing for an audience of men who make war.

The timer is set on my oven. Everything is right. I am a rich woman. I, who can squander a morning such as this, am a rich woman. The leaves burn orange and red on my sugar maple, planted by Lawrence's now dead, thank God, father. A glance outside reassures me. Fat, frost-encrusted pumpkins lounge upon garden earth. I wonder when it's to become a beachhead, when I, too, shall know the taint of ordnance, the stench of death, its promise of blood. Like menopause, there's no remedy, no stopping war.

On with my bread baking. On with my woman's venue. On with my body and my dissipating, concrete sexual desire that really isn't man's but woman's because we're the godhead, son, and you goddamned well better remember it. Being characteristic of wide-hipped, premenopausal women, I value nothing so much as release from hot flashes, night sweats and strange attacks of mood. From sons who can barely wait for their mothers' deaths and the Buick's keys. We've grown heads hard as pig iron and vaginas bereft of tears. *Don't tread on me*, my epitaph will read, lest I explode the ground beneath your feet with my wrath. Wrath at your meaningless disagreements. Your *war*. At your missiles that point death at each other, and by proxy at me, and then back at yourselves. War is men's venue. Damn you all to hell.

The dough is risen. *Perfect*. Fat and brown as Buddha's belly. I oil the pans, two so I can freeze a loaf for later. That's another thing I'm thinking about as I putz around my little kitchen with a dead woman's mixing bowl. What about the kitchens of women who live in war zones? Do these women have freezers where they store extra loaves of bread? Do they even cook at all? I watch the news, although I don't believe it, which means I'm ignorant and smart – equally. On TV, these women are never, I mean *never*, shown in their kitchens. I can't seem to get to know them. Mustn't their attire make cooking unbearably hot? I'm told the clothes protect them from the heat. And from the wrath of men who say women who dress whorishly cause earthquakes. Funny thing, I don't feel any shifting in the tectonic plates when I rake leaves in my bra and panties.

Still, in glimpses of the insides of those kitchenless TV homes, I see no freezers. The media provokes me. Show me those women's freezers, dammit. Show me their appliances. I stare at my Whirlpool freezer, a big, bulimic old thing – a coffin with all that dead meat and arrested decay stuffed inside. There's clouds of Cool Whip imprisoned in plastic bowls. And a salmon, a ten-pounder cut into inch-thick slabs, plus enough chicken to sink a destroyer – or feed an entire school of children.

I'm spoiling myself with yet another cup of coffee. Who's counting? I sink my knife into the moist flesh of the just-baked loaf, hot and steaming, and hand Dally a piece slathered with butter. She smiles and her dim old eyes, clouded now with cataracts, smile at me. *Thank you*, they say, as my son never has – not once – *and please may I have another?*

"No, Dally, we're on diets." But then, "Oh, what the hell. Here. What can another slice of bread hurt at our age?"

We gobble it down. I want to ask Dally *her* opinion on things. Bread baking. Aging. War. Sorrow. I don't, though. I figure she's had enough of me. I grab her leash. "Thanks, old gal, for sharing my morning. Ready to go take a pee?"

Wake Up, O Sleeper
By Brad Pauquette

WE SIT ACROSS from each other at the table in the middle of the bar. I guess you could say that neither one of us looks the part. We both wear flannel, work boots, just like most every other guy in town.

"She used to sing these old hymns," I tell him. "Just the two of us."

He just looks at me.

"Used to read from the Bible in this poetic voice," I stop and clear my throat, blink hard. "Nobody ever read it like she did. She felt it so much I could even feel it."

He leans his head forward and spreads his hands on the table. "Look," he blinks slowly, "I ain't your therapist, or your damn priest."

I swallow my spit hard. Look down at the table, pick again at one of the scratches there with my fingernail.

"What are you gonna do to them if I say yes?" I ask.

The man laughs, a single wheezing hack of a laugh, like air squeezed out of a bellows. "What do you care?" He's thin, younger than me, clean shaven. Mellow green eyes peer out at me.

I try to meet his eyes with a steely glare, but I know how it looks to him. A desperate old man – soft and desperate, and my gaze falls back to the table.

My mind returns to that day. The day I buried Charla. Died six days after she was born at home.

The midwife said she was healthy. I guess she wasn't. When Lisa held that little girl's body in her arms, she said it was just as well. That's how she felt back then, that's the day she came to feel that way. That wasn't my Lisa, but then all of a sudden, it just was.

We buried the baby's body in the woods behind the house, at the foot of the beech tree. The one that you can see from the other side of the hollow. It stands a hundred feet tall, a white obelisk reaching to God.

We sat in silence in the house after that, drinking hot tea in the mornings as the golden rays of spring sun peaked over the hills. It was something we didn't talk about much, just like it never happened. Like the past nine months just never was, a long winter that your mind just as soon forgets to embrace the blooms of spring.

I'd think about her after that. Thought how Charla might'a liked those daisies that peek up early where the sun makes a soft oasis of green at the bottom of the hill.

Two weeks later I went into town for the PO box and found Charla's birth certificate and social security card waiting for me. The ones the midwife had mailed away the paperwork for.

I almost pitched them in the trash right there. When I saw the crick in the distance on my way home, I thought I might tear them up into a million little pieces and scatter them into the waters. I pictured those little bits getting lost a thousand places between here and the Pacific Ocean. A bit stuck to a rock here, another on a branch down in Granite County, another burrowed into a sandy river bottom somewhere in Oregon.

But instead, I brought them home, and stuck them in a coffee can on my workbench in the barn.

I found a big white stone in the woods a few weeks later, big as an early watermelon, big as my strong young back could carry. I carried it back there and put it in front of the tree over her grave. Marked it for my Charla.

"Look, pops. It's two ladies we need, why you want to know more than that?" he stares at me and then seems to deflate. "You didn't do this before."

I look down at the table, and cock my head ever so much, set my jaw. The varnish on the surface is old and scratched. You can see where it's been slathered on a time or two before.

Lisa was always telling me just breathe, just feel the place. The first Lisa did at least. That's why we lived in the hollow. That's why we didn't see nobody. That's why it all worked. *We're surrounded by friends,* she used to say. She'd spin in the meadow, her hands outstretched to the trees, the birds, the creatures. She'd laugh. How she'd laugh. She was right, I didn't need no other company besides her.

Until Charla. Then she was a shell. I lost two that day.

Silence between two old lovers is more lonesome than being alone.

I hear the place, the bar. I feel it now. Monday afternoon. Outcast hour. Drunk mumbles at the bar. Young guy shoots pool by himself in the back, probably pretending he's at work, probably doesn't have the nerve to tell his pretty young wife that he actually ain't got no job.

Lisa told me once, got up in the dark of the night and came out into the living room where I sat in front of the fire. Had our old King James Bible next to me, even though I never opened it after Charla. I liked to run my hand across it, feel the worn leather grain under my palm.

"I buried God under that Beech tree," she said. Was all she said. Then she left again, silent as a shadow, her nightgown brushing across the floor like a whisper.

The boys had gone easy. Before Lisa died. Some things are easier when you have someone without a heart on your side.

It was like the universe lined up for how I met that man. He drove into town, a pickup truck just like mine. Hired me to build a half million-dollar barn, talked about a property out over the pass. Gave me a check for it, signed the invoice for the work complete. We both knew I'd never do the work, that there was no work to do.

I slid the paperwork across to him. The boy's social security cards, birth certificates, medical records, homeschool records. Then he just loaded them into his truck and left.

I stood in the parking lot and waved goodbye. Got in my truck and drove home. Saw that crick in the distance, thought about each of the four birth certificates I drove across that little bridge. How I'd cared for those pieces of paper like they was real children.

"You sell 'em?" Lisa asked when I came in the door. "You get the money?" Her face was still pretty and sweet as the day I married her. It was her eyes, only thing that lost their life. She showed her age in the whites of her eyeballs. I nodded.

She grunted, a smirk on her face. A rheumy twinkle in those dark eyes.

That was the last thing she ever said to me, the last time I saw any life in her eyes. In that smirk, even the shell was gone, the way the acorns litter the ground through the spring but by July they're just gone. Gone in the wind.

Two days later I found her body hanged in the woods. She had climbed up a tree with a bit of rope from the workshop, dropped six feet from a branch thick as a man's leg, twenty feet up. Her feet dangled just above my head. I imagined her standing tall on that branch before she let herself go. Arching her back like a reed bends in the wind, displaying her body to her friends the trees through that cotton dress before she fell. Neck broken by a silent *chunk* that even the birds couldn't hear. A branch like that wouldn't give an inch for a hundred twenty pounds.

Her face, her body, the same young woman I'd married at the courthouse three states away. Same woman I'd held tenderly in the cold our first year in that cabin, before I knew how to split the wood to keep the fire all night long.

My face carried the wrinkles of both our thirty-five years together.

Just breathe. Listen. Feel the place.

"One older, one younger. That's the request I got," the man leans in. "This is really a business where it pays to not ask too many questions." He puts his elbows on the table and leans in. He looks country, but there's city in his voice. I hear it peeking out from behind the cool eyes and expressionless face.

"Older?" I ask and shake my head. "You didn't tell me that before."

"What's it matter?" he spreads his hands, palms up. "You got girls. Females what's important, she'll make it work."

"How old?" I ask without fervor, patiently.

He guffaws, rolls his eyes, throws up his hands.

I buried Lisa's body next to Charla, in front of that big Beech tree. Found a stone, not unlike the other. A big white one, big as I could carry. Charla's feet pointed east into the clearing, Lisa's south into the woods.

When the grass was tall and I was up the hill at the cabin, those two white stones looked almost like children sitting in the field, side by side the way small children do. When I squinted my eyes, I could see white shirts above the sway of the grass.

Way I figured it, Lisa'd always been buried front of that tree.

She could say it was God we buried that day. But it wasn't God that left me with those shovelfuls of dirt, *shink shink*, into the hole.

I didn't report it to nobody. I just put her in the ground there. Let it be. Like it never happened.

"How old?" I ask again.

"Perfect?" he asks, then he shakes his head. "I don't know. One sixty, another thirty-five." He holds up his hands as if directing traffic. "But look, I've seen her. We can make thirty-five, forty work for both of them. I mean really, this woman ages like a goddess. Kind of a time is of the essence, age not so much, situation."

He's waiting for me to respond. I wait and listen. Breathe. Feel the place. The pool balls clack in the back. The drunk mumbles.

"You do have two girls, don't ya?" he asks, leaning forward again.

"They got a place to go?" I mumble.

"What?"

"Do they have a place to live?"

"Look, questions aren't –"

"Just tell me."

He shrugs, looks around. "We're working on it." He laughs now, I sense him change, lean in close, inviting me in. "Just two ladies need a clean start. It's unfortunate really, sometimes we just need an opportunity to put the past behind us. You know what I mean?"

A chance to put it all behind you.

John, Anthony, Patti, Charla. I guess you could say it was her idea, but I raised all of them myself.

Year after year, in the evenings I'd help them with their homeschool, tuck it neatly away. I'd help them submit their names in radio contests and grand prize giveaways. They opened savings accounts about ten years old, I put a little money in here and there.

When they finished their schooling, I put a little notice, just some text, in the local newspaper.

I hired them each on at my contracting company when the time came.

W-2s, file taxes. Didn't pay much, but there's value to the family business.

Sometimes I'd catch Lisa watching me from the doorway as I worked with them.

It had all been her idea, but she never wanted to help. When she found Charla's birth certificate in the barn. She told me how easy it was, her voice dull and pragmatic. Just a little form, that's all it takes, and you've got another baby – another social security card, birth certificate – "that's what a person is, right?" she said.

For the first time, I look him straight in the face.

"They can come to the cabin," I mutter, my voice faltering in my throat, like a sail that fails to catch enough wind.

He smiles big now. "You startin' a hostel?"

I shake my head. "I'm cashing out." I lick my lips and stare into my beer. "They can have it, might as well pick up the whole thing. Brand new lives."

"Look, I'm just –" he stops short. "I got cash for the papers. That's all I need."

I just look at him, raise my eyebrows ever so slightly. "If it's a fresh start, they can have it. I don't want no money this time."

He smiles. "Why not?"

I shrug. "Just a little cash for the house, that's all."

I give him directions rather than an address. Tell him everything's there. *Fresh starts.*

"They deserve it," then I ponder a moment. "I deserve it."

He shrugs and laughs, shakes his head.

"You gotta help me load something, though."

"That's a deal."

I drive home and ruminate on the way. Barely see the roads even though I know it's the last time I'll ever see them.

I wasn't crazy about it. I didn't read them bedtime stories. It was just a job, a retirement plan.

They're not real, I tell myself. *Paper don't make it real.*

Sometimes I considered giving them bedrooms. Decorating a room, taking pictures of it, just another piece of evidence that they really existed. But they didn't. They never did.

You'll make yourself crazy, I told myself. Aside from Charla, not one of them was real. Just paperwork we filled out, just a fake life we pretended to raise to sell to somebody that might need a new one. "An immigrant probably," Lisa told me, "somebody that just needs a chance."

That night before he comes, I stand in the living room. Ain't no pictures on the walls to make it mine.

Two manila envelopes sit on the table. Charla's is fat. All her papers, school records, newspaper clippings. All of it right there. A whole life up to the age of thirty-five.

Lisa's is thin, just the social security card, birth certificate, a few pictures I found from when she was a kid. I look around, the whole house is a testimony of her life. Empty. Dark. Lonely.

I say goodbye to the place before he gets there.

Next morning, I stop at the little bridge over the crick. Lower my tailgate. One at a time, I pull those white stones out, wobble to the side of the bridge, and toss them over. The first one, Charla's, splashes in shallow water. The second cracks atop it, splits in half, falls to either side of the rock. Half of Lisa upstream, the other half down.

I look over the side and see them next to each other, water rushing around the three parts. Rushing past. Like time moved around our little hollow, left us alone with her friends the trees.

I climb back into my pickup truck and shut the door behind me. Pull away from the cabin, the hollow, the little crick that held all my secrets.

Patti sits in the seat next to me, just papers in an envelope. Atop it sets the old King James. I put my hand gingerly, lovingly on the worn black leather, feel the warmth from the sun on my palm.

"Wake up, O sleeper," I mutter to myself as the dust clouds the road behind me and the ancient poetry seeps into my heart. "Rise from the dead."

Number 385712

By George Pallas

LARRY DAYTON SAT on the edge of the bed and watched the sunlight shine through the narrow slit of a window and reflect off the polished floor. He'd cleaned that floor yesterday and now, with the bright daylight exposing it with glaring intensity, he could see that it had been a well-done job. Look though he might, he saw no streaks or missed spots, only a uniformly clean and sparkling surface. His best cleaning efforts notwithstanding, tiny bits of dust danced around in the stark sunlight. Well, there wasn't much he could do about the dust, Larry decided. He smiled and mentally gave himself an attaboy while, in the upper bunk, Oscar Carlson snored quietly.

Before long, it would be time for the count and after that, breakfast. While Oscar slept, Larry availed himself of the toilet, a completely open fixture that offered zero privacy. Then he scrubbed his hands and face and brushed his teeth at the small metal wash basin. Every morning was virtually the same. Larry was almost always awake before Oscar stirred. And he always had the lower bunk, a metal bed with a thin mattress, bolted to the wall. If prison life consisted of numerous routines, Larry had established his own routine within that routine.

Oscar was awake now and slid off his bunk to stand on the floor. He was tall, six-foot-eight, but very slim. His close-cropped hair had enough flecks

162

of gray in it that it contrasted with his dark brown skin. Oscar preferred the upper bunk because the lower had no space for his feet to hang over the edge. The drawback was that it was so close to the ceiling that he couldn't sit upright on the edge.

He looked over at Larry, grinned and said, "Another beautiful day in paradise!"

Oscar had been Larry's cellmate for a week, but it seemed he was always in a cheerful, even playful, mood. In all his time in prison, Larry had never encountered such a good-humored inmate, much less shared a cell with one. Today he simply grunted in response, but grinned as he did so.

The count bell rang as Larry was putting on his shirt, blue denim with his number, 385712, stenciled above where the left breast pocket would be if the shirt had pockets. He and Oscar sauntered over to the bars at the front of the cell and stood where the guards could easily see them. After a bit, the clanking of opening cell doors indicated that the count was complete, nobody was missing, and the inmates were on their way to breakfast. Prison food might not be anything to write home about, but it was usually nutritious, and Larry was hungry enough that he eagerly awaited his turn in the chow line.

After breakfast, guards marched the prisoners back to their cells. It was easy to lose track of days in the repetitive tempo of prison life, so Larry glanced at the calendar he kept on the small desk he and Oscar shared. Today was Sunday. Sundays meant there was no work in the office where Larry and Oscar both had their assigned jobs. Their fellow inmates assigned to the kitchen or laundry details were not so lucky, but he and his cellmate could look forward to a day of leisure. Or idleness. In prison, free time usually meant boredom, so Larry sometimes envied the men who had to work on Sundays.

Oscar sat in the chair provided for the small desk in the cell, about the only place in the nine-by-twelve-foot enclosure his tall frame *could* sit. Larry positioned himself on his bunk. While he searched his small collection of books for something to read, he recalled the first time he met Oscar, a week or so ago. In the penitentiary, it isn't polite or even necessarily safe to ask an inmate why he is in prison. But Oscar had brought up the subject himself.

"Name's Oscar Carlson. I just got here from intake."

"Ever been in before?"

"First time. How 'bout you?"

"Been here nearly twenty years," Larry said wistfully.

"Damn! I drew ten but I'm hopin' I can get out before then."

Larry's expression brightened. "I've got less than a month left, then I'm done."

"Good for you! Whatcha gonna do when you're out?"

"I've got a little money. Very little, actually. I'll find a place and live on that while I look for a job. I used to be an HVAC technician."

"What's that, air conditioning stuff?"

"Yes. The letters stand for heating, ventilating, and air conditioning."

Oscar ran a hand over his close-cropped hair while he digested this. Then he abruptly switched the subject. "I bet you're wonderin' how come they sent me here."

"You always wonder, but lots of prisoners don't like to talk about that."

"Aw, I don't mind. Since you and me, we're going to be bunking together, I'll tell you straight out. It's like this. I had a decent job. I was an accountant."

"I never would have guessed that."

"What, you don't think a Black man can be an accountant?"

"I didn't say that."

"No, but you thought it, didn't you?"

"No, I actually didn't. I'd pegged you for a basketball player."

"*Another* stereotype! Since I'm Black, I must be an athlete, eh? I'm sorry to bust your bubble, but there isn't an athletic bone in this skinny body."

"I'm sorry."

Oscar laughed. "Don't worry 'bout it. It's funny – sometimes, the things people assume about you because you're Black."

"So, you were an accountant."

"Yes. I was good at it, too. Maybe not as good as I thought I was, but good. I was the head accountant for a small company. I had a lot of freedom and precious little oversight. That's how the trouble began. I thought I'd figured out a way to enhance my salary, so to speak." He used his fingers to put air quotes around the word "enhance."

Larry hung on every word. "Were you desperate for money?"

"In a way. I had three ex-wives on me for alimony. After I paid them, I hardly had a dollar left for myself. Plus, after a while, the job got to be a little boring. Small company, you know, not much new or changing. Figuring out a way to slide some money my way was sort of a game, a challenge. I thought it would be easy, and it was – at first."

"But then they caught on, right?"

"Damn straight. The owner got suspicious about something or other and brought in an outside auditor. She found out what I'd been doin' in no time. I hadn't paid enough attention to what would happen if somebody besides me got to going over the books. And she went over 'em with a fine-toothed comb."

"What happened then?"

"I tried to bluff it out. I pled not guilty and went to trial. That didn't go so well, and the judge sent me here for a ten-year stretch. So, I get here, and what job do they give me? I'm going to be an accountant in the office!" Oscar laughed heartily, enjoying the irony.

"You don't seem upset."

"I'm not. It was a stupid thing to do, but it's not like I had much of a life besides keeping the books and paying my ex-wives. Prison will at least be a change, and it'll sure get those damned women off my back!"

Their conversation had drifted off into other directions and Larry took care that it didn't circle around to how he became inmate Number 385712. He thought of it often himself, though. Mostly at night when he tried but couldn't go to sleep. The hell of it was that he didn't even remember doing what sent him to this place; he'd learned about it from others.

The first part was clear enough. Unforgettable, in fact. He'd come home from work to find Shelly waiting for him near the door with a dead-serious look on her face. She started in before he even got the door completely shut.

"I'm not going to drag this out, so I'll get to the point. I'm leaving. I'm divorcing you so Don and I can get married."

Things had been a little tense around the house lately, but nothing had prepared Larry for this. He could only stare at her, speechless, as she continued. She ranted for a bit about how miserable she'd been lately, and then the coup de grace.

"You know, I never knew how lousy, how *inept* you were in bed until I made love with Don."

Now Larry's mouth dropped, giving him the look of a largemouth bass out of water, gulping air. Before he could recover enough to say anything in response, Shelly flounced out of the house and drove away. Slowly, Larry collapsed into a sitting position on the living room sofa. Shelly's leaving had been a knife to the heart, but her crack about his sexual ineptitude brutally twisted it.

Hurt and anger fought inside him until Larry felt he couldn't breathe. He encouraged the anger because the hurt was too painful. He wanted to go somewhere, anywhere, just so he wasn't here in this house. Mechanically, he went back to his car and drove off. He drove aimlessly – and fast – for over an hour until, on impulse, he pulled into the parking lot of a little dive bar he'd come to.

There he sat, slugging down Old Grand Dad until he lost track of both time and the number of drinks. This is where the memories started to get fuzzy before disappearing completely. He vaguely remembered leaving money on the bar and going out to his car. But after that – nothing. He learned later that he started driving fast and aimlessly again. Where the road he was on intersected a highway, he blew through a stop sign. His car clipped the back end of another vehicle and knocked it into the path of an oncoming semi-truck. Four teenage girls were in the car he hit, and they didn't have a chance. As is often the case with drunken drivers, Larry suffered only moderate injuries. The cops found his car in a ditch with him passed out in the driver's seat. He woke up in the hospital with his wrist handcuffed to the bedframe.

Many nights, after lights out, the footsteps of a passing guard or the clanking of bars somewhere in the cellblock would keep Larry awake. As he struggled in vain to sleep, his thoughts invariably drifted back to that night two decades earlier, the night his troubles began. He had absolutely no memory of the wreck. Not surprising, since his blood alcohol level had been .25. But his lawyer, an owlish-looking man named Berry, had told him in precise, chilling detail what had happened and what evidence the district attorney planned to introduce if the case went to trial.

Four teenaged girls died in the crash. They were heading home after seeing a movie and stopping for pizza. Carrie Cross was 18, a senior at Robert Patton High School. Melinda Walters and Susan Slaton were both 17 and friends of Carrie's. They were also students at Patton High. Valerie Cross, only 15, was Carrie's sister, on her first outing with the "big girls." In the color portraits Berry showed him, all four girls sparkled with the vigor and promise of youth.

"If you go to trial," Berry said, "the D.A. is going to have poster-sized blowups of these four girls' pictures. The jury is going to be looking at them through the whole trial. And when they hear what happened to them, their hearts are going to harden, and your goose will be cooked. You *can't* take this to trial."

"So, what do I do?"

"I managed to work a deal. It was tough, because the D.A.'s up for reelection this fall, but he's willing to let you plead to second degree murder. Brace yourself, though. This deal will probably come with significant prison time."

"Wouldn't it be better to take my chances with the jury?"

"No," Berry said. "Take the deal. Otherwise, you're never going to see daylight."

So, Larry took the deal. He drew four twenty-year sentences, one for each of the dead teens. At least the district attorney conceded that the sentences could run concurrently. Shelly filed for divorce even before Larry left the county jail. With her soon-to-be-ex-husband going to prison for causing the deaths of four innocent young women, she had no trouble with the courts. Larry's heartbroken parents both died soon after. His father went first, suffering a heart attack while mowing the lawn barely two years after his son and only child entered the penitentiary. His mother lived another year in declining health before she, too, passed. His parents' friends from their church planned both funerals. Prison authorities didn't see fit to allow Larry out to attend either one.

When his first shot at the parole board came up, Larry was hopeful that, with his good prison record, the board would grant him parole, but a unanimous vote against him shattered that hope. Subsequent chances for parole were the same. Every single board member voted against him, determined to keep him behind bars for the entirety of his twenty-year sentence.

Daily, Larry's old life slipped away, receding from his grasp if not his memory. It was, he often mused, as if his life outside the penitentiary had never existed. No one visited. No letters came. No one from his past, not friends, not relatives, not coworkers ever so much as sent him a postcard. He supposed he was dead to them and, eventually, they became dead to him, too.

...

On a bright, sunny early autumn day, with the air slightly cool but not cold, Larry finally walked out of the penitentiary. His jeans and denim shirt were similar to what he'd worn inside, but this shirt had pockets and neither pants nor shirt had any markings to indicate they were prison issue. He was no longer Number 385712; he was Larry Dayton again.

The "gate money" the state gave him was laughably small and completely inadequate, but Larry did have a little money saved from his prison account. There was no money from his parents. Most of their savings had gone to pay for their funerals and the rest plus the proceeds from selling their house had gone to the families of the four dead girls. The court had forced Shelly to give him half the money she realized when she sold their house and that, too, went to the girls' families.

When his release began to seem like a reality, Larry had pondered whether he should go back home or settle somewhere else. The idea of a fresh start in a new city appealed to him but in the end, he decided that his chances might be better in his old hometown. Maybe the friends that forgot him when he was in prison would renew their friendship if he were physically back in town. If nothing else, he'd at least know his way around.

In prison, time seems to stand still, yet it keeps moving outside the walls. So many things were different than they were twenty years earlier. For instance, at first Larry puzzled over what the small, thin boxes were that people kept starting at, poking with their fingers, and putting to their ears. He was stunned when somebody told him they were phones. Higher prices were another thing. From the time he bought the bus ticket and throughout the trip back, he couldn't help but notice how much prices had risen in the years he'd been away. The ticket itself had put a larger dent than he expected in his small nest egg. And every gas station they passed, every place they stopped, he suffered sticker shock anew. The gate money that seemed paltry at first now looked ridiculously, impossibly miniscule.

And now, for the first time in two decades, Larry had to put a roof over his own head. Jobless and with meager funds, he knew he would find his choices limited. At first, he considered a halfway house. But priority for space in halfway houses went to parolees and Larry was not a parolee. He decided to try an area of town where some people with large houses rented out rooms.

One, with a "Room for Rent" sign in the yard was an older style multi-story brick home. A covered porch, a veranda really, extended across the front of the house and around to the left side. It sat on a sizeable lot whose trees would shade it in spring and summer. Not so much now, though, since they were shedding their leaves.

Larry walked up the steps and rang the bell. He heard movement inside and waited patiently until an elderly woman finally opened the door. Her lime green turtleneck sweater clashed with her short gray hair. She peered at him through glasses with thick lenses that she wore perched near the end of her nose. Despite the glasses and her bent-over posture, Larry decided she wasn't as old as he first thought. Perhaps in her early sixties.

"Yes?" she asked.

"I'm here about the room." He motioned toward the sign in the yard.

"Five-fifty a month, in advance. No smoking, no liquor, no drugs, no pets, and no women."

Larry winced inwardly at the dent $550 would make in his wallet but tried to maintain a poker face. "Those conditions won't be a problem."

He was about to ask if he could see the room when he noticed her staring intently at him through her thick lenses. She adjusted the glasses, then said, "Don't I know you?"

"I don't think so, ma'am. I haven't been in town for a while."

She kept staring until recognition flashed. "I *do* know you! You're that guy what murdered them four girls!"

Larry was momentarily speechless, then stammered, "I… Yes… I was involved in something like that. But it was twenty years ago, and I've served my time."

"One of them girls was my niece! I don't care if it's been a hundred years, you're not putting up under my roof!"

With that, she slammed the door hard enough to rattle the windows. The rattle had barely died down before Larry heard a deadbolt shoot into place.

Slowly, he turned and climbed down off the veranda and made his way to the sidewalk. As he turned to continue up the street, he looked back at the house and saw the curtains of one window suddenly fall back into place.

The old crone had been watching him. As accustomed as he was to being constantly watched in prison, this felt substantially different – and more than a little creepy.

Larry worked his way through the rest of the neighborhood. A few houses advertised rooms for rent but, upon inquiring, he found that the owner of each knew all about his being in prison and why. Not one would even consider renting to him. Apparently, the old woman from the first house had made a flurry of telephone calls to her neighbors.

It was almost dark when Larry finally found a room to rent. It was in a rather seedy motel that catered to the by-the-week crowd, although he suspected that some of the rooms rented by the hour, as well. At least no one recognized him there, and the owner even asked his son to drive Larry to the bus station to retrieve his suitcase from a locker. Trudging around town on foot – he had no other transportation – left him so bone tired he skipped dinner and flopped into bed. The mattress was lumpy but no less comfortable than what he'd slept on in prison. If he did have dreams that night, he was so tired he didn't remember any of them.

• • •

As an HVAC technician before going to prison, Larry specialized in the large systems that kept office buildings and shopping malls climate controlled. But HVAC technology was something else that had changed over two decades and not just a little. He did manage to land a job with an HVAC company, but as a janitor. He hoped that he'd be able to brush up his skills and eventually get into back into working with HVAC systems. The work would be more satisfying, and the pay would be significantly better.

On Friday of his third week on the job, Larry was sweeping a floor when his boss called him aside. Supposedly out of earshot of anyone else, he told Larry he'd have to let him go.

A stunned Larry managed to stammer, "Hav… haven't I done a good job?"

"Yes, I have no problem with your work."

"Then why are you letting me go?"

"It's just that… ah… business is in a little bit of a downturn and we need to cut some staff. You're our newest hire, so you drew the short straw."

"But I need this job! I'm barely getting by as it is."

"I'm sorry, Larry. Stop by the office and pick up your paycheck. I got 'em to put in an extra week as severance. They don't normally do that for people who've only been here a few weeks."

Larry supposed he should be grateful for the extra week, but it was hard to feel gratitude. He put away the broom he'd been using and went to clean a few personal things out of his locker. When he shut the locker door with a bit more of a slam than necessary, he noticed Carl standing nearby. Carl was one of the few employees who seemed to pay him much attention.

"That bit about a downturn was bullshit, you know," Carl said.

"Oh?"

"Yeah. Listen, thing is, some of the guys got together and told the big boss they don't want you workin' here 'cause of your, ah, trouble. It ain't right, but there ain't nothin' you can do about it. Long as they say they laid you off 'cause of bad business, you can't do nothin'."

Larry swore under his breath. "I guess this damned thing is going to follow me around like an albatross."

"What's an albatross?"

"It's a big sea bird. A curse in part of an old poem."

"Well, my friend, I don't know 'bout no curses, but you sure ain't got many friends here." Carl stretched out his hand, in which he held a twenty-dollar bill. "Here. Take this."

"I don't need your money, Carl."

"Take it. Take it! I'm fixed okay right now. It ain't much, but I got a feelin' you're goin' to need it."

Larry accepted the proffered bill. "Thanks, Carl. You've got a good heart."

"Pay me back when you can *if* you can. If you can't, don't worry 'bout it."

"Take care of yourself, Carl. And thanks again."

• • •

His small motel room seemed even tinier to Larry that night as he pondered his situation.

He'd never felt so alone before, buffeted by forces beyond his control. You didn't have any freedom in prison, but you had a place to sleep and you didn't go hungry. There was not one single person, he realized, that he could call on for help; he'd have to get through this on his own. All he needed was a chance to get back on his feet. Maybe, he thought, coming back home hadn't been the best idea after all. He supposed if it came down to it, he could go to a men's shelter. Shelters were supposed to be awful places, but they were probably no worse than prison. They might even be better.

His first task was to find a job. He needed money to pay for the motel room and to buy food. Not having transportation other than his two feet and the city bus system limited the geography of his job search. Not having a telephone added to his difficulties. But by Monday morning, he had a list of potential employers and a plan to apply at every one of them that would accept an application.

Larry started the week with high hopes, but by late Friday afternoon, the flame of hope had all but died, and he had to vigorously fan the embers to keep it barely alive. It had been a crushingly discouraging week. At least nobody had chased him away. But nobody hired him, either. With no immediate prospects for employment, he had to hoard his dwindling cash and manage it very carefully.

Trudging back to his little motel room, tired and footsore, he picked up a sandwich and a bag of chips at a small deli he passed. That would suffice for dinner, he decided. Passing a little park, he noticed the trees were now bare and decided that summer was over for sure. As if to underscore his conclusion, a chill breeze kicked up and made him shiver. He'd be glad to get back to his room, even if it wasn't much larger than his prison cell had been.

Fumbling for his keys, Larry looked up and saw that a small tan and white dog blocked his doorway. The animal gave him a pathetic "puppy face" that immediately tugged at his heartstrings. He'd always liked dogs, but Shelly wouldn't abide animals of any kind, so he hadn't had one since he was a boy. This one was a mutt; it was impossible to tell how many breeds were in its makeup. It had longish fur that was in serious need of a brushing. Larry reached down to stroke it and felt its ribs.

"You look like you need some loving, and maybe a warm place to sleep tonight. Why don't you come in and stay with me for a while?"

The dog began to wag its tail slowly and followed Larry inside, where it immediately jumped up onto the bed.

"May as well make yourself at home, since I see you already did," Larry chuckled. Then, determining that his guest was male, he said, "You look like a Roscoe. I'm going to call you Roscoe if that's all right with you."

Roscoe's tail waved back and forth, which Larry took for agreement.

"I don't have any proper dog food, but I guess I can share part of my sandwich." He moved the desk chair over to the side of the bed, sat down, and proceeded to break off small pieces of the sandwich and offer them to Roscoe. Fortunately, the sandwich was on a large hoagie bun, so he could feed a little to the dog and still have enough left for his own dinner.

"You're probably thirsty, too, aren't you?" Larry took one of the motel's drinking glasses, filled it about two-thirds full of water, and set it on the floor. Roscoe immediately lapped it greedily until the water was almost gone.

"I don't know what I'm going to do with you tomorrow, but at least tonight you can stay with me."

Roscoe stared at him with his soulful brown dog-eyes.

"You see," he explained to the dog as if he could understand, "you probably don't have a home, but I'm in a bit of a fix myself. I'm running out of money, and I need a job. But I can't seem to find one. Nobody in this town wants to hire me."

Roscoe thumped his tail while snuffing up the last crumbs from his share of the sandwich.

"When I was in prison – *you* don't mind that I was in prison, do you? Anyway, when I was in prison, almost all I could think about was getting out. But who'd have figured that being out would be so damned much harder than begin in? It's no wonder so many people released from prison make that U-turn that takes them right back inside the walls!"

Roscoe was a good listener, but he didn't offer much in the way of advice.

Finishing his part of the sandwich, Larry stood up and started pacing the tiny room. He paced silently for a while, then spoke.

"Roscoe, here's what I think we're going to do. I'm paid up here until tomorrow night. Then, bright and early Sunday morning, you and I are going to walk over to the Greyhound station and hop on a bus. It doesn't matter much where we go. We don't have to go far, just far enough to get away from here, to some place where nobody knows who I am." He reached over and

173

scratched Roscoe behind his ears. "You're my dog now, Roscoe, so you're going with me. From now on, we're a team."

With that, Larry began to pack his meager belongings into the suitcase he'd managed to score when he left prison. It *had* been a mistake to come back home. Prospects would be better somewhere where he was a stranger. There was just enough money left in the kitty for a bus ticket – if he didn't go too far, for another week or two's rent for a place like this motel, and even a few meals. He could probably scrape enough together to buy Roscoe some real dog food and maybe a brush to groom his coat.

"We may be down, Roscoe, but we're not out."

Number 385712 was going to stay right here in this dingy motel room. The man who got on the bus with his dog Sunday would be Larry Dayton, his old prison identity left behind forever. If sheer determination could make it so, he would arrive in a new city as a whole man, not a former prison inmate.

"Get ready, Roscoe," he said to the dog. "Day after tomorrow, we're going on a new adventure, and won't it be fine?"

Axman

by Steven Kenneth Smith

THE AX CONNECTED with a solid *thunk* as he swung it down, but the bone didn't separate. He'd missed the joint. Sloppy. Must be fatigue or something.

Josh swung again, pivoting at the hips for maximum power. The head went spinning down the alley. That's better. He dropped the ax, stripped out of his blood splattered hoodie and sweatpants, and dropped them next to the body. He turned his latex gloves inside out as he stripped them off and dropped them into a plastic bag.

He left the alley without checking if anyone saw him. That would look suspicious. As he walked down the lamplit street he picked up a fast-food sack laying discarded on the sidewalk. He dropped it into a trash can a half block later. The bag containing the gloves had made it inside first.

At Market Street he boarded the bus and sat near the back. With a practiced bored expression, he worked his shoes off without touching them with his hands, then took a thin pair of flip-flops from his pocket and put them on.

When the bus reached the north end of the route he got off, leaving his shoes behind. Two blocks south he caught another bus heading downtown. He got off at Fairfield Avenue and walked home from there. It was almost midnight when he arrived. He entered through the garage and stripped off the rest of his clothes. They went into a plastic barrel containing a detergent solution, and he showered before going to bed. He fell asleep almost immediately.

• • •

"How has the last week been for you?" his therapist, Dr. Havland, asked.

Josh smiled. "Pretty good, actually. I had a date that went basically okay last Friday night." He shrugged. "Nothing actually *happened* if you know what I mean. We just went to dinner and saw a movie."

"You mean you didn't have sex afterwards by 'happened,' I suppose."

Heat rose to Josh's face, and he squirmed in his seat, giving a little laugh. "Uh, yeah. No sex."

"Mr. Gibson, despite what you might see on TV or in the movies, it isn't typical to have sex on a first date. It's also almost never desirable, from a long-term standpoint."

"Yeah, I know," he mumbled.

"What you've mentioned so far sounds normal. Is there anything more you'd like to say about what did happen?"

"Well, I don't think she liked the movie very much, but dinner seemed to go okay."

"Why do you think that?"

"We saw *Zombies Forever,* and she sort of flinched and made this noise when they killed one of them."

"I see. How was dinner better?"

"I tried to keep from dominating the conversation, like you said to try. She smiled a few times."

"That's a good sign. Are you going to see her again?"

"I hope so. She said I could call her."

"It's Tuesday now. Why haven't you called her already if you like her?"

"I wanted to talk with you first."

Dr. Havland straightened his glasses and looked up from his pad at him. "Josh, you don't need my permission to call a woman on the phone."

"But what do I say to her?"

"Whatever you want. It's customary to start with 'Hello,' but you're the one dating her, not me."

"That's not helpful."

"I'm your therapist, not your social secretary."

He sighed. "All right. I'll call her."

"Okay." Dr. Havland nodded. "Good luck."

• • •

At the end of the hour, he left the office and bought a newspaper from a vending machine on the sidewalk. A frontpage story reported the latest of the "Axman" murders that had occurred the night before. There were still no solid leads to the murderer's identity. The latest victim, like the previous four, had been a homeless man. The city was trying to accommodate more people in shelters that were already overcrowded, but there just wasn't enough space.

He set the briefcase on the dining room table as he came in and dropped the newspaper on top. He checked his watch. Four-thirty. Still too early to call Marsha. Too early for dinner, too, so he turned on the television and found a channel showing a *Law and Order* re-run.

At five-thirty he dialed Marsha's number.

"Hi, Marsha, it's Josh. Hey, I just wanted to say how much I enjoyed our date last Friday and ask you out again."

"Thanks. What did you have in mind?"

"I can be flexible. Is there something you'd like to do?"

"Well, not another zombie movie."

He nodded, then realized she couldn't see him and cut off the gesture. "Okay, why don't you choose the movie this time? I mean, it's your turn." He gave a nervous laugh.

"All right, let me check what's available. Is Friday night at six good for dinner?"

"Sure. Where do you want to go?"

"I'll think of something. I'll let you know Friday."

"Okay. Thanks, again."

He hung up and pumped his fist. Yes! A second date.

He put some tater tots in the microwave and fried a hamburger, rare. Pickle slices, ketchup, no lettuce. He finished watching *Law and Order* as he ate.

Too early to go hunting again. The police would be on high alert. Should wait a week or so. Still, he felt pumped by his success with Marsha.

He opened the concealed door behind a shelf unit on the back wall of the garage. Inside, hanging on a rack of hooks, were five axes. He smiled as he looked them over. One-piece solid steel construction with a rubber grip and a matte black finish. The 26-inch length gave enough lever-arm for a good striking force, and he'd hand-honed the edge to razor sharpness. He'd bought them one at a time at different stores around the state over a period of more than a year. Cash sales only.

They were a little awkward to carry concealed, but suspended from a holster he'd designed himself, they fit down his pant leg with the head at his waist. He walked with a practiced amputee-style limp while carrying them, and hardly anyone paid attention. They were too polite to take notice of a person's handicap.

After dozens of hours of practice, he could draw the ax into position in just over a second, do the deed, and be gone thirty seconds or less afterwards. The longest part of the process was locating an appropriate victim. Sometimes it took several days before he could find a derelict sleeping off his bender in a secluded spot.

Maybe he could try it again tonight. The moon wouldn't rise until after midnight, so it'd be nice and dark. A tingle went down his spine.

He shook his head. Too risky, and the winos would all be hiding tonight anyway. He closed the cabinet and went back into the house. He settled onto the couch to watch the local news. Didn't want to miss it.

• • •

Marsha ordered pasta primavera for dinner on their date Friday evening. Josh ordered a steak. She grimaced at the bright red center of his sirloin when he cut it. He wore a sport jacket and an oxford shirt, no tie. His short cut hair was neatly combed.

She'd selected a romantic comedy for their movie. As they ate, she discussed the director's previous films and some of the other prominent previous roles of the star players. Josh nodded and made occasional comments, but he didn't seem like much of movie buff. Then she mentioned that the leading man had just entered an alcoholism rehab program.

Josh had been looking down at his plate while he cut his steak and snapped his eyes up to her face. "Really? That's bad."

"I think it's good that he's getting treatment. He's a talented actor, but I guess he likes to party a little too hearty."

He scowled. "Treatment can't hurt, I guess. But by my experience, once a drunk, always a drunk."

Marsha raised an eyebrow. "Experience?"

Taking exaggerated care to place his fork and knife on the table with the plate exactly between them, Josh said, "My father was an alcoholic. Used to slap me around a lot when he drank. Then, when I was sixteen, he came home drunk and beat me with an axe handle. Broke my arm. By the time he got out of prison, I was long gone."

"Oh. I'm so sorry."

"Don't be. He wasn't much of a father, but I've learned from his example." He took a sip of his iced tea and set the glass back on the table, precisely on the damp ring it had made on the tablecloth. He picked up his fork and stabbed the steak with more force than necessary as he reached for his steak knife. Some red juice seeped from the steak.

Marsha grimaced again and turned her attention to her pasta.

• • •

After the movie they strolled along the lamplit streets downtown to a coffee shop near the theatre. She took his hand, and his face flushed.

As they sat with their coffee she asked, "How'd you like the movie?"

It had bored him. Not enough action, and he couldn't get past the idea that the male lead was a drunkard. "It was nice. A beautiful story."

She smiled and nodded. "I love a movie with a happy ending."

He smiled back and hid his eye roll by bringing up his coffee cup to take a sip.

• • •

Josh walked her to the door of her apartment after taking her home. She took her keys from her purse, then turned to him and gave him a quick peck on the lips. His face flashed hot, and his ears roared. She slid the key into the lock.

"Thanks for tonight. Call me, okay?"

"Okay."

She closed the door behind herself. The deadbolt slid into place with a muted click.

He stood there for a second, staring at the door knocker, then turned and forced himself to not run to his car.

Back home he ripped open a new package containing black sweats and a hoodie. A little early to go hunting again, but the urge could not be refused.

•••

Two hours of limping along the back streets had been unproductive, and the busses would stop running soon. Josh was about to despair of finding a suitable target when he saw him. A bearded man sat on a grate behind a restaurant, half in the shadows.

A quick glance up and down the street confirmed no one was nearby. He pulled on latex gloves and crept up to the sleeping bum. A bare bulb over the restaurant's back door gave a dim light, sufficient to aim. An empty liquor bottle lay beside the man, near his outstretched hand. Yes, this was the one.

As he drew the ax, the drunkard stirred. His eyes opened and went wide just before the ax connected. The head came off and rolled behind a dumpster.

Josh shook as a powerful orgasm took over his body. He grunted. *That* was new. The ax fell to the ground.

Still shaking, he stripped off the hoodie and sweatpants, fumbling as he worked them off over the erection that strained the front of the thin cotton trousers under the sweats. Semen soaked the front of his pants, but he figured no one would notice in the dark. He dropped the sweats and hoodie by the body and stuffed the gloves into a bag. The restaurant's back door opened.

Josh flattened himself against the building as a guy wearing a dirty white apron came out and tossed a bag of trash in the general direction of the dumpster. Josh held his breath. The door opened again. The guy reappeared and threw out another bag of trash.

Josh waited for what seemed an eternity but was probably only a couple of minutes. The sticky wetness in his briefs had started to chill him. He took a deep breath and left the alley. Just before he reached the street someone shouted, "Oh, my God!"

He smiled.

•••

Detective Marc Welsley ducked under the police line tape and approached the officer at the scene, a young man, maybe mid-twenties. A couple of techs collected evidence. Occasional flashes from their cameras lit the alley behind an Italian eatery with a surreal strobe-like quality. The ambulance still blocked the entrance to the alley. A couple of EMTs stood next to it.

Marc shook hands with the officer – J. Bullfinch by his name tag – and they exchanged greetings. "Another Axman murder?"

He nodded. "Yeah. Same as the others."

Marc shined his flashlight toward the body. No head. He noted an empty whiskey bottle nearby. There was always a liquor bottle of some sort. "So, abandoned ax and discarded sweats and hoodie? We'll trace the ax from the manufacturer to stores nearby and process the clothing for DNA. Might get a break."

"Already bagged and marked," he grimaced. "Something was a bit different, though."

"Yes?"

"There was a damp stain on the front of the pants. Looked like semen."

Marc raised an eyebrow. "DNA. Good. Well, make sure to keep your report to the bare facts. We don't want the paper to print any of the particulars. This asshole has the city in a panic already."

"Okay."

Marc took a cursory look at the body again. "Where's the head?"

"Haven't found it yet. You suppose he took it with him?"

"Could be, but he's not done that before. Who discovered the body?"

"Dishwasher," the officer said, nodding toward the restaurant's back door. "He saw it when he took out trash. He's a mess. A young kid, just eighteen." He pointed to an odoriferous pool by the body. "The vomit is his."

Marc nodded. "Okay, well, I better go talk to –"

"Found it," one of the evidence techs shouted. "It's behind the dumpster."

...

"So, how did the week go?" Dr. Havland asked. "Anything noteworthy?"

"I had another date with Marsha, and it went well. She chose the movie and the restaurant for dinner beforehand, and she seemed to have a good time." Heat came to his face. "She kissed me goodnight."

"How did that make you feel?"

Josh squirmed in his seat and turned his face to stare out the window. "It was nice. I mean, it was just a little kiss, but she smiled." He turned back to the doctor. "I'm seeing her again tomorrow."

Dr. Havland nodded. "I'm glad things seem to be going well in terms of you developing a relationship."

Josh nodded. The rest of his hour passed with Dr. Havland asking more questions and Josh making carefully ambiguous, though seemingly encouraging responses. After a year in therapy, he'd learned the sorts of things Dr. Havland wanted to hear.

...

On Wednesday, Josh knocked on Marsha's door at 6:00. She answered, but instead of taking her purse and coming out, she invited him in. She wore casual clothes, a pair of slacks and a cotton top, instead of the skirt and blouse she'd worn on their other two dates. His face burned as he entered the apartment.

"Uh – where would you like to go for dinner?"

"I think I'd rather stay home tonight. I'm just really nervous about that serial killer running loose."

Josh shook his head. "I don't think we have to worry about him. He only targets drunken bums."

"Did you see the news the other night? The last murder was the same night as our movie date, and practically next door to the theatre."

It had been eight blocks west and two south from the theatre. He met eyes with her.

"Is that right? Wow."

"I can cook some pasta and make a salad, and maybe we could watch something on Netflix. Is that okay? I don't want to be out at night with that maniac loose."

He nodded. "Okay, that's fine. I don't want you to be uncomfortable."

"Thanks. Would you like something to drink?"

"Some water, or maybe iced tea if it's no trouble."

• • •

Josh insisted on washing the dishes after dinner while Marsha looked over the prospects on Netflix. As he put a paring knife into the dishwasher, the tip caught on the edge of the basket, and he cut his finger as he tried to slide it into place.

"Shoot," he said. He wiped his finger on a dish towel and inspected the wound. Not too bad. The bleeding was already slowing down. He applied pressure a little longer and checked again. The bleeding had stopped. He finished loading the dishwasher.

As he looked for a place for the olive oil, he opened a cabinet and froze. A couple of partially full bottles of liquor stood in a cabinet by the microwave, a bottle of bourbon and one of vodka. A few shot glasses sat upside down on the shelf beside them.

He clenched his teeth and set the olive oil on the counter. The dish towel lay draped over his shoulder. He wiped his face with it and dropped it by the sink. He balled his fists, then, as if forcing himself, he opened them and took a deep breath.

She was one of them. A drinker. And he had *liked* her.

He ran fingers through his hair. His eyes flicked toward the knife block, but he pulled his gaze away. Got to get out. Now. Rolling his sleeves back down, he entered the living room while buttoning the cuffs, not looking at her.

"Have you seen, *The Princess Bride*?" Marsha asked.

"I have to go. Thanks for dinner."

"What? Is – is something –"

The door slammed behind him as he ran to his car.

• • •

He found himself back home without remembering the drive there. The image of the liquor bottles stuck in his mind as if tattooed on his retina. She had *kissed* him.

The keys shook as he unlocked the door.

He opened the hidden cabinet in the garage and considered the four axes hanging there for a long time. He imagined taking one to Marsha's apartment, her wide eyes as he raised the ax, the thud and crack as the bone separated.

He shook his head. She and he had a history. There'd be a trail back to him. He thought about going hunting again but rejected the idea. To soon after the last one, and the moon was out tonight.

His phone rang. He pulled it out and checked the caller ID. Marsha Welsley. He rejected the call.

Hill Street Blues would be on cable soon. He made a pot of tea and settled in front of the TV.

• • •

Marsha stared at the phone's display. "Call refused." What happened? She thought things had been going well. Although her first date with Josh had been a little weird with the zombie movie, the second one was a lot better.

Then he dropped her with no word of explanation. She shook her head. Before she'd refused any sexual advances, this time. She wiped a tear from her cheek. They always drop me eventually. Something must be wrong with me. Twenty-five and never had a serious boyfriend.

Her brother Marc would know what to do. She hoped he was free. His job as a detective had irregular, unpredictable hours. She waited, tension rising with each ring of the phone.

He picked up on the fourth ring.

"Marsha? Hi, what's up?"

She'd intended to ease into the story gradually, but she lurched into her account of Josh dropping her almost immediately. By the time she'd finished her opening monolog she was crying into the phone.

"Marsha, calm down," Marc said, but it didn't register with her. "Marsha. Marsha! Listen to me. I'll be right over, okay? Did you hear me? I'll be over as soon as I can."

He finally penetrated her grief. "Okay. Thanks." She sniffled. "You sure it's no trouble?"

"Of course, it's no trouble. About fifteen minutes, okay?"

•••

Marc knocked on Marsha's door only ten minutes later.

"What happened, Martian?"

Despite being upset, Marsha couldn't help cracking a smile at him using her childhood nickname. They took seats on the sofa.

"He just dropped me for no reason, right when I thought things were going well. We had dinner, he washed the dishes while I checked Netflix, and then he just left. Now he's not answering his phone."

Marc raised an eyebrow. "You had him here? In your apartment? Did he try anything?"

Marsha pursed her lips. "No, he didn't 'try' anything. Originally, we'd planned to go out for dinner and a movie, but I didn't want to go out with that serial killer loose."

He sighed. "Okay, Sis. You're a big girl now. Just be careful."

"Well, I didn't want to cancel the date, and the first couple went okay. He was polite and kept his hands to himself. He tried to reassure me about the killer, but he didn't object to staying home for the date when I suggested it."

"I'll bet. Visions of rumpled sheets dancing in his head, no doubt."

"He didn't act like that. He was nice. He didn't want me to feel uncomfortable and said not to worry about the killer because he only targets drunkards."

Marc froze. His brows furrowed. "He said what? Only drunkards?"

"Yeah, something like that."

"Try to remember exactly what he said."

She grimaced and nodded her head, "It was something like that.

'Drunken bums.'" She nodded. "Yes, that was the term he used. Why does that matter?"

"What's his full name and address?"

Marsha furrowed her brows. "Joshua Gibson. I don't know his address. I've got his cell number."

"Give it to me."

"Marc, what's going on?"

He took a deep breath. "Look Marsha, don't see him again, okay? At least not until I let you know. That thing about only targeting drunken bums? That's characteristic of the Axman murderer, but it hasn't been in the news reports. We haven't given them that detail."

Marsha's mouth hung open. She closed it and reached for her purse. "Let me get my phone."

He patted his pockets. "Damn. Didn't bring a notebook."

"There's a pad for grocery lists hanging on the refrigerator."

Marc hopped up from his seat and jogged to the kitchen. He tore a sheet off the grocery list pad. As he turned to go back to the living room, he noticed the dishtowel lying on the counter by the sink. He furrowed his brows. It wasn't like Marsha to leave a towel crumpled on the counter. She was too organized. Then he noticed the red spot on it. He stepped to it and bent to examine the stain. Blood. He was certain.

He called out, raising his voice. "Marsha, did you cut yourself this evening?"

"No," she said.

"You said Joshua washed the dishes, didn't you?"

Marsha came to the kitchen door. "Yes, that's right."

"Have you been in the kitchen since then?"

"No."

He pointed to the dish towel. "Looks like Josh left some DNA behind. Do you have a Ziplock bag?"

• • •

Marc waited while Marsha packed a bag with several days' worth of clothes and other supplies. She followed him to his house and after a quick explanation to his wife, Amanda, he left for the station with the plastic bag containing the towel.

It was after nine PM when he checked in and delivered the bag to the evidence room. The officer in charge was Charlie Hupp, a big guy who always had a smile for everyone. He looked up when Marc came through the door and grinned.

"Well, if it isn't Marcus Welby, MD. Didn't think you were working tonight."

Marc rolled his eyes, but he returned Charlie's smile. "Welsley, and you know that good and well."

"Yeah, I know. I just like pulling your chain. So what'cha got?"

"Hopefully a DNA sample and an ID for the Axman."

Charlie's eyebrows lifted. "Really? That a fact?"

"We won't know it's a fact until it's tested. Can you rush it through for a match with the other samples from the Axman?"

Charlie took the bag, but he shook his head. "Not without the captain's say-so. We haven't got those back yet anyway. Probably be another week at least." He took a pen and logged in the evidence. "What makes you think this is the Axman?"

"This guy my sister's dating knew more about the murders than has been in the news. C'mon, I really need this rushed."

"Get the captain to sign off on it, but good luck with that." He held his hand level over his head. "We're backed up to here with DNA test requests."

Marc sighed. "Okay." Captain Anders was a good man, but very, "by the book." He finished filling out the form and handed it back.

Charlie looked it over and gave Marc a smile. "Looks good. See you later, Marcus Welsley, PD."

Marc huffed a laugh. "Yeah. Later."

• • •

"So, what have you got on this guy?" Captain Anders sat behind an oak desk with several neat stacks of paper on it. Morning sunlight streamed through the window behind him, making Marc squint.

"Just that he told my sister the Axman only targets alcoholics. That detail hasn't been in the news."

"That's it? You haven't questioned him yourself?"

"No, sir. Not enough probable cause to bring him in for questioning."

The captain leaned back in his chair. It creaked. "So, what makes you think rushing this sample is justified?"

Marc grimaced. "Sir, he's dating my sister. Well, at least he was."

Captain Anders raised an eyebrow. "Was?"

"Something spooked him during their date last night. He left abruptly and hasn't been answering her calls."

The captain sighed. "I can appreciate your concerns, Marc, but you don't really have anything. It's a stereotype, but it's not that big a leap for a civilian to assume that a homeless person is an alcoholic." He leaned forward, resting his forearms on the desk. "We'll process the sample you brought for matches in the database, normal priority. Best we can do."

$$\bullet \bullet \bullet$$

Josh left his therapist's office next Tuesday afternoon wearing a placid expression, but inwardly he seethed. Dr. Havland had sided with *her*. He said many people can drink responsibly, and that Josh didn't have any reason to feel betrayed since he hadn't asked her if she drank before he dated her. He shook his head as he approached the bus stop. He hadn't asked if she picked her nose or smoked crack, either.

He raised his eyes to the clouds. Looked like rain soon. Not good for hunting. Tomorrow night be better. The front should pass by then.

$$\bullet \bullet \bullet$$

Wednesday evening Josh watched a *Law and Order* rerun as he waited for darkness to fall. No rain forecast and the temperature was moderate. Good hunting weather.

Finally, the sky was dark enough. He switched off the TV, changed into his hunting clothes, and chose an ax from his cabinet. He slipped out of the house by the back door and kept to the shadows as he made his way down the alley behind his home and worked his way toward the bus stop.

• • •

Marc drove an unmarked car through the streets downtown, looking for anything that seemed out of the ordinary. Or too ordinary. Or something. Relying too much on instinct was unwise. Could get you into trouble. Ignoring instinct was as bad or worse.

Up ahead a man emerged from an alley. An above-the-knee amputee he guessed, based on his limp. There was a VA hospital in town, and it wasn't unusual for there to be Vets around being fitted for prostheses.

He almost passed by, but then it struck him. The man was wearing black sweats and a hoodie, just like the ones discarded by the Axman murderer. Didn't have an ax, though. He stopped the car, called in his location, and requested backup. He stepped out.

The man flicked his eyes up at him as Marc approached. Before Marc spoke the man said, "Hi, buddy. Could you spare a few dollars so I could get something to eat? I ain't had anything all day."

Marc was momentarily taken aback, but he recovered quickly. He held up his badge and said, "No, I don't think so. Could I see your ID?"

"Sure, Officer. I've got my VA card right here." He reached for the pocket at his side.

Almost before Marc could react, the guy pulled something long and dark from his side and swung it at him. He jumped back but it grazed his chest just under his nipples. Pain exploded. He fell back on the grass beside the walk and the man swung again, straight down at him. Marc rolled to the side and the weapon buried itself in the dirt. He pulled his service revolver and got off a shot while the man struggled to free the ax. Marc had no doubt it was an ax. The shot went wide. Too quick. He tried to level the gun. Not fast enough.

The perp kicked at Marc's gun, sending it flying off into the darkness just as a squad car turned the corner and lit up the siren and lights. The perp looked up at the car and fled into the alley.

The car stopped by Marc and two officers hopped out. One of them chased the Axman and the other pointed a gun at Marc.

"Freeze! Hands on top of your head."

Marc complied as well as he could with his injury. "I'm police. Detective

Marc – Welsley. My badge is on – the sidewalk over there." He nodded to indicate the direction and groaned. Breathing felt like knives stabbing his chest. "I'm hurt."

The officer spared a quick glance that direction and took a cautious step toward the black badge wallet lying face down a few feet away. He kept his gun pointed at Marc the whole time. He flipped the wallet over to reveal the badge and keyed his radio.

"Officer down, Market and Tenth streets. Need an ambulance and backup. Suspect is still at large."

Marc heaved a sigh and laid his head on the grass. Just after he heard sirens, everything went black.

• • •

Josh pulled off the hoodie as he ran and tossed it to the shadows. He turned the corner at the center of the block and crouched behind a dumpster to strip off the sweats. A few seconds later someone ran past, taking the route straight through instead of turning the corner after him.

Josh tossed the sweats into the dumpster and exited the alley, keeping to the shadows but not rushing. At the street he turned right and entered the first open business, a tavern.

He worked his way through the crowd to the bar and ordered a rum and coke. A guy standing next to him seemed engrossed in a baseball game on television. Josh struck up a conversation and got some details about the game.

The batter hit the ball.

"Yes!" the guy at the bar shouted. "Home run!"

Josh clapped his shoulder and raised his glass. His neighbor clinked it with his, but he failed to notice that Josh didn't drink afterwards.

Some commotion disturbed the bar as a couple of police officers entered and asked about suspicious characters who might have entered recently. Josh said he hadn't noticed anyone, but he'd been watching the game and could have missed him.

• • •

Though it made his skin crawl to be among that many people consuming alcohol, Josh stayed at the bar for an hour, taking occasional simulated sips of his drink. When his neighbor asked, Josh told him he was visiting the area on business. He was vague about the type of business. Sales.

At the game's end, Josh left the bar and boarded a bus heading uptown. He entered the house through the garage like he usually did, dropped his clothes into the barrel, and showered. Sleep evaded him at first, though. He hadn't worn gloves when he drew the ax, and now the police had his fingerprints. He didn't think they were on file anywhere, but now, one mistake, and they'd have him.

• • •

Lights glared in Marc's eyes as he woke. The beeps and bustle of a hospital surrounded him. He tried to rub his eyes, but his hand tangled with an IV line and the pull of a dressing on his chest hindered him. A face appeared above him, a woman with short-cropped black hair.

"Try to keep your right arm still for now," she said, pulling it back down to his side. "You've had surgery to close your wound and repair some muscles. You're going to be fine, but you need to heal. You lost a lot of blood."

Marc blinked in the light. "Did they get him?"

"Who?"

"The Axman. One who did this."

"I know nothing about that. There's a detective waiting to talk with you outside."

He dropped his head. "Okay. Send him in."

She frowned. "When the doctor says it's okay, you'll see him. Not before."

Marc considered her. She was a small woman, but her expression brooked no argument. "Okay. I'll behave."

"Good. Your wife and sister are outside, too. We'll move you to a room soon and you can see them then."

• • •

Josh tuned the radio to the local news as he made breakfast. The lead story was of his encounter last night:

"The police fought with the Axman serial killer last night in an incident that left a detective hospitalized in good condition. Detective Marcus Welsley stopped a man for questioning, who then attacked him with an ax. The suspect fled on foot and a subsequent search of the area failed to find him. Detective Welsley reported that the suspect had the ax concealed down a pant leg and walked in a simulated limp to deflect attention from it. Citizens are advised to be cautious..."

The radio was still making noise, but Josh had stopped listening. Marcus *Welsley*? A relative of Marsha's? He ran fingers through his hair. How many things had he touched at her apartment?

His hand shook as he sipped his coffee. Calm down. There was no reason to think Marsha would have connected him to the killings. Still, the possibility gnawed at him. He turned off the radio. The toast still sat in the toaster, cooling, neglected while he ruminated.

It was almost time to leave for work, but the more he thought about it, the more he thought he needed to do something about Marsha's apartment. He pulled out his phone.

"Consolidated Claims Processing, Kevin Ratcliff speaking."

"Hi, Kevin. Josh here."

"Hi, Josh. Everything okay?"

"No, I don't think I'm going to make it in today."

"Oh?"

"Something nasty and intestinal. You don't want it running through the department."

"No, I guess not. Just take it easy and keep us informed."

"Okay. Thanks."

He turned off the phone and stuffed it back into his pocket. He had a few glass pop bottles in the recycle bin and a can of gasoline in the garage. That should work.

• • •

Marsha's phone rang as she took readings on the DC calibrator. She put the probes down and pulled out her phone. Her landlord's number showed on the caller ID.

"Hello?"

"Miss Welsley, this is Mason Franks. Did you leave something on in your apartment?" Mr. Franks never seemed to be calm, but now he was in a purple-veined panic.

"No. I haven't been there for more than a week. I've been staying with my brother."

"Well, I just got a call from the fire department. The place is on fire. You better get over there right now. I'm heading there myself." He cut the connection.

Marsha stared at the phone, her mouth hanging open. A co-worker across the bench tapped her forearm. "Trouble?"

She pulled her gaze from the phone. "Yeah. My apartment's on fire."

"Oh, my God! Go. I'll tell the boss what happened."

• • •

A ladder truck sat parked in front of her apartment and firefighters sprayed on water as Marsha arrived. No flames showed, but acrid black smoke still billowed from the windows. Tenants of the other three units in the row of town homes stood by the street, shock painted on their faces. Mr. Franks stood near them. A police car parked in the street sprayed the area with flashing blue beams.

She stepped up to Mr. Franks. "Was anyone hurt?"

He glowered at her. "Just me. All the others got out safe."

"Well, thank God for that."

A police officer approached. "Are you Ms. Welsley?"

"Yes."

"I'm Officer Helmsman. Well, it seems you've made an enemy. The crew chief just told me it looks like someone threw a molly through your kitchen window."

Marsha furrowed her brows. "A molly?"

"A molotov cocktail. A homemade firebomb."

"Oh, God."

"Have any idea who might have done that?"

"This guy I was dating broke up with me suddenly, about a week ago. He's the only remote possibility I can think of. I never thought he could be violent, though."

The officer wrote down Josh's name and cell number and asked a few more questions. He gave Marsha a business card and went back to his car.

Marsha pulled out her phone. She hesitated, but Marc had insisted that she keep him informed, even though he was in the hospital. She pressed the hotkey to call his cell phone.

• • •

Marc set down the phone after his sister disconnected. Oh, shit. That asshole was targeting Marsha. He shook his head. Hard to think. The demerol clouded his mind. What was the officer's name? Helmsly? Helmford? No. Helmsman.

He woke up the phone and entered the number for his office.

"Marc, that you? How are you feeling?"

"Andy, the Axman is after my sister. He firebombed her 'partment. You've got to get her pertecton."

"Whoa, Marc, slow down. I can hardly understand you."

"Axman fire-bombed Marsha's a-part-ment. 'Member? Told you this guy she was dating knew stuff he shouldn't? Got his DNA. Need to get Anders to rush the test."

"Okay, Marc. Just take it easy. Is she okay? How'd you hear about a firebombing?"

"Marsha called me. My sister. Yeah, she's fine. Wasn't home when it happened. Officer Helmsman's at the scene."

"Okay, let me check the dispatcher log." Keys clicked in the background. "Got it. Yeah, Randal Helmsman, fire at Corning Ave."

"That's it."

"So, this guy knew too much, and now there was a firebomb?"

"Helmsman tol' her someone threw in a molly."

"I'll talk to Captain Anders. Where's your sister?"

"At the scene. She been staying wif Mandy and me."

"Okay. I'll get the captain."

• • •

The other tenants dispersed as friends or relatives came to collect them. Marsha shook her head. She should go see Marc. He was definitely not himself when she called. Probably on pain meds. Otherwise, she wasn't sure what to do. Insurance. Needed to call her agent.

Another guy remained nearby, scrolling through the display on his phone, frowning. He was a few years older than she, maybe in his early thirties, with sandy brown hair cut medium long. Could stand to lose a few pounds. He lifted his face from his phone, and they locked eyes.

He lifted an eyebrow. "Are you okay?"

Marsha shrugged. "No, not really. I'm Marsha. I guess we were neighbors."

"Carl Davidson. I guess we're not neighbors any more. I'll need to find another place to stay."

"Yeah, me too. I've been staying with my brother, but eventually I'll wear out my welcome there. I'm Marsha Welsley." She offered him a hand, and he shook it. "Have you got a place to crash in the meantime?"

He held up his phone. "That's what I was looking for just now. Anything but staying with mom." He cracked half a smile. "You offering? Your brother got another spare room?"

Heat rose to Marsha's face. "No, not offering. No offense."

He laughed. "None taken. Wasn't being serious. My renter's insurance'll pay toward a hotel for a few days. I was looking for something cheap that doesn't have bedbugs." He stuffed his cell phone into his pocket. "Well, I've got to find a pharmacy on the bus line and then get some lunch. Nice meeting you." He grimaced. "Sorry. I guess the circumstances weren't very nice." He started walking toward the main road.

Marsha watched him go for a couple of seconds, then shouted, "Carl –"

He stopped and turned toward her. "Yes?"

"I need some lunch, too. Could I drive you?"

After a second's hesitation, he stepped back to her and met her gaze. He pursed his lips.

"I'm a diabetic. My testing kit and meds are probably destroyed, and I can't get in to retrieve them anyway. Before I get lunch, I have to go beg for some insulin off cycle from my insurance allowance. It could take a while."

"I don't mind waiting. It'll be easier if you go to your regular pharmacy, right?"

• • •

Joshua Gibson watched from his car a block from the building. The fire trucks and police came and did their things. Nothing looked out of the ordinary. They'd determine it was arson, but there was no link back to him. He'd used gloves, and the shoes he'd worn were in a dumpster a block away.

At a supermarket near his home, he bought an anti-diarrheal. From what he'd told Kevin, that would be expected. Back home, he squeezed a couple of the pills out of their blister packs and flushed them down the toilet.

That should do it. No way they'll get fingerprints in that charred mess. A glass of iced tea calmed the last of his jitters. He turned on the television.

• • •

Andrew O'Cleary sat at his desk first thing that next Tuesday morning. He sighed. Too many hamburgers yesterday at the Memorial Day picnic. Going to have to log some extra time in the gym to work those off. He took a sip of coffee and then hit the play button on the answering machine. One message stood out:

"This is Officer Hupp in the evidence room. We got results from the DNA samples from the Axman that Detective Welsley wanted. Thought you'd want them right away."

Andy left without hearing the rest of the messages and ran to the evidence room.

Charlie Hupp glanced up when Andy burst through the door, smiled, and held up a finger. After a short search he pulled a sheaf of papers from a stack on his desk and handed it over.

Andy flipped through the sheets and smiled. Got him. Lifting his gaze from the sheets, he met Charlie's eyes. "Thanks, big time. You rock."

Charlie's grin widened. "Luck o' the Irish to ye."

As Andy walked back to his desk, he called Marc's cell. It went to voicemail.

"Hi, Marc. This is Andy. Wanted to let you know, got the DNA results for the sample you got from your sister's ex-boyfriend, and it's a match for the Axman. Thought that'd bring you some joy. Catch you later."

He stuffed the phone into his pocket. Work to do.

• • •

At 8:40, Josh Gibson had pulled the car out of the garage and was half-way down the block on the way to work when several cars passed him going the other way, one of them a police car. He stopped at the intersection and watched in the rearview. The cars stopped by his house and people hopped out, some of them heading around the house from both sides.

Police. Somehow, they'd found him. Marsha. Had to have been through Marsha.

He pulled through the intersection and turned at the next alley. If they knew where he lived, they knew where he worked. At the next street he turned left and continued to a bank. He stopped at the ATM and took out the maximum cash he could, $200, then got a credit card advance for $500. Wouldn't go far, but he couldn't risk going inside the bank for a face-to-face transaction.

At the back of a parking lot, he parked next to a car similar to his. Using the tool kit from the trunk he swapped license plates with the other car, then moved to a secluded spot in an alley nearby and pulled out his phone.

If Marsha filed an insurance claim, he could probably find it on the list from the online system at work. Most of the local companies used their service. It took only a few minutes to find it. The contact address was different from her previous address. Either she got a new apartment, or she was staying with someone.

He took the Beretta 950 from the glove compartment and slid it into his pocket. It wasn't very powerful, but it was easy to conceal. He didn't like guns – they were noisy and impersonal, but they had their uses. Marsha would regret turning him in, but only for a short time.

• • •

Dr. Hall stood at the foot of Marc's bed with her arms crossed in front of her. She frowned. "No, I'm not releasing you. Your wound's infected. Trust me, neither you, nor your loved ones, want to ignore that."

"So, send me home with some pills."

"There are all sorts of drug resistant bacteria in hospitals. We're going to make sure it's responding before we consider that. Might have to hang an antibiotic drip."

Marc winced. "C'mon, they're closing in on the Axman. I should be with them."

She lifted an eyebrow. "Oh? Because they're incompetent?"

"No, they're good. But this is personal."

Dr. Hall shook her head. Straight black hair framing her face barely moved. "You need to stay here. Maybe you don't realize how close you came to dying. A little deeper and you'd have bled out before the squad arrived."

Marc sighed. He pursed his lips and glanced out the window, then met her gaze again. "Whatever."

"I'll take that as consent. Someone will be in soon to get a sample of the discharge, and I'm starting you on Cipro in the meantime. Might change that based on the lab results."

• • •

"I have no idea where he is. He didn't call in, and he's not answering his phone." Kevin Ratcliff shot a nervous glance from Detective O'Cleary to the uniformed officer behind him, and back. A couple of other officers searched Josh's cube. "That isn't like him. He's always been reliable before."

"Has there been any change in his behavior recently?"

"Not that I've noticed. He's always been kinda shy and private." He tilted his head. "He called in sick a few days ago. That's sort of unusual for him. Said he had the flu or –" He stopped a second when the evidence techs removed Josh's computer. He glanced at the search warrant lying on his desk. "– Or something." He gulped. This was not going to look good on his weekly report.

• • •

Marc tried to watch television but couldn't concentrate. Andy had called before dawn to say they got a positive ID on the Axman, but then: silence. He checked the clock. 3:13. Surely something would have happened by now. His phone sat on the tray table and kept drawing his eye. Shouldn't interrupt Andy if something's going down, but either it'd be over by now or something went wrong. He dialed Andy's number.

"Hi, Marc."

"Hi. Any news?"

Andy sighed. "He got tipped off. Wasn't home or at work. He withdrew a chunk of cash this morning about the time we were breaking down his door. Got an APB out for his car, but he's probably out of the city by now. They stopped a car matching the description of his and with his license plates, but there was a seventy-six-year-old lady driving it. Just about gave her a heart attack, I guess. He must have swapped plates with her."

"Dammit. Where'd he work?"

"Consolidated Claims Processing. They subcontract for a number of insurance agencies to process claims, check for insurance fraud, and such. Everyone there says he was a great guy. Quiet and kept to himself."

"Great guy. Yeah, right."

"They're working over his computers now. Nothing useful yet."

"Okay. Keep me in the loop, will ya?"

"Will do, but you just concentrate on healing. Gotta go. Another call coming in."

Marc disconnected and set the phone down. He looked back at the TV, but after a moment he shut it off. Something Andy had said bothered him, and he wasn't sure why. He sipped some water.

Consolidated Claims Processing? Marsha had submitted an insurance claim. That meant Gibson knew where she was staying. He picked up his phone. Marsha's phone was off. It went straight to voicemail. Mandy's did, too. She was always forgetting to charge it. He called Andy and left a message.

He stared at the closet. Mandy had brought him some clean clothes yesterday when he told her he might be going home. Careful not to strain his wound, he climbed out of bed and closed the door to the room.

• • •

Marsha picked up Carl after work Tuesday afternoon. It turned out that he worked in the same industrial park as she, and they'd been having lunch together regularly. He was a good conversationalist, polite, respectful, and intelligent. He laughed easily and had a great sense of humor. Today they planned to have dinner together.

"I'm a little nervous about meeting your sister-in-law," Carl said. "I hope she gives a good report to your brother. I don't want any trouble with the police."

Marsha laughed. "You'll be fine. I just need to change. We'll only be there a few minutes." She smiled wider. "Marc might be home. He said he could be getting out today."

Carl's eyebrows lifted. "Now, I'm really nervous."

She parked in the driveway and led him to the house, opening the door. "Mandy, it's me and Carl."

Amanda met them in the front room and took Carl's hand. "Glad to meet you."

"Is Marc here?" Marsha asked.

"No, they're keeping him another day at least. His wound got infected."

"Oh, shit. Is he okay?"

"He'll be fine."

The front door flew open. Amanda spun toward it, "What the hell?"

Josh stood in the doorway, a gun in his hand.

Carl grabbed a lamp from the end table beside him and threw it at Josh. Josh flinched, then shot at him. Carl fell, clutching his belly while Amanda grabbed Marsha's hand and pulled her toward the bedrooms. Another shot behind them missed. Amanda opened the top drawer of the nightstand and searched through it.

Josh appeared in the bedroom doorway. "You shouldn't have turned me in, Marsha, but I guess I shouldn't expect loyalty from a drunkard." He raised the gun.

Carl slammed a heavy glass vase onto Josh's head from behind. Josh crumpled to the floor, and Carl slumped to his knees a second later. Blood dripped from a wound in his belly. He collapsed on top of Josh and rolled off, groaning.

Amanda screamed.

Marsha hurried to Carl's side and scooped up Josh's gun. She pressed on Carl's wound.

Carl gasped and heaved a ragged breath.

"You, okay?"

"I'm fine. Hang on, we'll get you help." Marsha twisted toward Amanda. "Collect yourself, dammit, and call 911."

Marc appeared in the doorway clutching his side. A red blotch showed under his hand. He held up a phone. "Already did that." He turned to Marsha. "Give me the gun."

Marsha gave it to him one handed, keeping pressure on Carl's wound.

Amanda rushed to him. "Marc! What are you doing here?"

"Being too late to help, obviously. Glad you managed. I came in just in time to see this guy whack that asshole." Marc plopped onto the bed. "Thanks, guy."

Amanda stroked his brow. "You damn fool. I love you."

Josh moaned and tried to push himself up. His eyes flickered open.

Marc pointed the gun at him. "Please, Mr. Gibson, give me an excuse to shoot you."

Josh locked eyes with Marc, then he let out a whoosh of air and collapsed.

Sirens sounded in the distance.

Parquet to the Past

By Mike Sieminski

HOW DID I end up here?

I stand up in the foyer, dust off my shoulders, and follow the parquet steps up to the kitchen, my joints stiff.

"Mom?"

The warm vanilla sugar scent of home is replaced with a stale, quiet air. My mom isn't in her chair by the window, coloring with her favorite set of colored pencils or doing word searches. She isn't listening to her Abbey Road or White Album CDs. Her chair is gone, the only music a melodic ticking from our strawberry wall clock.

"Grandma?"

I follow the floor back down to the landing. The bright yellow walls I painted with my sister look faded with time, tar, and nicotine.

"Mom, you in the basement?"

I walk down, careful not to trip on the loose flooring or the gold step protectors my brother hastily installed.

"Mom?"

I look in the corner of the basement. She isn't doing laundry or hanging sweaters on the clothesline; she isn't there to greet me.

I turn and almost knock over our cheap plastic game shelf. There's only one board game resting on it. *Where's all our other games? Where's Huggermugger? Balderdash? Rubik's Race?* I grab Life and look at its cover – an image of a mom, dad, and two kids playing, smiling. It's a cheesy picture, my sister and I joke about it all the time, but now it's covered with dust, the family's faces and clothes drained of color.

I flick on the light to the other side of the basement, made livable by the frayed, mint-green carpet from our living room and the wood paneling my brother and his friends nailed to the cement walls. I expect to see a centipede scamper across the wall, looking for a dark, damp shelter. But he's not there to greet me. *Where is everything?* My bed is missing and the couch we found last year on someone's tree lawn is gone. *Where's the plush gold chair and the big-screen Curtis Mathes? Where's my Alice in Chains and Kelly Gruber posters?*

I exit the finished side and glance over at our utility sink where I wash my hair and where my friends sometimes piss during parties. In the ceiling across from the shower is the laundry chute – where my clothes appear dirty and somehow always reappear clean in my closet and dresser. But there are no clothes. The hamper is gone!

I walk to the opposite side to the furnace area, my lungs now feeling heavy, tight. Under the cobweb-ridden window sits our giant 1950's freezer, made by steelworkers at Frigidaire and built to last a nuclear holocaust. As I open the door, a sharp pain shoots through my wrist, but there's nothing inside but metallic-smelling ice crystals. The pantry shelf adjacent holds only a can of French-cut green beans and a can of disgusting cream of mushroom soup. There's no boxes of raisin bran or Honey Smacks, no cans of Boost, Maxwell House, or Busch. *Where's the extra rolls of paper towels and toilet paper?*

"Mom!" I try to run up the stairs, but my legs don't move quick enough – I stumble, banging my hip and knee against a step. I limp through the kitchen towards the dining room.

"Grandma? Where are you?" I shout, grimacing. My grandma isn't in her recliner watching Matlock or Murder She Wrote, her chair and entertainment center are gone – the only thing left to watch is our baby-blue clock on the wall. Her bookshelf and Funk and Wagnalls encyclopedias are also missing.

"Mom! You up there?" I yell upstairs towards her bedroom, my voice fragile, shaky. "Anybody home?"

I walk past the bathroom into my grandma's bedroom only to find nothing there. No vanity, bed, dressers, no family pictures on the walls, only Venetian blinds hanging halfway down the windows.

I hobble into the bathroom and splash water on my face. In the mirror, I'm frightened to see the man staring back at me. His hair is thin, gray. His face dry and dying, covered with wrinkled skin drooping from his chin and neck like a chicken's.

"Dear God!" I cry. "Mom, are you home? Please tell me you're home!"

A Tummy Rub for Gaffney

By Stephen Kyo Kaczmarek

"GAFFNEY, get your pacifist ass up here!"

I stuck my head through the heavy-duty hatch, eye-level with Fitch's dirty combat boot.

"Yes, corporal?"

He thrust a mylar dispatch satchel in my face. "Get this to General Carnahan."

"That's… that's on the other side of the kill zone."

Fitch had a potato face, his expression like a permanent stink resided under it. But he was bigger and had the stripes.

"No shit. Well, you elected noncombat duty over infantry, philosophy boy. Hope you're enjoying it."

My insides tightened up. I started to shake.

"There's thousands of Xanti out there. How am I supposed to get past them in one piece?"

Fitch grinned at Sergeant Homan, who leaned his bulk against a 20GW blast cannon. The two of them had menaced me since I'd transferred in weeks ago, they the skulking, merciless stoats, I the frightened, fluffy bunny. Their special project.

"Were I you, conscientious objector," Homan opined in Texan drawl,

"I'd run really, really, really fast."

They laughed.

I looked toward the blazing twin suns and gulped. Beyond the high fortress walls lay miles of powder blue desert in every direction. Major Whitaker would send physical dispatches whenever he feared the Xanti had broken encryption codes. A vehicle was too conspicuous in the light of day. That's why dispatches normally went over at night.

But maybe a man staying low or hugging rocky outcroppings could make it.

Maybe.

• • •

A half mile out, I stopped to catch my breath, insides on fire. I rested against a purple Xantian rock, wiping my salty brow. I imagined Fitch and Homan watching me through high-power binoculars, taking bets on how far I'd get.

Suddenly, a white flash blinded me. There was no sound. When I could see again, the outpost was gone – just gone.

Then came tingling on my skin, intensifying until I passed out.

• • •

The defining feature of a Xanti is the tentacles – two long feelers in front, twelve stocky ones at the sides, and a kind of tail in back. The massive, cerulean creatures undulate on the stocky tentacles, using the tail to stabilize their locomotion in what should be an impossible way. It's a wonder to see.

Their faces, if they could be called that, consist of two wideset, glossy black eyes and a wet slit for a mouth. Nature has a sense of humor, as their expression is cast in perpetual smile.

This one looked positively jolly. His voice was rich and melodious, as though a jar of honey had learned to speak.

"Comfortable, Mr. Gaffney?"

Oddly enough, I was. The examination table was a warm hand cupping my nakedness, but my brain was also swimming happily in sedatives, enough not to question why they were speaking English or not dissecting me.

"Yes, very. Am I a prisoner of war?"

"Hardly, sir."

"Then I can go?"

"Well," he said, drumming four tentacles together like nervous fingers. He hemmed and hawed. "I'm afraid that's a different matter entirely, for you see, well, there's no easy way to say this. The fact of the matter is there's nowhere for you *to* go."

"What?"

If a Xanti could look sheepish, this one did.

"I'm sorry to be the bearer of bad news, but your comrades have been neutralized."

I sat up dizzily. Behind him, technicians went about their business, adjusting whirring levers and tapping blinking, multi-colored buttons with tentacle tips. If it served a purpose, I knew not what.

"Neutralized?"

"I'm afraid they're gone, Mr. Gaffney."

"You… destroyed them?"

"We neutralized them."

I couldn't think of anything to do except try to hit back with words. So much for my pacifism.

"There'll be reinforcements from Earth."

"Yes," he said, letting out a slow breath, "about that…"

When I stopped crying, he motioned to one of the technicians, who flipped a switch. I went all soft and sleepy. The jolly one daubed my forehead palliatively with a damp towel. At that point, I couldn't have hated the Xanti if I'd wanted to.

• • •

It took weeks for me to begin to come to terms with being the last human in the universe. I mean, how do you wrap your brain around it?

It didn't matter that the universe had dealt me lousy cards – knock knees, dull features, and thinning hair, for starters. I'd have to grow to be average height. A woman I briefly dated – my longest romantic relationship – left because, in frumpy-dumpy Maureen's words, I was "boring and too poor to make it tolerable." She took my dignity and my Ficus, Fred.

If there was an existential punch, my glass jaw was there to take it. I was a skid mark on the road of life.

It didn't matter if most humans I'd met were more like Fitch and Homan. I never wanted Earth and its people, cruel and foolish as they could be, "neutralized."

On a rare mild afternoon, I just wanted to take a walk. But where to? This was not my neighborhood. Not even my planet. And the Xanti lived in long, identical rows of what can best be described as gigantic adobe huts. Thousands and thousands, each like the last. Below them, a vast network of tunnels and work and storage chambers – skyscrapers in reverse. A single, crystalline tower rose in the center of the city, a great arrow pointing to where Earth had been. Or perhaps a middle finger to its memory.

It was then that it really hit me, all at once, a tsunami of never-agains.

Never again Christmas mornings, baseball games, lounging by the pool, chicken noodle surprise, long drives in the country, lazy Saturday afternoon movies, that fresh smell after mowing the lawn, eating peanuts out of the shell, browsing in shops around the corner, a fresh piece of pie at dinner, finding a new painting at the museum. Neighbors with fingers and toes. All the seemingly inconsequential but consequential things on Earth, gone with the planet itself.

I went outside and screamed.

Xanti went about their business, looking at me askance. Eventually, one stopped to shush me with a tentacle to his mouth.

In the dark depression that followed, H'Rondtha, as my, what, benefactor was called, tried his best to help me adapt to this new life. It started with pills – all sizes and colors. It grew to frequent talks together.

"You'll always have shelter and sustenance," H'Rondtha said one bleak evening, jolly looking as ever, "and want for nothing."

"Including freedom?"

H'Rondtha looked into the distance, as though the answer lay out there in the blue desert. The delicate folds over his eyes wrinkled.

"Freedom is an illusion, Mr. Gaffney. I think you've come to understand that by now."

"Then let me out, please."

He gestured at the door, not unkindly. "There are no locks here, sir. No bars on the windows. Walk beyond the city's edge, and no one will stop you. But where will you go? What will you do?"

I nibbled my bottom lip. He was right, of course. Where was there for me better than this?

I guess I would have to make the best of it.

"So, now what?"

"Now," he said proudly, "I want you to meet my daughter."

The door whooshed open, and a smaller, softer version of H'Rondtha loped into the room.

"Oh, father," Ch'Notssas said jubilantly, "he's adorable!"

She gathered me up in her tentacles and hugged me to what would have been a cheek in a human. It was warmer and drier than I'd expected. She smelled a little like fresh cantaloupe.

At that point, I understood, indeed, I wasn't a prisoner. I was a pet.

• • •

"Why didn't you kill me, too?" I asked, sporting the oversized, frilly blue sweater his daughter knitted for me. It had fifteen arms – eleven stuffed with batting – so I looked like a novelty version of a Xanti.

"Neutralize," H'Rondtha corrected gently. "The truth is, the Council wanted to. They're politicians, always looking for easy solutions to complex problems. But I'm a scientist, Mr. Gaffney. My scans of your brain revealed that unlike your comrades', your aggression level was minimal. In fact, it barely registered at all, which led to a conundrum: How could I support neutralizing someone so clearly not a threat? I must ask, though, why with so little desire for combat would you become a soldier?"

"I was drafted."

"I see," he said, reflecting on the concept. "Well, it just wouldn't seem right to destroy you, would it?"

"Neutralize," I said.

H'Rondtha came as close to laughing as a Xanti could get.

"Very good, Mr. Gaffney! Very good!"

For this, he offered me a tasty, mascarpone-cream-flavored treat from a pink bowl on the mantle, just out of my reach.

"But what of Earth?"

"Yes," he said in a low voice. "I'm afraid I couldn't do anything about that. You see, scientists can only influence the military and politicians so much, even among Xanti."

That touched on a question I'd had for some time.

"Your technology is obviously superior to ours. Why not prevent the war in the first place?"

H'Rondtha rubbed what should have been a chin.

"You humans were having such fun! Nothing motivates your species to action like war. It's in your race consciousness – well, except yours, of course. And since no Xanti was ever actually harmed by your primitive weapons, we were satisfied to indulge your fantasies of conquest. To a point, that is. You see, timing is everything. We had an election. Reformers took over political leadership and, against progressive voices like mine, saw you as a nuisance. Even a last-minute filibuster could not stop the bill being passed, and, well, you know the rest."

"So, Earth was legislated to death? That hardly seems taking the moral high ground," I mumbled.

"No," H'Rondtha said. "If it's any consolation, I filed a stern protest the very next day. They'll think twice before doing such again."

"Did you save anything from Earth? Anything at all? A plant? An animal? Some human DNA?"

"Only you, Mr. Gaffney. In this respect, you are now rarer than diamonds and sapphires."

"Which I'll bet you can manufacture, can't you?"

Rather than reply, he offered me another treat, this one like a chocolate and raspberry ganache. While I chewed, his eyes measured me.

"What would you say if I could double, maybe triple your life expectancy, Mr. Gaffney?"

"How?"

"As you've seen, our science is far more advanced than yours. The process is actually relatively simple – a modification of your DNA to keep the proper protein sequences from fragmenting with age. We do it all the time. Why, I'm more than 700 of your Earth years old. Of course, there's always a limit to how much we can do."

Two or three lifetimes. Who wouldn't want that? Maybe the last, loneliest survivor of his species, that's who.

I shrugged.

"What would I do with the extra time?"

He kept trying to cheer me up. "Maybe there are other humans somewhere. Who knows what's out there?"

The Xanti had visited thousands of worlds in their eons of existence. When I asked on how many of them human life had been found, H'Rondtha could only say, "Hope is but gossamer, Mr. Gaffney. We must give it air and breadth to lead our way."

"What does that mean?" I said, genuinely confused.

H'Rondtha looked at the floor. "Well, I'm a scientist, sir, not a poet."

A few days later – I assumed at H'Rondtha's doing – a kind of ceremony for me was held. The Xanti President gave a speech that started with how regrettable action against Earth was but culminated in a comparison to exterminators ridding a house of pests. He thrust a plaque into my hands. On it was an image of Earth and "SORRY."

Xanti don't applaud. Instead, they moan, raise tentacles, and undulate like a dashboard hula girl. So, I had to stand there with my plaque until thousands of Xanti finally stopped moaning and undulating at me.

• • •

One night, sitting in what might be considered Ch'Notssas' lap and looking up at all the stars the Xanti had visited, I admitted, "I'm lonely."

She was petting me with her softest tentacle, careful not to slice my flesh with any of the minute hooks dotting it.

"But why? You have your toys and your little human house. Don't I give you enough attention?"

"Oh, no, it's not that," I assured her, not wanting to be cross to a child, which despite her size and strength, she was. "I appreciate your love and affection. But it's different than being with another human. You understand?"

"I think so," she said. "I'll tell father."

The next day, a life-sized doll of a woman was delivered to my house.

"No, sweetie," I explained to her, "that's not quite what I meant."

She looked vexed and not a little disappointed. She'd been a bad mother.

"Let me talk to father."

"How about an android, Mr. Gaffney?" H'Rondtha offered.

"I don't think it would be convincing."

"You'd be surprised how skilled our engineers are. Some are bona fide artists."

"But I'd still know."

"Yes," he said, "I suppose so."

I'd been ruminating about his offer of increased lifespan. It had given me an idea.

"What about making a woman?"

"You mean an actual human woman? I appreciate your faith in our abilities, Mr. Gaffney, but we're yet to be deified."

"Hear me out. You wouldn't be creating a woman from scratch but using my DNA as the basis."

H'Rondtha was intrigued.

"Assuming we could do this – and that would be a questionable assumption, wouldn't the results be rather, er, too familiar?"

I thought about telling him the story of Adam and his rib producing Eve or a dozen other stories with similar foundations or even that biologists assumed all human life stemmed from a single female in Africa, but he'd know all this from when the Xanti had scanned Earth and, among other things, learned English.

"All humans already share 99% the same DNA," I said. "And maybe desperate times really do call for desperate measures."

H'Rondtha said he would bring it to the Science Council, but before then, I'd need to talk to one of their psychiatrists.

Dr. K'Gictept was very much what I'd expected – exact, probing, monotone. He asked me first to explain how I saw myself.

"I've always been a loner. Unmarried. Only child. When drafted, I was excited to see other worlds, make friends. Perhaps meet a girl."

"This is important?"

"It's not to you?"

"We reproduce by artificial insemination, Mr. Gaffney. Then the males raise the offspring while the females go off somewhere. Otherwise, they devour the male after first vivisecting them."

"Guess that answers the question of who pays for dinner," I quipped.

He scribbled something on my medical chart.

"Tell me about your mother."

"What do you want to know?"

"A memory that has stayed with you. Whatever comes to mind."

It popped into my head so fast, I winced. "Well, one day I got teased in school, so I asked my mother if I was ugly. In her patrician, middle-class honesty, she told me, 'Your face has character.'"

"How did that make you feel?"

"I was seven. How do you think it felt?"

"Tell me what you'd want in an ideal mate."

"Kindness and sensitivity."

"Attractiveness?"

"Please."

"What do you think you have to offer her?"

I hadn't really thought about it. "Companionship, for a start."

"You believe you'd be a good companion?"

After a lifetime of loneliness, I said, "I do."

We did word associations: Love (joy). Trust (important). Loyalty (necessary). Happiness (everlasting). Sex (hopefully).

Not long after, they scraped cells not from my rib but my gums and went to town. I knew enough about science to stay out of the way.

• • •

They had accelerated her growth to be in her 20s. She didn't look one bit like me, thank goodness. I inherited every weak, recessive trait. But she had gentle, sculpted features, bright eyes, lustrous hair, and an athletic physique. She was, in short, beautiful.

H'Rondtha was quite proud about the results.

"Maybe I know some poetry after all," he said.

"Thank goodness you didn't clone me."

"We considered it."

"So, what changed your mind?"

"Eh," he said.

H'Rondtha moved on. "There were some challenges with her genetic matrix."

"Matrix?"

"You see, parthenogenesis is known to many species, but not humans. You do have your genetic eccentricities. Anyway, we had to splice in gene samples taken from another species, the Strrmph in the K Galaxy."

"Are they... human?"

"More or less – like your Coke to your Pepsi. Or maybe Mountain Dew. Bipedal, mammalian. Much further along in the evolutionary current, but we made adjustments. That's the spice in the recipe! Trust me, you'll hardly notice the difference."

I didn't like the sound of that. I noticed right away her intelligence – she absorbed a lifetime of education in mere weeks. It turned out that she was talented, too. She could sing like a golden-throated Veery – perfect pitch – and draw in exacting detail from memory.

They let her pick her own name.

"Destiny," she said.

H'Rondtha winked at me and shooed us into my cottage in the back yard. It was four spare rooms and hastily assembled from wood they'd synthesized in the laboratory – not much, but bigger than my old apartment in Cleveland.

"Do you like it?" I said.

She surveyed things with a steady gaze, pausing momentarily on my plaque.

"You find this comfortable?"

"I've grown used to it." I gestured nervously – pheromones or something about her heavenly scent made my coordination wobble. "Please."

She sat at the tiny kitchen table, somehow looking formal in a simple setting. I put a plate of synthesized pasta primavera in front of her. She sampled it.

"Do you like it?"

"It is adequate."

An uncomfortable silence floated between us.

"You understand why you're here?" I said at last.

"You requested a mate."

"Well," I said, "that's not all. I mean, I'd like a friend, too."

"What is the purpose?" she asked, taking in her surroundings again.

"Of friendship? Well, support and understanding. Companionship. We do things together, share experiences."

She studied me.

"What do you do?"

The question caught me off guard. My impulse was to answer I'd been a soldier and a grocery clerk before that. But I understood she was asking for more.

"Well, I suppose I read. Garden a little. I like taking walks and looking at the stars. Or at least I used to."

It all sounded so terribly insufficient under her expressionless gaze.

"Where do I sleep?" she said, pushing her empty plate away.

"We, um, only have one bed. Is that okay with you?" When she said nothing, I asked, "But isn't it early to turn in?"

"You have a regimented schedule?"

"No, but it's still light out," I said, gesturing to the window.

"Show me the bedroom."

I took her there, uncertain what might follow. My mood lightened when she stripped, her nakedness so undeniably impressive I trembled. She pulled back the covers while I clumsily shed my pink jumper and slippers. I got in next to her warm, supple form.

But she was already asleep.

After a month of platonic cohabitation, it was clear she just wasn't interested. I might be lonely, but she was independent.

H'Rondtha was sympathetic.

"Attraction is mostly about biology, Mr. Gaffney."

"She's literally made out of my DNA," I said, crestfallen. "How do you get rejected by yourself?"

"Unfortunately, our science doesn't yet confer the ability to make people fall in love."

"Great. I feel like a donated organ that didn't take."

H'Rondtha patted me on the head and gave me a treat – vanilla mousse.

I found out the source of our problems. Destiny convinced the Xanti to give her a shiny new spaceship, with which she planned to visit the K Galaxy. Like an alien salmon swimming upstream, she was determined to find her Strrmph people.

I made her a memento, a kind of animated photocube with 3D images of our brief time together. Before slamming the cockpit canopy down, she handed it back to me.

"Weight restrictions," she said.

I watched the tiny ship lift off and roar skyward, a receding dot against the cold, cloudless sky.

H'Rondtha started to say something, but I just shook his tentacle. He didn't offer me anything, not even a treat, but with sad eyes watched me heading for the tall tower at the center of the city. I think he understood.

There, on that windy ledge, I felt certain for the first time in nearly a year. My life had come to this moment. Somehow, I always knew it would.

And that's why I leapt.

• • •

"Putting him down might be the merciful option," the veterinarian said.

Perhaps because his science had failed me, H'Rondtha nodded gravely. But bless her three massive hearts, Ch'Notssas interjected.

"No, father, no!"

Oh, yes, please, yes.

H'Rondtha looked torn. In the end, love won out, and they patched me up.

Love.

I couldn't help but think of the apathetic universe circling above us, and that far distant planet now only a silent, insignificant hole in it. I wanted to go there and erect a public notice:

Let this be a warning to all about the choice between love and hate, for here once existed a lush, beautiful world billions of years in the making, gone in an instant, testimony to the perils of greed, folly, and hubris. It was home to morons who believed in peace through superior firepower. Now they are in eternal peace. They thought they could step onto other worlds and squish that which was already there. Only they found smarter beings with bigger appendages and many more of them.

> Signed, Orson T. Gaffney, unremarkable final member
> of that silly little species known as Homo sapiens.

"You'll be fine soon," Ch'Notssas said, stroking the cast holding in my shattered spine and ruptured organs. "Remember, the best days are always ahead of you."

I didn't argue. What good would it do?

Besides, with that ridiculous white cone around my neck, I couldn't even turn my head to speak.

Editor's Note

MANY MEMBERS of the Ohio Writers' Association were instrumental in the production of this anthology. First, I would like to thank the president of the Ohio Writers' Association, Brad Pauquette, for his support of this project. I would also like to thank the anthology production team for all their hard work throughout the process, especially Juli Ocean, Devon Ortega, George Pallas, Madison Pauquette, Bre Stephens, Joseph Torchia, and Khadija Zahoor. They put countless hours into this project, and I owe them a tremendous debt. Thank you to Devon Ortega for her brilliant developmental editing. Thank you to Bre Stephens for her meticulous copy editing. Thank you to Columbus Publishing Lab for our cover and interior layout. Lastly, I want to thank our Ohio authors for crafting such engaging stories and sharing them with the Ohio Writers' Association.

—Emily Jones, Editor

Author Biographies

DIANE CALLAHAN strives to capture her sliver of the universe through writing fiction, nonfiction, and poetry. As a developmental editor and ghost-plotter, she spends her days shaping stories. Her YouTube channel, Quotidian Writer, provides practical tips for aspiring authors. You can read her work in Consequence, Short Édition, Translunar Travelers Lounge, Riddled with Arrows, Rust+Moth, and The Sunlight Press, among others.

CURTIS A. DEETER is an internationally published author of fantasy, science fiction, and horror. He runs an independent publishing company and creative community called Of Rust and Glass. When he is not writing, he enjoys spending time with his family, discovering new music, and taste-testing craft beer at local breweries.

CARNEGIE EUCLID is a writer from Cleveland, Ohio. He has an MFA in Creative Writing from Ashland University. He has been a finalist in the Owl Canyon Press Short Story Hackathon and appears in the anthology *Where the Ride Ends.*

JOE GRAVES grew up in Hicksville, Ohio, as one of seven kids, but now lives in Columbus, Ohio, with his wife, Allyssa, and their son, Finn. He is the lead pastor at Central City Church. He enjoys almost anything creative but loves storytelling the best, currently exploring the intersection of faith & science, technology & nature, and issues of justice through the science fiction genre.

KRISTA HILTON earned her MFA from Colorado State University and teaches writing online for several universities from her home base in Columbus, Ohio. Her fiction has recently appeared in The Valparaiso Fiction Review. She is currently working on a novel.

BRIAN R. JOHNSON is a lifelong Ohioan and recovering photographer, who has returned to his love of writing. He wrote his first "book" in the second grade, continuing on to poetry and short stories in high school, before taking a hiatus from writing for over a decade. His first novel is currently being revised and edited. He writes with his co-writer and co-conspirator Elora Lyons. Together they can occasionally be found streaming their writing and editing adventures on their Twitch channel: add_descriptor. For more information, Brian can be reached at add.descriptor@gmail.com.

EMILY E. JONES lives in Ohio with her husband and three children. She received her B.A. in philosophy from The Ohio State University. She has been published in Altered Reality Magazine and Dark Fire Fiction. Emily is also the creative director of theworldswithin.net, a website for short fantasy and science fiction stories.

STEPHEN KYO KACZMAREK is a writer and educator in Lewis Center, Ohio. Much of his writing has been for nonprofits, education, and business and industry, and he also co-authored the textbook *Business Communication: Building Critical Skills*. More recently, he began submitting fiction to publications. Steve's online work in multiple genres is available at *Five South Journal, Every Day Fiction, The Ohioana Quarterly, The Columbus Dispatch,* and more. He has several other stories under review, as well as a completed novel manuscript under revision.

STELLA LING is an Asian American writer, poet, healer, and artist. She is the founder of the Wilmington Writers Collaborative, started in 2006, member of the Wright Library Poetry Group, Tower Poets, and Orinda Writers Group. Her work is featured regularly on WYSO Radio *Poet's Corner*.

BRIAN LUKE is formerly assistant professor of philosophy at the University of Dayton, currently organist and choir director at Northwest United Methodist Church in Columbus. He is author of Brutal: Manhood and the Exploitation of Animals (University of Illinois Press, 2007) and co-author, with Barbara Luke, of The Complete Crimes of Donald Trump: Part 1, Crimes of Race and Sex (Carriage House Press, 2020). Brian and Barbara live in Marysville, Ohio, in their "empty nest" of five cats, twelve hens, six goldfish, and one golden retriever named Finn.

ELORA LYONS is a Texan through and through. She is on her second stint in the Midwest, this time landing in the Buckeye state. Reading has always been one of her passions. Her love of books led her to share that passion with children by hosting book fairs and spreading the joys of reading and books to future generations. That love of reading brought her to the other side and now she writes and edits with her co-writer and co-conspirator Brian R. Johnson. Together they can occasionally be found streaming their writing and editing adventures on their Twitch channel: add_descriptor. For more information, Elora can be reached at add.descriptor@gmail.com.

MARY MCFARLAND is a writer, speaker, editor, and techpreneur. She writes suspense, true crime, SF, mainstream fiction, fantasy, and nonfiction. A Golden Pen award winner, she is published in both the novel and short story genres. She writes full time at Mucky Manor, her organics farm and winery in southern Ohio. She is also CEO of Red Girl Digital, a digital marketing firm exclusively serving authors. She is launching an upcoming thriller in November 2021. Mary is a member of Ohio Writer's Association, West Virginia Writers, and River Valley Writers (RVW). Find Mary at: marymcfarlandbooks.com, redgirldigitalmedia.com, and facebook.com/authormarymcfarland.author.

D. WAYNE MOORE is an artist, a writer of fiction, and a creator of unusual things. He lives in Columbus, Ohio, with his wife and two neurotic cats. Above all else, he enjoys spending time with his family, hatching new ideas, and standing in an ocean doing nothing.

DEVON ORTEGA obtained a bachelor's degree from The Ohio State University and a master's degree in creative writing at Ohio University. She was the recipient of the 2011 Gertrude Lucille Robinson Award for her poetry series, "Tavern at Ten." Her poetry has appeared in Barren Magazine, Azure Magazine, Door is a Jar, and several anthologies. She currently lives in Pickerington, Ohio, with her husband and four children.

GEORGE PALLAS was born in Chattanooga, Tennessee, and grew up in the Nashville area. He moved to Ohio after graduating from Vanderbilt University and began a career in information technology. As a writer, he has two short stories to his credit and is in the process of publishing his first book, *Stalking Horse*, a mystery novel. He also writes about historical true crime in his blog, *Old Crime is New Again* at georgepallas.com. George lives in downtown Columbus, Ohio, with his wife, Sharon, and his dog, Sheldon Cooper.

BRAD PAUQUETTE lives in Zanesville, Ohio, with his wife, Melissa, and their five children. He is the co-founder and director of the School of Kingdom Writers, a nonprofit training program for Christian writers. Learn more about Brad at BradPauquette.com.

DAVID M. SIMON is an ad agency creative director by day, writer and illustrator by night (and weekends). He writes for both adults and kids. His short stories have appeared in several anthologies, including the forthcoming *Heads and Tales*. His first novel, a fantasy adventure for middle-graders titled *Trapped in Lunch Lady Land*, was published by CBAY Books in 2014. His work has also appeared in everyone's favorite dentist office magazine, *Highlights for Children*.

STEVEN KENNETH SMITH is a fiction writer, a poet, a musician, and a retired engineer. His poetry has appeared in many journals and anthologies, and he has short fiction published in both English and Esperanto. His debut novel, *The Great Disruption*, is available on Amazon and in bookstores in Granville and Bexley, Ohio. As a resident of central Ohio since age 5 and a graduate of Ohio State University, his ties to the state are secure. He enjoys backpacking and is a former regional champion on the Mountain Dulcimer. He's been a performer at the Ohio Renaissance Festival since 1992.

MIKE SIEMINSKI lives in Westerville, OH, and is a graduate of The Ohio State University. When he's not writing, he's working his day job as a nutritionist, raising his twins, exercising, and watching TV shows about aliens or cryptids.